MAR - - 2022 *SH*

Acclaim for Pawan

Coinmar

MW00721314

Winner: 2016 eLit Book Awards for Literary Fiction (Bronze)
Winner: 2016 Readers' Favorite International Award (Honorable)
Finalist: 2016 NIEA Award for Humor
Finalist: 2016 IAN Book of the Year for General/ Literary Fiction

"A business firm that turns violent...a conspiracy in the works...and a spy among the coworkers. Coinman is an incredible and an unforgettable journey." --*Readers' Favorite*

"Originality is often elusive, yet that's exactly what Pawan Mishra delivers." --*BookViral*

"Mishra's debut comic novel is an absurdist tale of office and personal politics set in a small town in northern India." --*Kirkus Review*

"A quirky, heartfelt novel about finding your identity - and keeping it." --*SPR*

"As a study or allegory of the workplace, Coinman stands as a rather intriguing and good satire." --Misanthropester, *Musings on Popular Culture*

"This story holds its own in the story world." --Ana Meyer, author of *Marie*

"Refreshingly unique, humorous, and honest! Mishra's eloquent writing style is itself a feast for lovers of literary fiction." --Nelou Keramati, author of *The Fray Theory: Resonance*

"The story of Coinman is like an Indian meal, with so many rich spices that contribute to the complexity of the overall flavor. One to be eaten slowly, and savored." --Catyana Falsetti, author of *Facing Death*

"This story is a modern day parable. It is laced with psychological insight, pithy wisdom, and is an astute parody of the dynamics of office politics and group-think." --Ginger Bensman, author of *To Swim Beneath the Earth*

"The book is a brilliant linguistic muddle and a stunning display of stylistic somersaults. The style of the novel is an intricate mosaic

i

fashioned with care. The most striking aspect [of this book] is its apparently bottomless and amazingly diverse fund of linguistic humor of all possible kinds. 5 stars." --*The Bibulous Bibliobiuli*

"This story was a breath of fresh air to read. The author weaves together humor and insight into the nature of humanity to create a masterful piece. A must read!" --Sara Angelo, author of *Drift*

"Coinman is a story that is similar to an exotic meal. Too many books these days are your boring meat-and-potatoes stories, while this novel is a breath of fresh air for your taste-buds." --John Autero, author of *The Scorpion*

"Original, imaginative and full of India's culture, Coinman: An Untold Conspiracy is a book that will stay with you long after you've finished reading it." --Rebecca McNutt, author of *Smog City*

"I've never read sarcasm like this before from such a young author. For me, sarcasm is the best thing served on plates by this book. I just loved that." --Titas, Blogger

"Pawan Misha isn't your typical author, that's why I loved this book. Pawan adds puzzle piece by puzzle piece and it starts to come together as a fun comical masterpiece." --Kate Fennell, *251 Things to Do in Tofino*

"Prejudice takes a plethora of forms. A recent example of the outcast can be found in Pawan Mishra's Coinman. He masterfully weaves laugh-out-loud humor into this very quirky, very creative and very original story." --Kenneth Preston, author of *The Passing of Each Perfect Moment*

"Mr. Mishra uses long sentences, quality words and phrases that convey thoughts and feelings precisely and conjure vivid images. An engrossing and entertaining novel which also offers useful moral lessons to readers." --Getty Ambau, author of the series *Desta*

It is an insightful, funny, and beautifully crafted mockery of the ridiculous and bureaucratic social oddness that is working in an office. --James Hockley, author of *Fear's Union*

Coinman

An Untold Conspiracy

PAWAN MISHRA

Lune Spark L.L.C., Morrisville, NC

Lune Spark L.L.C.

PO Box 1443, Morrisville, NC, US, 27560

www.lunespark.com

Email: coinman@lunespark.com

Phone: +1 (919) 809-4235

Ordering Information: Quantity sales. Special discounts are available on quantity purchases by corporations, associations, and others. For details, contact the publisher at the address above.

Or visit www.coinman.info

Cover design by: Shahrukh Ehsan Romario

ISBN 13: 978-0-692-47567-6

ISBN 10: 0692475672

1. Fiction 2. Humor 3. Satire

First edition

(Updated on Sep 15, 2016)

DEDICATION

To my dad,
the late Mr. Chandra Prakash Mishra,
for teaching me to live to the fullest and fight till the very end,
and for inspiring me every day through cherished memories.

Contents

COINMAN

1. The Cacophonous Plight

*I*t all began with high expectations.

I couldn't believe at first that Sage Mangal, our esteemed master at the ashram, whose personality I can't promise to make you very familiar with, had trusted me with a task of such ambition.

"A lack of emotional engagement in the affair affirms higher credibility," Sage Mangal had explained when asked why he chose me, Sesha, over many others, for pulling the pieces of Coinman's story together after the latter's departure from the ashram.

In short, it was the lack of my prior acquaintance with Coinman that had won me this prize.

His Politeness also bestowed me with the divine power to find almost everything that I needed to find. Such was this power that I could enter invisibly into past situations, could be at multiple places at the same time, and could even float in someone's mind without their discovering. Before you ask, Sage Mangal did meticulously bar my access to certain activities and places—for example, the bathroom where one of the main characters in our story spent a major part of his life. The sage agreed in advance to bear with any compromises that my lack of full access might potentially introduce to the story.

I could ramble on forever, but this is all I wish to convey to you about me and my job. I will assume that you wouldn't want to know more than that either; not only will it make my job simpler, but it will also fulfill my wish to remain largely invisible. Honestly, with the kind of story I am about to embark on, I know you couldn't care less about me. So let's get to the story without further ado.

Jangle jingle! Clink clatter! Ding-a-ling! Ring-a-ding!

The mind-numbing sound of relentlessly jingling coins was something the people of the office, the center stage of this story, hadn't quite learned to live with yet. Not only when the possessor of the busy coins, Coinman, walked, but also when he stood talking—or engaged himself in doing anything else, for that matter—his left hand constantly fondled the coins with tenderness.

The coins occupied an eternal place in the left pocket of his trousers and, regardless of where he dwelt or what he did, constantly slithered through the narrow spaces between his fingers.

When an activity adamantly demanded participation from one of his hands, he strategically let the activity claim his right hand to allow the left one an uninterrupted opportunity for the recreation. If such an activity insisted on his left hand, he transferred the coins to his right pocket ahead of time to allow his right hand to continue feeding his mind. Once the exceptional engagement was over, the left hand impatiently looked forward to the return of its possession. If there was a momentary delay, the left hand hurriedly tried to enter the right hand's den, making the coins feel nervous, just as a princess would on seeing two equally adept princes fighting to claim her hand.

When an activity required continuous use of both hands, like welcoming a delegation from another firm with garlands, he tackled such desperate scenarios by the means of a last-minute absence. There were rare yet difficult off-the-cuff occasions, too, when it was unavoidable that he stop the action in his pocket, such as a sudden request to hold a big chart with both hands for a few minutes for a colleague's presentation. Faced with such calamity, he immodestly excused himself for biological breaks, which, despite not fooling anyone, did not provide anyone enough justification to raise an official protest.

The office was located in a small town somewhere in northern India; in a four-story building where it occupied the second floor, where all the managers sat in private offices, and the first floor, where the rest of the staff sat at desks in a large open hall.

Far back in time, beyond a recall of the exact date, unable to put up with Coinman's interminable daylong feat, colleagues at neighboring desks had started shifting their positions away from him; inch by inch, each day. It caused some sort of a ripple effect throughout the entire arrangement. The staff, without a spoken word, synchronized the move, over several months, with such a constant and slow pace that it was hard to spot it at any given point.

When Coinman first spotted the continuous movement, he stayed calm initially, for he wanted to observe for a few more days to confirm his findings. Past embarrassments from his premature findings had left him wiser.

Satisfied with the constancy of the move, he felt comfortable loudly announcing its progress every day to his neighbors. The minute he reached the office, he threw his bag on his desk, flew to nearby desks with the wings of curiosity, and bent down to take notes on the tiny spiral-bound notebook that he carried in his shirt pocket. Spiral-bound notebooks did not misbehave during his right-hand-only writing endeavor the way the sewn or case-bound notebooks did, like closing repeatedly without support from his coin-engaged left hand.

The futility of Coinman's verbal attempts to convince his neighbors about the unfaltering motion of the desks made him carry a small measuring tape and a white chalk to mark the daily progress. At the end of each day, before leaving the office, he marked the location of each neighboring desk by drawing boundaries around its feet, accompanied by a date and time. He did the same on the following morning, as soon as he came to the office. He realized within a few days that one of these two marks was redundant but wasn't quite sure which one. He decided to continue only with the morning mark.

But that did not solve the issue entirely. Since the desks were moving extremely slowly, two consecutive marks still overlapped with each other.

To crack this challenge, he started bringing high-quality thin marker pens. The hard-nosed desks had to accept defeat and move visibly thereafter.

"There, you see? That mark. This one, right here. Look at the overnight distance. God!" he would exclaim, flying from one desk to other, pining for his colleagues' approval.

Seeing no impact on his cold colleagues, he saw no point in trying to win them over. He started removing marks from the previous day while adding the new ones in the morning to continue tracking the direction of the movement for his own record.

At times he chuckled to himself, in a loud voice, "The poor desks are so impatient to leave. God help the atmosphere here!"

Ratiram, the reservoir of wisdom, the most widely revered man among the first-floor inhabitants, had been discreetly keeping an ardent eye on the move. He was one of those who are not born handsome, but develop charming features with age by continuously engaging their brains with intelligent thoughts.

Ratiram announced one day that the move had racked up to the threshold of management's endurance for untidiness. He astutely explained that if the move continued any further, management was no more going to avoid acknowledging it publicly; and in that case, it was inevitable that the response would involve ABC, Andar, Bandar, and Chandar, the three most dreaded individuals in the office; the supreme powers who came from nowhere to establish discipline when chaos crossed their limits.

The announcement compelled an immediate shudder among the crew because ABC's involvement had never been without a few expulsions. The move stopped right then and there. But by this time, a belt of circular empty space had formed around Coinman's desk.

Coinman felt relieved from his self-assigned burden of tracking the move. He used the circular empty space around his desk for his post-lunch brisk walks.

"Chew it well and walk like hell; else the lunch will make you swell," he chanted in a low voice during these walks, followed by a loud laugh every single time, implying to his unsmiling colleagues that a good joke doesn't necessarily need appreciation from others. One can freely laugh at one's own deserving jokes.

A later development was his exclusion from the meetings run by the denizens of the first floor. Initially he continued to attend the meetings without presenting any signs of awareness of any restrictions. But he understood soon that everyone was secretly jeering at his pretentious ignorance. So he finally decided to stop attending these meetings. He was afraid that if he reacted to the situation, it might blow things out of proportion. Now at least he could continue with his interests freely outside the meetings. Who could tell? If he voiced his objection, he could jeopardize his pocket sport.

"On the other hand," he thought, "there is hardly anything of importance that happens in these meetings." He smiled to himself as he remembered Ratiram telling him once from his soapbox, "These meetings are conducted as a means to spend official time and money on eating and gossiping. The agendas are so ambiguous one cannot make out in the end if the objectives are met or not. Some of the associates wait for these meetings to complete a power nap, while many others only allow themselves to turn into yawning machines."

Coinman could not help a laugh to himself every time he remembered how Ratiram had summarized it: "A meeting is a collective tacit confession of participants' unwillingness to work."

The coin-stricken souls at the office used as pain-killers some fabricated tales about Coinman's buffoonery, yet these pain-killers were not good enough to make even a dent in the constant trauma the coins caused. The mind-paralyzing sound of the coins, mixed with the hatred against him, evolved to a stubborn assessment in their minds that Coinman was perpetrating the most unbearable experience they'd ever known.

The tenured associates had been somewhat successful in exhibiting numbness toward the turbulence caused by the jingling coins. A newcomer like Hukum, though, found it very challenging to live under the metal chimes hanging above their heads.

Hukum shared his experience with everyone within a few days after his joining. "It was like a sudden installation of huge copper chimes into my brain. These chimes slam together unbearably, causing an indescribable feeling in my chest area that's several times worse than a thousand nails raking simultaneously across a chalkboard."

Understanding a newcomer's challenge very well, old associates always acted early to lend a kind hand by trying to elevate his soul with their own stories, explaining how they were able to eventually cope with the phrenic tsunami.

The common source of suffering brought them all closer as personal differences gradually melted and evaporated in the scorching heat of coins. Whining about Coinman every day, they started noticing merits in each other. It was like suddenly discovering an ocean a few steps away from one's house. Many even took the office companionship home, where their respective families found opportunities to get together and talked excitedly about otherwise mundane affairs of life.

Sadly enough, no one felt obligated to Coinman for being the main cause of the grand social platform. Instead Coinman's smile penetrated them, his laughs annoyed them, and his existence offended them.

They wanted independence from coins at any cost.

"I swear by the self-assurance with which elderly men sitting in public tilt sideways to allow the gas to escape loudly," Hukum announced, during a gossip session, "allow a man to sit on your shoulder and he will instinctively take a leak in your ear. Instead of tolerating him, we must figure out a way to protest. Someone needs to take the lead so that it's not everyone's but no one's."

2. The Autonomous Arena

*E*ach life is yet another chance given to humanity, but it was not even a half a chance in Coinman's case. God surely must have been undergoing some sort of mental metamorphosis when he dispatched Coinman to the world. This was how his colleagues often described Coinman in a nutshell to anyone who had no prior acquaintance with him.

Coinman was of average height, dark, shy, and lean but healthy. His looks often misled people in judging his age: some believed him to be as young as thirty, and some thought he was as old as fifty. The former perceived him as a young man who looked older for having been through hardships, while the latter thought he was an old man who looked younger for having lived a contented life. The rest either did not have an opportunity to express their opinion or did not deem the subject worthy of their reflection.

His chin was in a funnel shape, tapering down to form a very thin verge at the bottom. In addition to this extraordinary appearance, his chin vibrated whenever its owner was excited, positively or negatively—two times every five seconds, in quick succession. The two successive vibrations occurred at such speed and within such a short span that there was an ongoing debate at the office, behind his back, as to whether it happened once or twice. Each vibration made his chin contract, go up, and then relax back to its usual form. People often wondered if other children his age used to annoy him on purpose, just to enjoy this rare demonstration of a chin's low tolerance to its master's stress.

Time had eroded a large section of hair on his head. What had once been a dense jungle of black trees had become a barren island. The large, shiny bald area in the middle of his head was surrounded by a perfect circular band of black hair, just like a monk's tonsure. It was as if a black ribbon had been tied in a circular fashion to guard his shining bald head against evil eyes.

He wasn't the kind heavily invested in keeping up outward appearances, but the kind who believed in inward well-being, and hence did not pay much attention to the things that embellished his outward appearance. He generally wore loose, dull-colored clothes. These clothes, if his colleagues were to be believed, had served his father for a few years before serving him. If it had not been for his belt, which was admirably dependable for keeping the trousers from slipping beyond the territory of decorum, those loose trousers would have left no stone unturned to flow with the gravitational force. His walking style was discussed in great detail as well: a gait that made it seem as if a narrow open sewage line passed right between his legs.

The office unit belonged to an old private firm run by one of the ancient business families in the region. While the interior of the second floor was state-of-the-art, the interior of the first floor was too aged to keep secret the necessity for a comprehensive repair. The thirty-plus years of marriage between the ceiling and the cement plaster showed signs of weakness by the plaster's frequently developing cracks and holes. Now and then a small portion detached itself from the ceiling, took flight, and attacked the proceedings below without a warning. Whenever this happened, everyone at once gathered around the site of the impact. If the plaster happened to hit a living being, it made the occasion even more special. A few pinched the victim while a few playful types took the opportunity, depending on the range of playfulness of the victim, to pat him gently on usually restricted areas, putting on an act as if clearing dust from his clothes. The victim turned into an instant celebrity for the rest of the day.

On a few occasions, when the plaster came out during lunchtime and landed in someone's lunchbox, the mob took hold of the lunchbox from the proud owner and went on to complete two rounds within the office in a procession, interchangeably carrying the lunchbox on their heads. They passionately dramatized the proceedings, behaving as though they were carrying a coffin to the graveyard, constantly chanting a dirge indigenous to the office; the leader asked the questions and the rest answered in unison.

"What is life?"

"A lousy puzzle with missing pieces."

"Is there a God?"

"Yes there is, yes there is."

"Who bestows life?"

"He does, He does."

"And who takes it away?"

"Damn! He does, He does."

"Whose turn is this today?"

"This one is done for, surely done for."

"What shall we ask now?"

"Rest this lunatic soul in peace, yes, in peace."

They then surrounded one of the trash cans, seriously chanting mantras used during sacred offerings to God, and thereafter emptied the box into the trash can before returning it to the honored owner.

The interior office walls were painted light green, and the long-standing furniture matched the color well. Devoid of aesthetics, the overuse of the dull green color in the room couldn't have been deliberate. Therefore, it seemed that the furniture had acquired the color of the wall by way of continuously absorbing it for years. And it was a possibility that there was a rapid back-and-forth transmission between both sides in order to achieve a joint convergence on a perfect sameness in color.

The office area on the second floor was very small compared to the first floor. The elevator opened up right opposite the reception desk, behind the waiting couches. There were office rooms for managers on both sides of the reception area. The biggest and most luxurious room on the right side of reception belonged to Jay, the unit head. A similar-size room on the left was reserved for ABC, and was kept locked at all times because ABC's visits to the office were very rare, and entirely undesired because of the casualties caused by each visit. No one knew the exact roots of the sovereign power ABC savored.

There were several other office rooms on the second floor, occupied by important-looking people who were chanced upon only in the elevator, and whose source of importance was thus not known to anyone.

The tables on the first floor were always full of files. These tables appeared to be yearning for a break after several years of service. Not many at the office treated them with the respect they were worthy of. What if these tables did not watch over the important papers while the associates were away? One can easily guess how ill-behaved these papers could become at times—especially with the companionship of electric fans.

Ratiram not only knew but also felt deeply in his heart how immeasurably vital these tables were. These were simply his bread and butter. Hypothetically, if the tables were to go away for any reason—of whatever nature it could have been, presumably of the kind that invariably caught ordinary people like him unaware—he had no doubt in his mind that his job would follow them.

Ratiram, who had started his job as a janitor at this office during the olden days, had gotten a promotion ten years later to become a junior administrative assistant and had held the same position ever since. His job description wasn't formally documented, having been shaped over the years by all and sundry. Still undocumented, it included doing anything that the associates could think of within the purview of office boundaries and the market outside. The majority of his work was to move files from desk to desk, from one person to another. With the files, he also moved gossip.

Even though Ratiram's was the lowest rank in the office, he was the most respected person on the first floor, immeasurably gifted with intellectual wisdom. Everyone found a friendly listener in him. He was an artist who molded his behavior and conversation as it worked best for the other party—just as a great musician improvises her notes with a fellow musician during a class performance.

Hukum and his gang were second only to Ratiram in the art of relentlessly keeping the grapevine alive.

When Hukum joined, on his very first day at the office, his adroit eyes did not fail to notice that a group of three, Daya, Sevak, and Panna, always moved together. In gatherings of any sort, even those of a spiritual drift, he noticed that these three could be seen inaudibly sharing funny observations in a corner, accompanied by violent mute gestures. Even during the gatherings where a complete silence prevailed, such as those for listening to a speaker, they mutely mimed eloquent laughing gestures among themselves. It seemed that they found a lot of fun with every mundane thing. There was a dream team to be with! Hukum kept a curious watch over the group until he felt an irresistible desire for a friendship with them, and introduced himself.

The group of three received him enthusiastically. It was a mutual pull, as they later discussed during a drinking session.

Hukum's insertion into the group was so natural that within a week it seemed they had been together for a year. When Hukum went outside for a smoke, the rest of them accompanied him, even though none of the three smoked.

Who had been the leader of the gang of three prior to Hukum's advent was not known, but in a short period Hukum assumed leadership, without leaving anyone with hard feelings. On the first floor, they went by "Hukum's gang" or simply "the gang."

The gang apparently knew of a fascinating place that they candidly talked about ceaselessly without revealing its name or location. Others claimed, though, that it existed only in their fantasy world.

On occasions when the gang believed someone was eavesdropping on them, one of them let out a deep sigh of agony, calling out, "Let's take him to our holy den this time, I am sure his world view will transpose upside down." At this the gang would laugh uproariously and continue the big talk about the agony of not having been at their hangout for the past few days.

Once, in the past, people had felt the itch to know everything about the place and had made their best attempts in that direction, using various tactics, until a complete lack of success prompted them to ignore their curiosity and conserve energy. It was then, to increase the likelihood of the gang's revealing the details themselves, they embraced a belief that the place didn't even exist.

The gang shrewdly responded neither positively nor negatively to the notion.

3. Thus, Coinman

The most ironic thing in the world is having no say when your name is determined for the first time (which is also for the last time for most), because newborns are not necessarily known for speaking their minds.

But when a new name is acquired thereafter, it's generally not without a perfect harmony with one's will.

Coinman was an exception. At age twenty-five, he had gotten a new name, Coinman, without having a say. He had felt sad back then at in effect losing his earlier name, Kesar, yet quite helpless to do anything about it.

No one could ever recall who deserved the credit for inventing his new name. It was certain, though, that his colleagues had repeatedly started referring to him as "Coinman" behind his back during gossip sessions about his tireless fondness for coins; then, at a later point, this name sprang beyond the periphery of the gossip sessions to breach all facets of his life.

First the office openly started calling him "Coinman." Then one day the name mysteriously showed up on all his office records as well. It was as if someone, behind closed doors, had cleverly erased "Kesar" from every place it appeared and replaced it with "Coinman."

The first time his new name figured on an official document, in the office newsletter, he dismissed it as a joke played by his colleagues. But thereafter, all official letters bore his new name. In protest he returned all his letters to the mailing department. When his letters formed a big bundle and could no longer be accommodated in his mailbox at the office, they caught the eye of the mail manager, who immediately paid a visit to his desk to deliver his letters personally and wanted to know the reason behind his earlier refusals.

Coinman protested that these were not his letters, that they were for someone named "Coinman." The officer clarified that the administration pulled names from the employee database and advised him to follow up with the Human Resources department. Later, an executive in that department showed him that in their records, his name had been "Coinman" from day one.

"How could that happen?" Coinman exploded in anger. "Isn't the HR department supposed to help the employees, rather than harassing them?"

The executive pretended he did not hear him and said he failed to see the issue.

Helpless on this, Coinman took it up with his then-supervisor, who, to his relief, acknowledged this as a mistake and promised him to get it corrected. But the supervisor left the company the following week due to an unrelated matter.

"You can make any promises as long as you are not going to be there to fulfill them." Coinman confided in Ratiram, grinding his teeth.

Then he was introduced as Coinman to his next supervisor, who was appointed after much dust had already settled over the affair. That left no room for meaningful protest.

It was decided for Coinman by the stars above that he was to live the rest of his life with his new name.

Initially the new name seemed to force him into a different life filled with troubling glimpses of the past. He was inconsolably sad for several days.

His given name, Kesar, had been a birthday gift from his favorite uncle, Sukhi. Coinman recalled how his mother used to tell him the story of his name, and that until he was three years old, he went by several names. Spellbound by his innocent infancy, the uncles, the aunts, and the rest of his relatives had exhausted their respective warmhearted signature creativities in inventing these names: Tiktik, Peehoo, Kesar, Munna, Betu, Muaah, Puchcha, Chunnu, Chhona, Lal, Ladla, Laddu, PuchPuch, Happu, Paaru, and Daukast.

Daukast was his mother Kasturi's favorite, her own invention, for it partially incorporated her name as well as his father Daulat's. No one else liked it.

Uncle Sukhi came to their rescue. On Coinman's third birthday, Uncle Sukhi invited all the relatives to his own house. In the afternoon, after the guests were exhausted from playing games, chatting, and dining, Sukhi explained the gravity of the nameless situation and its potential effect on the child's future life if allowed to continue. He then conducted a poll by distributing a sheet of paper containing a list of all the prevailing names and asked everyone to tick the name of their choice.

There was a tie between Munna and Kesar for the top spot. The dilemma was short-lived after Uncle Sukhi declared, "The letter K always appears in the alphabet before the letter M. Given it's too late for experimenting with the surname now, if there is ever a situation where the alphabetical order of the first name is one of the criteria for a certain benefit, like assigning seats in a classroom, or standing in a queue, or assigning a roll number, or even determining a rank in the exam when all other criteria tie as well, 'Kesar' will outshine 'Munna.'" Everyone applauded the flawless logic.

"And before I forget to mention," Uncle Sukhi further declared, "the results of the state high school board examinations have just come in this morning, and you know what? A boy named Kesar is in first place. Can there be a more desirable coincidence?"

This sealed it. Kasturi added, to console the equal majority that favored "Munna," "I personally loved the name Munna. I promise that if we have another son in future, I am going to name him Munna."

Uncle Sukhi then labeled the child Kesar for the entire day, by putting a sticker on his forehead to cement only one name in everybody's mind.

With such an affectionate past behind his earlier name, Coinman felt a moral obligation to visit Uncle Sukhi; an apology over the phone was not proper penance for the fumble.

As he reached Uncle Sukhi's house, he saw, through the wrought iron gate, that Uncle Sukhi was sitting in his garden reading a newspaper. His left hand clenched the coins to stop the jingling sound for few moments. He silently opened the gate and approached Sukhi's chair with quiet steps. He covered his uncle's eyes with his right hand and wondered how to disguise his voice. He thought of holding his nose, but then rejected the idea, as that would have required him to free up his left hand from coins. Holding a handkerchief next to mouth was also out of the question for the same reason. He then thought of pretending a speech impediment, but rejected this because he had not practiced. He settled for muffling his voice by burying his mouth in his right shoulder and clenching his teeth at the same time.

Coinman's pondering over ways to modulate his voice had allowed Sukhi to grab at his hand for a few moments.

"Guess who?" Coinman said excitedly.

"Ramdin?"

"No."

"Shyamsundar?"

"No."

"Damn you, the grandson of your very own father-in-law!" cursed Sukhi in excitement. "Who the heck are you?"

"You have to guess."

"Only Ramdin and Shyamsundar stray here once in a while. I know of no one else who can visit this wasteland."

"Ta-da!" Coinman said, jumping to face his uncle, after releasing his eyes.

"Kesar. My son!" Sukhi shouted, and stood up to hug him. He appeared a bit embarrassed by his earlier teasing remarks. Sukhi held Coinman's hands affectionately to take him inside the house. He went into the kitchen and immediately started pumping the kerosene pressure stove to prepare tea, although Coinman noticed the tremor in his old hands dissipated a large fraction of the force he was trying to apply to the pump.

A retired clerk from the government water supply department, Uncle Sukhi stayed alone in his house. He hadn't married. Having no child of his own, he had always showered his share of love on the kids of his relations, and Coinman had received a lion's share. During Coinman's childhood, Uncle Sukhi had frequently visited the family to spend weeks just playing with Coinman, until his frequent visits caused fights between Coinman's parents, Daulat and Kasturi. During a particular visit, when Coinman was five years old, Daulat did not speak a word to Sukhi. Sukhi tried many times to strike up a conversation with him, but without luck. Kasturi too wasn't timely, either, with serving meals. Sukhi understood that Coinman's parents could not have allowed themselves to make a more explicit disapproval of his visits. He had left the house and never returned, even when Daulat had specifically invited him several times later.

Such delicacies are relationships.

Now that he was with Uncle Sukhi, Coinman did not know how to convey the purpose of his visit, so he suspended its mention until the opportunity surfaced on its own. Coinman stayed with his uncle for a week; they played cards, listened to old songs, went on long walks, and just sat in the park for long hours watching kids play.

At last, when Coinman was ready to leave, Uncle Sukhi kissed his hands and invited him to visit more often. He made no secret of considering himself indebted to Coinman for coming all the way from a distant city just to see an old man of no importance. The opportunity— probably the last one—was in Coinman's grasp to achieve the objective behind his visit; but his resolve failed him yet again. He couldn't bear the possibility of hurting Uncle

Sukhi. Uncle Sukhi forced a hundred-rupee bill into his hand before Coinman left.

With time Coinman came to terms with his new name. To bring uniformity to all references about him, he got his name changed accordingly outside the office, too: at banks, at government offices, on his ration card, on his barber's books, and everywhere else. He was formally honored by the neighborhood society for demonstrating a great spirit. He received broad applause during the award ceremony, when he summarized it all by saying, "What is there in a name? Mother Teresa—if she had been called by any other name, would it have mattered to the people she helped? Would it have made the reverential grand soul any less powerful? It's not the name but the character that is important. Can anyone ever change someone's character?"

Unlike the roots of his name, the roots of his profound interest in coins could never be traced with complete certainty. Everyone had to rely on a long-standing rumor that was universally promoted until it had acquired the status of verifiable truth.

The rumor said that his passion for coins dated back to the time when he was at the crawling age, when one newly discovers the mouth as a testing lab for everything that can fit in it.

Wallets were still in an evolving stage around that time, and most fathers instead used their breast pockets to carry money, bundled between other important paper chits. One day, home from the office, Daulat was struggling hard to take off his shirt after opening only the top two buttons, by stooping his head down to take the shirt off like a high-necked sweater—something that won him a lecture every time Kasturi saw it. As a result of his tussle with the shirt, despite his utmost care in putting his hand like a lid over his shirt pocket, its contents slipped to the ground. Coinman, a one-year-old child, who was crawling by his side, was completely captivated by the alluring sight of coins rolling to all sides. It was an instant crush, a love at first sight.

Laughing ecstatically, he scrambled to acquire the coins. But before he could reach them, Daulat collected all the coins—except for one that evaded Daulat's nimble eyes by rolling into a corner. The clever coin couldn't escape Coinman's admiring eyes, however. He pretended to be completely absorbed in trivial games until Daulat was out of sight. Then he crawled with lightning speed to the corner, ignoring the winter-cold marble floor. Within seconds the coin was in his mouth, where it voluntarily slipped farther down to salute his Adam's apple. Sensing the endeavor turning into a nightmare, the child howled as loud as he could.

Daulat ran back to him and, per the usual practice, rolled a finger in his mouth forcefully. He tried to drag the coin up, but the finger was not able to grab it well despite a bend at the tip. So he brought his second finger into play to form a pincer, not to the increased convenience of the child. This had an adverse outcome: the coin slipped much farther down and couldn't be reached with a finger. The father at once panicked and called the mother, the grandmother, and, above them all, the great-grandmother. The ladies of the house experimented with various remedies—a number of things that they had witnessed work in such cases. They made the child swallow melted clarified butter, turmeric paste, and, most importantly, the cow urine shake with crushed basil leaves. When the homemade therapeutic efforts of old and very old women in the house failed, Coinman was rushed to an emergency room.

A doctor examined Coinman and found that everything was just fine; the coin seemed to have made it all the way down. But the doctor was shocked when the family told him that Coinman hadn't had a bowel movement after swallowing the coin, because the X-ray and the ultrasound couldn't find any traces of a coin in his body.

"The best explanation science can provide," the doctor said, "is that the child's digestive system is exceptionally strong. I have never seen one that even comes close to this.

In short, his system has already dissolved the coin into waste."

But the most authoritative rumor at his office didn't agree with the doctor's finding. It instead said that the coin had actually gone straight to the child's brain and had instated itself there permanently. The coin had assumed the driver's seat in his mind to conceive and direct all his actions thereafter.

Being in a unique position to explain Coinman's absorbing addiction, the rumor quickly became, in most people's minds, fact.

4. The Gossipmongers

*O*n the first floor, the first rule of a rumor was humor.

The first-floor junta had this rule deeply inscribed in their minds through their own welcome program for new employees.

Thus Coinman was the best topic, one of the very few to easily prompt a rumor with humor.

The gossips around Coinman went on to speculate about him at almost ridiculously detailed levels. They wondered if he used the same set of coins all the time, or if he replaced them every day. They also speculated that his father had some sort of a derangement that was slowly spreading to Coinman's brain as well; that Coinman lacked courage to speak a argumentative word to his wife and agreed to everything she said; that he was having a secret love affair with a close relative, which was devastating his family life; that he'd had an abusive childhood; and that a local hooligan had once beaten him badly right in front of his house when he raised an objection to the former's ingenious attempts to target Kasturi, his mother, with intimately suggestive remarks—a verbal rape.

Daya, one of the top suppliers of such speculations, and who looked for opportunities to flatter members of his gang by publicly glorifying them, once claimed that Coinman had an exclusive inside pocket in the main pocket of his trousers to safely carry the coins. Everyone knew Daya hadn't done any investigation—it was just one of those fabricated stories shared in gossip sessions with the sincerity of one providing a verifiable truth.

The cafeteria on the first floor adjacent to the main hall, originally intended to serve tea and light snacks, was now used as a boulevard for brewing gossip sourced from every possible corner of the office, with a special affinity for matters related to Coinman. As soon as someone witnessed a marvelous act from Coinman, he got everyone to rush to the cafeteria at once to babble about it over a tea. The only exception was Tulsi, the only woman on the first floor. She did not join these gossip sessions because she had apparently been taught right from her early childhood, as Daya had once revealed to everyone, that when a number of grown-up men get together in an informal environment, it is next to impossible for them to remain honorable enough for a woman's presence.

Coinman also skipped these sessions, unaware that he was their common theme. He had been to a session only once, when, under the influence of a momentary tide of curiosity, he fell in behind the folks rushing to the cafeteria. On seeing him enter, everyone had sunk into a deep silence. That had magnified the sounds of the sipping of tea and of the coins jangling in his pocket. He held on as long as he could, knowing very well that once outside, he wasn't going to try this again. He wanted only to stay till the end this time, to quench his mind once and for all about what really went on in these sessions that excited everyone to such a degree. Instead, to his disappointment, people started leaving, one by one. He left after everyone else and resolved that unless it was a matter of life and death, he wasn't going to join these sessions ever again.

It was hard to tell if the interesting proceedings on the first floor, including these gossip sessions, were secretly encouraged by the management because they built deeper bonds among the employees, or if they still had no clue about it all; they hardly came down to the first floor. When they wanted to have a meeting with someone, they typically called the person to their offices on the second floor.

Although most of the gossip sessions transpired quite spontaneously, a few participants attended more frequently than others. Hukum, Daya, Sevak, Panna, and Ratiram were just about always present. In fact, the associates on the first floor believed that nothing at the office happened without being on Ratiram's radar. Some of them facetiously said that God's calendar of events was provided to Ratiram before the events happened. They were not to be blamed because even when Ratiram did not attend a particular session, he somehow knew everything that was discussed.

Saarang, too, joined most of these sessions, but rarely spoke at any of them, as he suffered from a massive and incurable lack of self-confidence. On top of that, he was very lazy and self-centered, especially in matters related to romantic possibilities. During his college days, he wouldn't think twice before ditching an activity planned in advance with his best male buddies for the smallest prospect of a girl's company.

The other associates were also a regular in these gossip sessions, if they could altogether be considered as a single entity. Despite a few individuals missing now and then, the strength was generally consistent, governed by some sort of law of averages that Hukum was the first one to point out to the group.

The folks who missed a particular session would follow up with the ones who had attended. The ones who had attended seemed to feel handcuffed by social obligation, a byproduct of the evolution of cooperative venom against Coinman, to apprise the rest of the latest.

So when someone witnessed a "marvelous" act from Coinman, he quickly gathered the others and rushed to the cafeteria. This usually started a chain of stories. The overstated stories about Coinman were then tossed back and forth from mouth to mouth. Everyone was equal in these gossip sessions when it came to scoffing at Coinman.

The gossipmongers took this opportunity to show off their ability to generate good humor, ideas, and imaginary tales. The ability to speak well in these gossip sessions had long been a means of obtaining recognition and respect in first-floor society. Those who had it were listened to with respect, and their initiatives were better entertained in general, even outside the cafeteria's confines.

A few could never get ideas; their type, seen in abundance in mass employment, tried hard to throw something out just for the sake of active participation in these discussions, often putting the most emphasis on things of low relevance. Out of discretion and the wish to avoid fruitless conflict, none of the accomplished critics commented candidly on these sorts of ideas. They, however, took mental note of the donors of such ideas and adjusted their personal rating grid with the donors' new standing. This rating grid, maintained in their minds, was deemed very useful for them for possible future dealings with such individuals.

Close colleagues even exchanged notes on particular people's standing on their respective mental grids. In fact, doing this strengthened the bond of friendship between them. After all, nothing nurtures a friendship bond more than the ability to consistently bitch about someone else.

Ratiram was the most trusted source of information for certifying the veracity of a rumor. If someone inaugurated a new rumor that couldn't naturally convince others, Ratiram was requested to verify it. That provided Ratiram with yet another opportunity to demonstrate his scholastic stature. To steer clear of accidentally displaying a sense of pride, he would first start on a low agreeable note, and then slowly increase the rational touches before delving into profound analysis of the matter.

This was not entirely the same strategy he'd employed a few years before. His intellectual prowess hadn't been fully revealed yet then and, being a low-ranking employee, he knew such methods might hurt others' pride unintentionally.

So he had adopted a jovially dramatic method: he'd pretend to be Sherlock Holmes putting his audience in a good humor, free of rank pride, while he conveyed his findings in the most refined manner; he'd even contemplate the matter visibly by repeatedly putting his palm below his chin and fingers over the right temple. This way he washed away any possibility of bitterness emerging from his being able to discuss important matters more intellectually than others.

Through such thoughtful conduct, Ratiram climbed on the personal rating grids until he was openly declared the most gifted member by the first-floor society. No one could gauge the actual depth of his thoughts, yet everyone was a great aficionado of the captivating spells he managed to cast over them by way of disentangling complex matters and crisply articulating at the same time.

"Coinman lets out another legendary explosive from his hindquarters!" Panna, whose fabric of language often had vulgarity woven very artfully into it, called out to Daya at the top of his voice as he entered the office one day, throwing his bag to his table from a distance. Daya rushed behind him to enter the cafeteria. It was only a minute before many others joined them, too.

"This is really kick-ass, guys," Panna told them, settling on a chair. "Our Coinman is a rare gem. I heard this story from a clerk in my bank."

"I can't wait." Sevak dragged a chair right next to Panna.

"I needed to get some humdrum stuff done at the bank yesterday, and noticed the clerk was paying odd attention to our firm's name," Panna continued. "He even mumbled the name a few times. You all know me, how good I am in smelling the bizarre shit! So I yanked his sack a bit—by asking him if he was trying to make up his mind to buy our firm."

Hukum could not help laughing aloud and smacked his right palm against Panna's in a high five.

"He laughed at my joke, then asked me reluctantly if I happened to know someone called Coinman."

"This is getting freaky." Daya said.

"Yes, indeed; and a real trip, too," Panna said. "I was so damn excited on hearing this that I could not allow him to dillydally any further. But if I asked the details then, in Dullsville, the chances were high that the cheese hog wouldn't be able to tell me details properly."

"Get back to the story," Hukum said impatiently. "I don't care about the fatso. I want to hear about our own superman."

"Do you really have to blow this popsicle stand to catch a cotton-candy train?" Panna countered heatedly. "What's the damn hurry? The meat in the story remains uncooked until we slowly build it up. Why do you want to jump to the end so soon?"

"OK, all right. Carry on, I will filter the irrelevant part at the very entrance of my ear," said Hukum with a smile.

Panna clearly wanted to retort, but set his emotions aside to continue.

"All right. So I invited the fat-ass to my home on Sunday for a few drinks. The bastard did not open up until he finished half my stock of Scotch, but once he opened up, he seemed overly obliged to go out of his way to provide any information on Coinman that would please me. The butt-head even tried to guess things about Coinman."

"I wonder if they were aware of the power of complimentary alcohol during World War I." Ratiram commented.

"I am sorry," said Sevak, who had been twisting the top button on his shirt while listening. "But if we continue at this speed, it's going to take years to finish. That wouldn't be bad, though...we can have our grandchildren join in as well."

"This is not horseshit. It's a real story—I can't cut it short." Panna got up as though ready to leave.

"Hey, don't take it to heart, buddy," Saarang said. "We are just trying to have some fun here."

Hukum held both his ears in an apologizing gesture and motioned with his hand to request Panna go back to his chair.

Panna sighed and went back to his chair to continue. "Anyway, it turned out that Coinman had been to the bank to invest some money, the details of which are not significant to the story. Don't look so smug, Sevak—I am not cutting it short for fear of you."

Everyone laughed.

"So," Panna went on, "they gave Coinman a typical bank form with a huge number of terms and conditions. The representative who served Coinman told him that it was all regular stuff, and he only had to sign each page."

"Hold on here," said Hukum. "Do you mean to say that the fatso did not actually serve Coinman?"

"That's a very smart catch. You are right. The fat-ass heard the story from his colleagues—it's a big topic of discussion, it seems," Panna answered.

"We are becoming famous," Saarang said.

"Coinman insisted on reading the terms and conditions word for word, on all twenty-odd pages." Panna continued. "Coinman told them that without reading it fully, how was he to know that there was nothing objectionable in it? He asked the representative to imagine she was a crook in a masquerade who had curried favor with many of the bank officers to rob gullible people like him. He concluded that she would see his point, how a swindler could easily receive one's signature deceivingly on manipulated text. On hearing this from Coinman, she could not see any hope in arguing further."

"Wait a minute. Some honest advice," Daya put in. "Let's place an order for both lunch and dinner now. I am sure this story will go on till dinnertime."

Panna glared at Daya without verbally responding, and continued.

"The scumbags asked Coinman to take the form to his house, read the conditions, and give it back, but Coinman started arguing with them, saying that they did not like his presence in the bank. He then wanted to meet the manager of customer relations to complain that his presence seemed to offend the bank executives. And when the manager came to meet him, Coinman turned around and laughed. He told the manager that there was no issue after all—he only wanted to meet the manager to find out if everything was going fine with the bank, as some concerns were expressed in the morning newspaper about the institution's financial health. The manager dismissed any awareness of such news and inquired about the newspaper. Coinman shrugged and said he could not recall the newspaper. He offered to call the manager later, if he would share his phone number. The manager didn't seem to like this and left without a word."

Everyone was laughing by now. "Brilliant," Hukum said. "It's been a while since I last heard of something that hilarious."

"I really commiserate with the bank manager!" Sevak said. "The poor soul must have had a tough time sleeping that night. His laugh is the most unbearable thing—well, only after his coins. I have not had a chance to hear a devil's newborn's laugh yet, but I am quite sure it's very like Coinman's."

"Beyond a shadow of a doubt," said Ratiram, putting his cup on the table after the last sip, "and the best explanation I can think of behind such a laugh is not being able to form a good style of laughing because of a serious lack of opportunities to laugh. Each time he encounters a situation that prompts his laughing glands, he works hard to manufacture a better laughing sound than he did the last time, but, on the contrary, ends up with a coarser sound. If he just tried to build on his previous laughter, laughing more frequently, he might have developed a normal laughing style by now."

"That seems like good logic," replied Daya, "but has he not been observing others and seen how they laugh? Can't he see that his way of laughing is clearly singled out?"

"Goddamn it, that's why you are not Coinman!" said Panna with a chuckle.

"Hmmm...Coinman. Hee...hee...hee...Coinman!" All eyes rolled to Sevak as he blurted while trying to rub clean a spot on the table with his fingers, seemingly in his own trip somewhere at the moment.

"Someone please bring an ambulance from the nearest madhouse," shouted Daya. "We have a mental emergency here. Our noble pal Sevak has just been wickedly divorced by his mind."

"I am sorry for my brief absent-mindedness." Sevak said, smiling. "I swear, every time I hear this name it makes me laugh clear down to my bones. I feel victorious and comic, both at the same time, when I think about our role in dubbing him Coinman."

"Mr. Sevak, you are entitled to only one *sorry* per month. But you have spent four *sorry*s just today. You have accumulated concerning debt already and need to watch your spending habits immediately. We have decided to help and accept not more than two *sorry*s a month from you from now on," Hukum put in with mock authority.

"Why"—Daya had been waiting to respond to Sevak —"it is not that unusual. I happen to know this man called Sawaal Singh. He was born just five months after his mother's arranged marriage. So when he was born, people said that his mother had not really given birth to a human but to a question. His real name was Sanjog, the destiny, but people only called him "Sawaal," a question."

A laughter filled the air in the room.

"But the story doesn't end here." Panna wasn't going to give up yet. "Our esteemed superman was back to the bank the next day with his unfinished shit. His unsatisfied intercourse on the previous night with every paragraph in the agreement text was marked with yellow highlighter everywhere. The representative patiently explained the yellow poop. This incident has made our superman a legend at the bank, too. They now have a joke floating around.

Whenever they confront a brain-eating customer, they classify him in their records as 'Coinman.'"

"The legend of Coinman! We should make a movie, guys. I bet it's going to be an instant hit," Daya added.

The group laughed wholeheartedly.

"On a serious note," Hukum said, seizing the opportunity, "without putting our veterans here on the spot, it truly amazes me at times that despite the dolor that the coins cause us, we have been able to put up with the pain for so many years." He paused to assess the silent reaction, gauging the level of aggression the group needed to do something about it.

"This is no martyrdom that we are doomed to suffer for our entire lives," he went on more gently. "It's good that we are able to generate good humor out of this to somewhat reduce our anguish, but the coins torture us not only at the office but also at home. On the bus, in a taxi, while eating, playing, sleeping—I can hear that shameless, wicked sound all the time. It's like the coins have been placed permanently in our minds."

As soon as Hukum paused, Panna started clapping, in irony.

"What's new in this shit, other than smelling of utter futility?" Panna said with brutal pugnacity. "Are you just waking from a ludicrous dream? Or maybe you've just been time traveling. Hasn't it always been like that? Enlighten us, then—why this sudden melodrama?"

"You are right," replied Hukum, suppressing his irritation. "All I mean is—we've got to stop this now. We cannot go on suffering like this. If we believe in ourselves, we can stop it. It just requires some clever thinking, planning, and team effort."

Saarang had been trying to speak for the past few minutes; finally he gathered enough courage. "Coins jingling in that manner in the pocket are a sign of a poor man, and this may jeopardize the image of our company by leading outsiders to think that employees here are very poorly paid."

That proclamation deserved askance looks, and got them. Many of them immediately lowered Saarang's standing on their respective mental grids.

"That's my feeling, too," Daya said, ignoring Saarang's remark but responding to Hukum. "I feel the same as Hukum does. But what can possibly be done? I am no pessimist, but at this point, like always, it seems all bark but no bite to me. Once we go back to our desks, it will be another day tomorrow, and we will again completely forget about the present emotion. Do you have any tentative action plan, off the top of your head?"

"The perfect thing would be for all of us to hijack all his coins together," responded Hukum bitingly. "But knowing this would require a huge amount of planning, I suggest that we try a milder approach first. We should first try to open a dialogue with him to see if that can help. One of us should approach him and make him aware of our concern with his coins."

Daya immediately agreed. "Yes, many times a huge problem gets solved with a trivial move. It's only a matter of effort."

"But who would put a bell on that cat's neck?" asked Sevak, trying to gauge at the same time if he needed to shave by constantly running his left hand subtly over his lower face. "Hukum, why don't you go and talk to him about it?"

"Why not? And all of you could sit there and enjoy the exhibition. Are you guys not afflicted as much as I am?" Hukum countered. "It's a deadly sin to ask someone who has come up with a bright idea to carry it out as well. It's like getting penalized for doing something good. It's decided. We shall all go and talk to him."

"No, that will not be a good idea," said Ratiram firmly. "I hear you, Hukum, but if we go together, it may make it difficult. Firstly, he may panic by the enormity of our effort, and secondly, putting an excessively large team on a small and precise task could only multiply the unforeseen challenges. If you all have no objection, I can take this on myself."

"Ratiram, I completely agree on employing only one person in this task. But I apologize beforehand for countering your proposal. I suggest that you do not get yourself involved in this," said Sevak, while his left hand intimately massaged its owner's face. "If you do, we will lose a bridge to access Coinman's mind. He treats you as his best friend, in fact, and it's only to you that he talks about his thoughts with indubitable honesty. We would lose this secret channel if he finds out you are a part of this."

"So, here, it's all decided now." Hukum raised his right hand above his head. "I'll take it on myself. I know it will be tough, I have never had a word with him; but to settle this business about coins, I will do my best. Bless me, my dear friends."

"That's a great spirit," shouted Daya with excitement, performing an impromptu high five with Hukum. "Folks, isn't that impressive? How my precious friend maintains two complementary sides of him? On one hand, he is the master of wit, the perfect humorist, and on the other hand, he is so sincere toward his duties. Ratiram, we need a few words from you, buddy. Have you ever met a person with such vividly different sides? Isn't it a true mark of a genius?"

"Daya," cried Hukum, "this is no time for pulling my leg."

"No kidding," Panna said, and laughed.

"Stop. I really meant it. Ratiram—please say something."

All eyes immediately settled on Ratiram, who paused to think before he spoke.

"Sure. Hukum is a fantastic buddy," he said quietly. "The high degree of wit that he possesses is seldom found in a dedicated man." He took a deep breath, cast an empty look at Hukum, and continued, "However, I am not sure if demonstration of two completely distinct sides is truly indicative of a genius. If you talk in terms of likelihood, yes, a person with different sides probably has above-par chances to be a genius. But it's not injective."

"Injective?" Saarang caught the word.

"Yes. All I meant," Ratiram explained, "is that if you pick a genius, he would have two or more distinct sides. But if you pick a person with two or more distinct sides, the person may not be a genius."

"Got it. I understand it now. Thanks!" Saarang said.

"Saarang, dude," Panna said quickly, "can you now explain it back to us? I am not sure if I necessarily understood it."

Everyone knew that Panna was pulling Saarang's leg. But Saarang's face turned pale with nervousness. Thankfully, to his relief, Ratiram continued.

"As you know," Ratiram said, "even the most sophisticated personalities are not reasonable in all situations. Many of the best people have an entirely different side, a rather dreadful one. For example—keep it within the four walls—Jay, our beloved unit head, is an ideal man for all office matters. But I have witnessed a completely different side of him—a horrible one, if I may say."

Everyone was shocked at that. Despite the perfect setting in these gossip sessions to lavishly flout their supervisors, they had refrained from dragging Jay's name in. They had big respect for him for his sincere attempts to improve the workplace. They couldn't have been more impatient to hear Jay's mysterious side.

"It happened a long time back," Ratiram began, "when Jay was still a middle manager. He happened to make an urgent business trip to another city, and I accompanied him to help with all the running around. We had to put up in a hotel which had only one room available for the night. Back then we did not have many of today's conveniences—like another department taking care of the travel in advance—so we had to find lodging on our own and get it reimbursed later.

"Anyway, Jay was visibly uncomfortable with the idea of sharing the room with me. I wanted to help him out by offering to sleep outside at the reception area. Even though I knew very well that the hotel staff was not going to allow me to do that, I wanted to convey to Jay that I was willing to assist him as best I could. He declined my proposal to ensure no inconvenience to me, but I also figured out that if there was another room available, he would have paid whatever price to sleep privately.

"His reluctance in sharing the room really intrigued me, because, as you know, it's very common in our culture for two males to share a room with two separate beds. I am sure he would have had plenty of occasions to share his room with another male. So what could have made him so uncomfortable about it? He was also not a man who ever believed in ranks, hierarchy, or social class. I was very curious.

"After finishing dinner that we had ordered in the room itself, Jay opened a book and sank deep into it within a few minutes. On the other hand, I slept immediately, like a tired lion who returns to his house in the jungle from a wearing day trip to the city.

"I do not know what time exactly he went to sleep, but something strange happened that night—something that opened another facet of the human psyche.

"A loud shouting voice woke me up from my deep slumber. It was pitch-dark in the room. I rubbed my eyes, but couldn't see anything, not the tiniest spark. I pinched my left arm hard—I even hurt myself—just to make sure that I wasn't in a dream. It took about a minute to be fully in reality, and my ears could now grasp what was being said. Jay was swearing badly.

"I was horrified at first. I brooded over the possibility of him standing next to my bed, even feared he might possibly attack me."

"Come on!" Said Daya, "Jay can't harm an ant in his dreams."

"Daya, wouldn't you agree that when you witness one immeasurably unexpected act from someone, all your trust in that person flies in a matter of seconds?" Ratiram said.

"That horrible shit would make me suspicious of my own mother. I don't blame you." Panna supported the argument.

"No analysis, guys," Hukum said bossily. "You're spoiling the flow of this mesmerizing story."

"Then, Jay's shouting became more and more meaningful," Ratiram carried on. "He was naming people and seemed very offended by a certain girl who cared a lot about a set of individuals. I could not make much of who these people were. He was quickly changing the context. One moment he was shouting from the stands in a game of cricket, the next moment he had a complaint about his parents, and before you knew, he was confessing something to a vicar.

"By now I had a good idea of his location in the room. When it seemed safe to get up from the bed, and when lying down amidst this tornado was no longer possible, I courageously got up and looked for the switch for the light. Jay had operated it the previous night, so I could only make my best guess. I moved in the direction of the door with my hands stretched ahead of me to save me from stumbling. Luckily, I found the switch there and turned it on rapidly. The bright light pinched my eyes; and there he was, sitting in a yoga posture in his bed, with his back resting against the wall, still shouting. Surprisingly, that sudden intense flash of light had absolutely no impact on him.

"I went and stood in front of him with questioning eyes, but he failed to notice me. So I shook him by his shoulders. He gave me blank looks, stopped shouting immediately, and dropped onto the bed to sleep again. His instant dive into peace suggested that he was under some kind of spell.

"His behavior in the morning had no trace of midnight's big incident. But surprisingly, about two months later, he asked me if I had slept well that night. Unless he suspected something bizarre had happened that night, why would he ask me about it? Suddenly, after two months! In all fairness, I could deduce that he smartly timed this question so that if nothing had happened that night, I would not think too much of it. At the same time, he wanted to assess from my response if it happened, what he thought could have happened, so that he could apologize and grab the occasion to ask me to bury the secret forever. To make him comfortable, I told him that I slept so deeply that night I did not know where I was until I woke up in the morning."

"God bless you, Ratiram," said Daya, still wandering in the story. "I have felt at times that there is something unusual about that man. You know what? Sometimes I have a feeling that Jay is secretly in love with our golden girl, Tulsi."

"No. That's not correct," cried Saarang. "It's not true."

"Don't you think your tongue is straying in the danger zone too much today?" Daya teased Saarang. "Can you disprove Jay's love for Tulsi?"

"No," replied Saarang feebly.

"Then zip your lip, would you?"

"Daya, excuse me, but let's not bring our golden girl into this sort of conversation," interrupted Sevak. "She hardly speaks to anyone."

"Jay is no nitwit either," Panna added. "At the office, he wouldn't poke at a romantic possibility with a six-foot stick."

"All right, OK, fine, sorry, wrong topic." said Daya smilingly. "But the thought wasn't so unreasonable as to deserve a miniature revolt. One of my friends works for an electronics company, and they recently hired a young girl of twenty-three. It was a rumor that a senior executive of fifty had a crush on her. No one believed it until the marriage invitation went out. Many young hearts were broken; but the girl wasn't heedful of them in the first place. One never knows how these matters take turns. Sometimes, I feel that beautiful girls and money seem to go very well together."

"Whoa! Let's not doubleplus debase the entire good-looking female fraternity here." It was Panna's opportunity to play Mr. Nice, which he rarely was perceived as.

"Panna, firstly, stop going to cheap stores and start using branded earbuds," Daya retorted. "That's how we chat here. Remind yourself that I am not speaking on national TV. Secondly, I am not exactly the type of person who would think of a woman as loose if she has put on massive makeup, but also, I am not the one who wouldn't express himself for the fear of how others might think."

Sevak tried to mellow the conversation. "Also, it nauseates me how foolishly these pretty girls fall for those monkey sorts of guys. Hell, it's enough to make me lose sleep at night when I see a lovely girl in the market going with a ridiculous guy."

"I have a confession to make." Daya spoke contemplatively. "I feel sorry about a momentary lapse of my reason in associating our golden girl with Jay. I have appreciated how she has carried herself in the most elegant manner. There are a thousand beautiful women out there, but only a handful of them possess the grace required by such beauty to stop it from looking ugly."

This conclusive remark from Daya was given a standing ovation by everyone before the long gossip session was dismissed.

5. The Pizzazz

*T*ulsi's charisma, the Elysian dazzle, was the only other theme that could compete with Coinman's in the gossip sessions. Tulsi, beyond any perceivable clouds of skepticism, was the best living form of beauty known—the matchless delight, the most generous blessing granted to a human eyeball. Her beauty effortlessly managed to arrest the pulse of each heart at the office and keep it in a dreamlike cage where she could have a look at each at her will and derive pleasure that, it had to be said, was a touch malicious in nature. This is where the whole thing entered into a vicious cycle, for her proximity always inebriated the hearts, thus only deepening their desire to remain hostages in the cages so that they could booze even more on that beauty.

She had a mischievous pair of feet, not less beautiful than her whole self, slender, soft, with long thin toes unfailingly adorned with trendy nail polish, easily visible through her thin, flat sandals. She frequently meandered around on those restless feet through the office on the slightest opportunity, to walk, to cut, to tease through the devoted fondness that the office staff possessed for her. As she walked the narrow zigzag pathways among desks, one end to the other, everyone ogled her with eyes growing bigger by the moment.

During these proceedings at the office, when she walked through royally, almost doing an unreturnable favor to the ground beneath, and the men around, everything seemed to come to a halt. The splendor of her walk mortified everything else at the moment. She was no less than an angelic cynosure, viewers' unanimous choice among all other captivating distractions; the ruthless empress among indebted slaves.

During these magical walks, she was consummately aware of the starving yet modestly unclaiming eyes that moved in harmony with her motion. She never failed to seize the opportunity to add special effects to make the whole phenomenon look even more extraordinary: walking in slow motion as if gravity had bestowed an exceptional beauty allowance to her by reducing its strength to half; or running her hand slowly through her long, silken hair while smiling randomly into the eyes of the gaping faces.

The knocking sound made by vigorously leaping hearts at once transmitted her to cloud nine, a feeling she had become addicted to at an early age and could no longer live without experiencing a few times a day.

The freshness that Tulsi's brief walk brought to the place usually lasted much longer than the lovely sight of her. The impressed audience looked in the direction of her disappearance for minutes afterward, slowly turning back to reality with a heavy feeling hard to describe.

Every time she had her magical walk, she made every heart fonder. Everyone had a personal name to call her, but "our golden girl" was the most widely accepted one. As folks got home from work in the evenings, they rushed through their time at home, just as a reader skips through the uninteresting sections of a book, to be at the office again to provide contentment to their hungry spirits.

If by any chance Tulsi happened to be on vacation, or sick, or away for any other reasons, the office looked dull and heavy as a burial ground. To handle such situations individually, each of her fellow workers had installed a personal copy of her magical walks in his mind to take a look at when she was absent.

The deficiency of girls at the office wasn't to be blamed for the romantic emotions that dwelt for Tulsi in each heart;

Tulsi had an undeniable universal appeal. For instance, when she occupied a table in a restaurant, men sitting there slowly adjusted their seats to a good angle for an uninterrupted view of her beauty. Along the same lines, when she shopped in a street market, the shop she went in suddenly saw an incredible influx of customers. As she walked in the busy market, even the shopkeepers—who normally had ample opportunities to be face-to-face with beauty, and thus were more likely to grow somewhat indifferent to it—found it difficult to cling to a jaded attitude.

There was a recent rumor that Saarang, who did not have any advantage over others that called for a special mention, had lately been trying to establish a communion with Tulsi. That he'd recently started to cross Tulsi's path deliberately, during her magical walks, to make her notice him. There was no accompanying rumor about a positive reaction from Tulsi. Thus, no one paid any attention to Saarang's futile attempts; his persona was so minuscule compared to Tulsi's that giving any importance to the rumor would have seemed an unjust promotion in Saarang's social status.

As much as they were in the face of everyone else, Tulsi's magical walks weren't even noticed by Coinman. His lack of attention to her charisma irritated her. Only a fraction of her charm was enough to distract the soul of a spiritual counselor, so she was clueless about what it would take to impress Coinman. She started doing her own personal research on him; not because of her interest in him, but because of his lack of interest in her. She hadn't ever seen a man like him.

Coinman was constantly in a rush, rummaging through papers at his desk. Panna claimed once to have observed him for long enough to deduce that he shuffled papers completely uselessly to kill time.

Despite the fact that people at the office talked so much about Coinman, they really knew very little about him. No one could surely say what Coinman worked on each day or how much he worked except for his supervisor—who never came down to the first floor.

"How much more time are you going to take to complete that tiny task?" his supervisor had once asked him at his desk, making all eyes turn at once toward them.

Coinman, aware of the curiosity of his colleagues, did not respond immediately. He merely lifted his right hand and waved to the supervisor to wait while he searched for something important—among the papers lying on the table, in the drawers, beneath the table, in all corners of his mind. Growing very displeased, looking at his supervisor with accusing eyes, as though the supervisor had caused irreparable harm by interrupting in the middle of critical work, Coinman asked, "If it is of no inconvenience to you, can I explain that in your office, sir?"

Thereafter they went to the supervisor's office on the second floor. Coinman appeared again at his desk an hour later, smiling to himself. Thenceforth no one ever saw Coinman's supervisor at his desk.

Rumors said that when Coinman joined the firm, he was made to roam, boss to boss, desk to desk, and morning to evening, asking for work, but no one came forward to define his job. It was too late when someone tried to define his responsibilities years later during a company reorganization; by that time Coinman had started assigning work to himself and monitoring it himself. It was found that he set his own goals at the start of the year and neutrally assessed himself against them at the end of the year. He then sent his performance report to his official supervisor for his signature.

6. The Goatee Axiom

*A*cross the board at the office there was a belief, an unproved theorem, about Coinman's blind faith in Ratiram: that if one thought Coinman would willingly sip a cup of botulinum if Ratiram wished it, one still underestimated the reverence that dwelt in Coinman's heart for Ratiram.

Coinman relayed the information in his heart only to Ratiram, his best friend of the past few years and a guide in his own opinion, someone he shared everything with—his joys and anguishes, excitements and apprehensions, convictions and trepidations, triumphs and learning experiences. Such was the wavelength between them, Coinman fancied, that when Ratiram proposed to call him just "Coin," Coinman dearly subscribed to it, feeling that it brought a sense of brotherly care, a pledge of the hand of a true well-wisher.

"The world definitely would be a much better place," Coinman often cogitated, "if everyone had a friend like Ratiram."

What Coinman didn't know was that it was a one-sided brotherhood: Ratiram held a covert unfeeling intention in the companionship.

The gossipmongers not only anesthetized their minds to coin-trauma through stealthy gossiping about Coinman, but also took him for a ride, whenever they could afford to, through a flurry of unending hoaxes. Ratiram was considered a champion by all for employing the most outstanding hoaxes; he had over ten years of experience in successfully deluding Coinman without awakening his suspicion. In fact, he executed these hoaxes so well that Coinman rather thought of them as opportune ventures. Ratiram designed minor ploys, creating a wall of deceit around Coinman's vision, to trap him in situations that became delightful spectacles for the gossipmongers. This way Ratiram remained dear to both—to Coinman and to those who enjoyed Coinman's troubles.

As a teacher feeds the pupils on knowledge, Ratiram fed the whole office on Coinman's secrets. He found it very recreational to first maneuver Coinman into sharing his secrets and then relay them to the gossipmongers, after adding his own aromatic spices. He achieved paramount cerebral pleasure on seeing his colleagues enjoy these accounts. He ardently observed Coinman's activities from a distance to contrive ways around him, went extra miles to invent a fresh endeavor, and invested copious time pondering over its logistics. As his fellows devotedly looked up to him for these tidbits, Ratiram felt it little less than his duty to oblige them with the best fun he could bring.

As it happened, on this day Ratiram found Hukum's promise to speak to Coinman a timely development, one that immediately opened his mind's door to a new way to add another feather to his cap. On the following day he dropped by Coinman's desk during lunchtime, when no one was around.

Finding that Coinman was lost in his files, Ratiram hissed into his ears, "Find a few minutes, quickly. I've got a stinky alert for you."

Ratiram's voice had brought about a wave in the deep personal world Coinman inhabited at that moment, plucking him instantly from it. He raced his mind to retrieve what Ratiram had just said—as though from some sort of large, invisible communal memory that stored everything that had ever been said.

Nervously sensing something adverse, Coinman had all he could do to keep his chin from vibrating.

Ratiram slanted his forehead toward the ceiling, as though complaining to God about the unnecessary nuisance that people had created to badger Coinman. Then, looking straight at Coinman's face, he frowned as he spoke. "Don't panic as I say this. Someone is going to talk to you about your coins. Your colleagues aren't great fans of your coins."

The nervous malaise turned into anger. "Ratiram, I do not understand what damage I have done them," Coinman seethed. "I have drained my brain completely for a decent explanation. I haven't figured out what could cause such spite."

"Coin," said Ratiram affectionately, "don't take it to heart. The problems are here to stay. We need to find a way to deal with them."

"Ratiram, I always do my best to be nice. I know I am a person with habits—and quite honestly, I have tried hard in the past to part with my coin-habit but the results of my attempts were so unbearably painful. I would give anything to abandon this habit, if that could be achieved painlessly. Perhaps a topic for another time. The point is, what business is it of theirs to condemn my personal habits? Have I ever complained about Daya when he digs his nose for gold and did I mention the joint venture of his thumb and index finger in safely processing the gold?"

"Ick! That's actually funny, Coin." Ratiram laughed with his right hand on his stomach. "Coin—you are a genius."

Coinman's mood was relaxed, too. Smiling now, he said, "Ratiram—I know you are saying this to raise my spirits. I can't help getting frustrated sometimes. The way I have been treated here has often affected my behavior. In the past few years, I've changed from the jovial person I was to a timid and naïve loser who is waiting to be exploited."

Coinman looked away to let the emotional surge settle before he could speak again in a reflective tone, "The life has been perversely bad-tempered toward me. She comes to me, yells at me, spits right in my eyes, and disappears in annoyance without even saying good-bye. Sometimes, when she is in a kooky state of mind, she does not hesitate to remove my clothes just to make it a compelling sight for others."

"Coin, your sense of humor has been legendary today! To your point about life, you are fortunate to see her, in whatever form she breezes in. It's truly great that life is giving you at least something. For many, it doesn't show up in the first place. I am sure, for the amicable person you are, life will not only eventually embrace you but also kiss you on your forehead with her very own tender lips."

Coinman could not figure out an immediate response. He felt humbled by this. Anxious for a response, he hurried to speak the first thing that came to mind.

"Ratiram, as plain as I can be—I am not looked upon with much respect, and people haven't been generous in praising my efforts. On the other hand, I have not let slip any opportunity to praise anyone. My most original ideas are not well received. Others' mediocre ideas are published to the whole office with rewards! I have endured this silently for all these years. I don't want to sound defensive; this will help you see the full range of my grief."

"Coin, I understand, but you know, many times we fancy things are much more intense than they truly are." Ratiram dragged one chair from the inner circle of desks.

"I have even tried to look at the situation from a distance, like watching my own soccer game from the stands, but I did not notice a difference."

"Coin, I was just trying to alleviate your worries a bit. I do see your point."

"Thanks," Coinman said. "So now the next question is, how can I earn more respect without having to ask for it?"

Seeing that this launched Ratiram into deep brainwork, he added, "Of course, you don't have to answer now, you can take your time. I can wait."

Ratiram responded as if he hadn't heard the last statement from Coinman. "Coin, with the wolves around, your humbleness is your worst adversary. You look like someone who can entertain the pack at your own expense."

"I am afraid I don't understand that point."

"Let me elaborate." Ratiram was ready to build a mountain of fancied philosophy on the spot. "The mix of key behaviors that a given person demonstrates to others is set at his birth."

"Some examples will help."

"Here, but this is by no means a complete list: compassion, rebelliousness, affection, ignorance, secretiveness; or being uncooperative, impolite, resentful, unfriendly, selfish, grateful, honest, humble, arrogant, jealous, reliable, respectful, stubborn, or flexible. And so on."

"And maybe bullying, gossiping, too?"

"Yes, of course." Ratiram smiled. "So everyone, almost unknowingly, is always on the lookout for people who are suitable to receive a certain part of that proportion. This is where people find you a permanent receiver of humiliation, impoliteness, and insolence. They understand you as someone who can publicly be laughed at."

"So are you saying I look like someone they can empty their stomachs on every morning, irrespective of what they had at night for dinner?" Coinman was serious, but Ratiram couldn't help but laugh.

"Figuratively, maybe, but I wouldn't put it quite that way."

"All right, never mind. Whatever. Let's come to the point. What can be done to change this?"

"You need to find a way to look less gullible. In other words, you need to look more important and shrewd."

Coinman had not expected Ratiram to be so direct. He was silent for a few moments before he spoke.

"I do have a doubt. You have stated that everyone has his share of these conducts toward others, which I can relate to many people I know. But I can think of some cases where people possess an extreme quantity of one or two of such behaviors. For example, I know people who are always angry and who do not talk to anyone with respect. Where do these people spend their favorable emotions? On the other hand, I know people who are always pleased with others and are most polite to everyone. Where do they spend their impoliteness?"

"That's a very good question. It reaffirms your thorough understanding of the concept. To answer it, well, the people in your examples must have a secret channel, hidden from observers. Do not be surprised when some of them apply these on nonhuman beings. They might beat a dog, kill a pest, throw stones at a monkey, or give great affection to a squirrel. Some people have entirely different faces in their public and personal lives, which brings up the balance your question aims at. Some people are different in front of known people versus unknown ones; many of them even swear when they're with strangers, but are well-spoken with acquaintances—or, of course, vice versa."

"Well, I would try to notice these people more closely," said Coinman, "to get a glimpse of their secret spending of these behaviors. Now, what do I do about the villain of humbleness, and the unfair behavior allocation I was born with?"

"There are ways to make ourselves look much more important. Unfortunately, even when there are no takers for inner substance today, guileless people like you still believe more in inner substance than outer appearance. Let's talk in terms of our office perspective, for example, to make it easy to understand the concept. A person achieves a status here based on his outer manifestation. But when he is not able to perform to that status—maybe because of lacking inner substance—he is further promoted to the next level simply because of the combined effect of two reasons: one, since he cannot perform, someone is needed to be brought in who can do the job; and two, no one is ever demoted, as working at higher levels is always easier and hence demotion would mean a tougher job and lesser likelihood of succeeding. It's no secret that there is almost no work at the higher levels. So the best that can be done with him, given he is not able to function at a certain level, is to promote him further."

This shook the wisdom tree that Coinman had cultivated and nurtured, leaf by leaf and year after year. He looked at Ratiram, not quite willing to believe him. "But this is quite contrary to what I have learned during my life."

Ratiram smiled. The smile was that of a sage when he encounters a primitive question suggesting the questioner's lack of elementary knowledge on a subject. "It's a mass conspiracy—a secret brotherhood that ensures that the divide between the management and the workers only grows bigger. Please also spend a minute to ponder the importance of unlearning things in life while we spend most of our energy on learning things." He paused, picked up Coinman's water bottle, and drained it. "Sometimes one is led to be stupid by things that happen in this world, as these things have masks that one needs to develop a capability to see through. The moment one has that capability, one can start to unlearn what is necessary—or unnecessary, depending on how you want to interpret it."

There was another thing Coinman wanted to ask, and the time seemed right. Moreover, Ratiram seemed to be in a good frame of mind.

"Ratiram, please do not answer this if it feels distasteful. A question related to you has bothered me for a long time, and this conversation just refreshed it in my mind. I have always wondered why, despite being widely appreciated for the wisdom you have, you still have to move files. I am convinced, as would anybody else be in the office, that you can handle much bigger responsibilities."

The sage's smile repeated its stint on Ratiram's face. "Like I said, when you move up, you are seen as someone who cannot perform in the present role. I do my work pretty well, so the situation does not arise. Hope that answers your question. I am sorry for unknowingly digressing. Coin, your companionship is so pleasing that I end up chatting for longer than I expect."

"You need not feel apologetic, Ratiram. It is my good fortune that you digressed, if that's how you want to speak of it. Now, going back to the original conversation—tell me now what should I do?"

"Coin, there are a lot of ways it can be done. Some require a lot of hard work, dedication, and patience, while others create almost the same effect with little work. Some are even impossible to do, even though human beings would sacrifice anything if only someone could make them possible. I am going to suggest to you something that is easily possible and is also most effective."

Ratiram looked at the empty water bottle with disappointment, then continued.

"I can already see perfect goatee potential. You are destined to rule with a goatee's support. It is common knowledge now that a goatee has helped people, even ones without any ability or persona, in winning attention and respect. Why don't you grow a beard and then trim it as a goatee? A person with a poised goatee not only achieves a higher confidence level but also looks mature. The joy one gets out of wearing a goatee is unmatched.

"People often gauge your beard first to discern more about you. And if you have a good, healthy, and attractive beard, especially a goatee, you tend to make an instant good impression. A positive goatee sets the platform right in your favor even before you start a conversation. Many a time, you may not even have to speak, however difficult the situation; your goatee speaks for you. To tell the truth, the person conversing opposite to a goatee holder feels that goatee can look into his mind and read it like a book. And that hypnotizes him to tell all his secrets all by himself. A goatee is to beards what diamonds are to ornaments."

"That's really promising. I have one little doubt."

"There can't be a doubt. The goatee is well beyond the realm of doubts. Well, I am just joking. Shoot."

"All the benefits of the goatee that you have highlighted are extrinsic. Does that mean that the goatee doesn't improve the intrinsic part of an individual?"

"Not at all," Ratiram replied. "If you think that a goatee only creates an impression and does not help the personality of the beholder intrinsically, then you are mistaken. A goatee instills confidence in others about you, which induces enviable support to your fortitude, thus unblocking the path to the sincere wisdom which is desperate to announce itself through you and impress people around you in unprecedented ways. Does that click with you?"

"Yes."

"Lock, stock, and barrel?"

"Yes."

"Excellent."

Coinman was surprised that he had never considered goatee-ful life by himself.

"Ratiram is glorifying the goatee a bit dramatically," he thought to himself, "but everything he has said makes perfect sense."

Seeing that Coinman was lost in his thoughts again, Ratiram plucked him again from his world. "Here is a tip for you. The period while you grow a full beard can be pretty unexciting. You can make it a little more interesting by observing people who have goatees, seeing how they look, and comparing their faces to yours. The best places to find such people aplenty are high-profile shopping malls, management schools, and offices of high-paying firms. You can even take some pictures for reference later. If someone objects, tell him about your noble goatee intentions, accompanied by a compliment for his goatee; I think you'll be all right. Hey, let me quickly get some water."

Ratiram was back within few seconds, gulped more water from the bottle, and asked, "So remind me, where was I?"

"You were talking about how to spend the lull time while the goatee grows slower than the movement of a snail on a concrete road."

"So, basically, that's about it. Now go get the goatee of your dreams."

"While you were away to get water," Coinman said, "I had an idea. If you don't mind, may I run it by you?"

"I am at your service."

"What do you think about earrings? I am sure that earrings, coupled with a goatee, would double the impact."

"Well, earrings, without a doubt, suck. But if you want them, I wouldn't stop you." Ratiram sounded a bit agitated.

"I am sorry, Ratiram, I did not mean to irritate you. Sorry for such a stupid proposal."

Ratiram smiled. "It's fine, Coin. You are responsible for your own looks in the end. Feel free to make your own decisions." Ratiram intentionally made his statement a tad melodramatic, deviating Coinman's mind from earrings.

"Ratiram," Coinman said, his chin trembling, "I didn't know it might hurt you that much. Look, I am sorry! You know how much I care about your opinions."

"Hey, I got you," said Ratiram, smiling. "Remember, it's an insult to a goatee if we put it in the same class as earrings. If nothing else, the goatee is a gift from God, while the earring is a gift from man himself."

"You know," Coinman said, "sometimes thoughts come to your mind and, if you are with a close friend, you express them without much thinking. That's exactly what happened here. I am glad you did not mind it at all."

Later that afternoon, Ratiram collected everybody and recited the interaction word by word.

"Coinman with a goatee!" Daya cried. "What a sight that will be! And he thinks that he'll have the look of a wise man, and strangers will insist on a photograph with him."

"And the girls will drool over him"—Panna laughed madly—"and he will have his face buried so deep into honey pots that the bugger won't be able to even breathe."

"Better be his friend now and share the adventure with him." Sevak winked at Panna's commentary.

"But why wouldn't you let the nutsack go for earrings as well?" Panna questioned.

Ratiram replied calmly, "Yeah, that would have been fun. But allowing his ideas would have instilled a germ of self-confidence that could have multiplied eventually to guide him to trust his own thoughts. Then he would have started caring less for my advice."

Everyone nodded in agreement.

7. The Lady in the Veil

*C*oinman's ménage consisted of four living souls beside himself—his father, Daulat; mother, Kasturi; wife, Imli; and distant-cousin-cum-maid, Shimla. The house enjoyed two bedrooms that belonged to the two couples, and one hall of which one corner turned into Shimla's bedroom each night when she arranged her homemade mattress as soon as she was done with the day's housework. She usually went to sleep after and woke up before everyone else.

Shimla never forwent wearing a veil when she stepped outside the home, or if someone visited the family. People outside the family wondered if the veil was forced upon her by the house or if it manifested her voluntary surrender to social engagements. She spoke very softly, if at all. Such was her speech that it could not have caused any soreness to the most sensitive soul; it would, rather, have soothed it like soft music. When there were family invitations, Shimla rarely came along to the event; she stayed at home to finish the pending work.

Shimla's advent into Coinman's family had been a planned move, to serve a mix of humanitarian and personal objectives, and no one could have guessed at that point the far-reaching consequences it was to give rise to as time went on.

The prologue to her entry to the family dated back to the time when Kasturi was in the seventh month of gestating Coinman—a high-attention and high-priority stage of a pregnancy—a time that requires utmost care in bringing one life safely to the world without losing the other.

Daulat and Kasturi had scanned though all the relatives for a woman who could provide the necessary support during those delicate days. They judged each prospect on a number of parameters: availability, forbearance, simplicity, sincerity, devotion, integrity, contentment, respect for elders, pleasant face, cleanliness, plausibility of staying for a longer duration, and—it must be admitted—level of destitution in current life and likelihood of grumbling about the neighbors. Shimla not only surpassed all relatives in her cumulative score; she also outdid all of them on each individual parameter. This, combined with Kasturi's philanthropic objective, made the decision easier.

Katori, Shimla's mother, was Kasturi's distant cousin; the relation was an uncle's wife's mother's nephew's cousin's niece sort of thing, which no one was really interested in accurately tracing, as long as it provided them a bedrock for a mutual companionship that prospered for five years when their families happened to be neighbors. Even when Katori's family moved to another nearby city, Kasturi often visited her, almost once every month—although only during afternoons, when Katori's husband, Adham, was out at work, because of his screwed-up mind.

Kasturi loved Katori's three daughters, but her favorite one was Shimla, who was silent, meticulous, and good at household work. Whenever Kasturi visited them, she brought gifts for all three girls, with a special one for Shimla. Shimla's childlike heart was so touched by this that she carried a noble image of Kasturi even later as an adult.

Kasturi showered immense affection on the family to offset the maltreatment the four females of the family received from Adham. During the time they were neighbors, Kasturi often discussed the issue intensely with Daulat, opinionating that Adham should be sent to the darkest of the prisons, no arguments entertained, and without a possibility of release.

Despite Adham's unfaltering savagery, Katori declined Kasturi's secret offers to summon police protection, reasoning that she didn't wish to raise her kids without a father.

Adham was addicted to executing punishments—he knew nothing more satisfying—so he made sure someone was always up for punishment of some kind. He was a chicken in the outside world that turned into a lion on entering the house.

Shimla was twelve years old, and her younger sisters were eight and six, respectively, when Kasturi became aware of Adham's animosity for the first time.

Adham looked for an opportunity of any kind to enforce punishment; and if there was none, he converted absolutely normal things into such opportunities. When he ran out of reasons, he typically resorted to punishing his daughters for things like not receiving their last punishment in the right spirit; for being found not studying when he entered the house from work; for burying their heads entirely in books, disregarding his entry into the house; for wearing dirty clothes; or for wearing clean clothes that were supposed to be worn only for parties.

The reasons for Katori's punishment included the ones for the daughters, plus many more. She could also be punished for not starting the cooking before he entered the house from work; for meeting a neighbor's wife; for inviting someone to her house; for keeping no control over the children; or for keeping too much control over the children.

The punishment often started off with one person, and then traversed through the rest—completing multiple such cycles. Adham very proudly demonstrated that the human was an animal once and rediscovered his origins regularly in everyday life.

While his favorite punishment for his wife was caning with a long dry twig from a neem tree, his little girls had to stand below the spout of their rusty hand pump, entirely naked, summers or winters, while he pumped the water. "It teaches the little girls at an early age how bad are the two extremes of anything," Adham had said to write off Katori's protest against his bestiality when he was, a rare occurrence, in a happy mood. The only traces of relative kindness in his devilish behavior emerged when he used only half the force he used on his wife in swinging the twig on his eldest daughter, Shimla.

Sometimes he returned home fully drunk, and grabbed Katori by her long thick braid to drag her from the couch to the floor. She would grab the other end of her hair to save her scalp. But still, at times she blacked out with pain— fortunately, as it turned out, because then he left her to herself for the lack of resistance.

As a result, the mother always bore swollen ankles, wounded hands, and a perforated soul. The children were afraid, quiet, and depressed. Adham left the house for a few hours after he completed a punishment, as a boastful criminal proudly leaves the scene of the crime. Often, as soon as he left, Katori called Kasturi. Kasturi was thus a constant eyewitness of the aftermath of this man's brutal conduct. On each occasion she wept heartily and embraced the mother and the daughters.

Thus, when Kasturi needed to ask for Shimla to aid her during her pregnancy, she asked Adham directly, during one of those rare occasions when he was happy by his standards. She knew that asking Adham presented a better chance than asking Katori; if she had asked Katori, Katori would in turn have asked Adham, who would simply have turned down the request as a pointed demonstration of the insignificance of Katori's existence. When Kasturi asked him directly, it worked for two reasons—firstly, he did not get much time to formulate a response to the request; secondly, being a chicken to outsiders, he could never easily say no to them. He did not say yes, but couldn't say no. Kasturi did the rest by skillfully converting this lack of denial into his agreement. The only condition that she had to agree to was that Shimla would never come back to Adham's house. She was dead to him.

Katori's sadness about not being able to see Shimla in the future was trivial compared to her happiness that Shimla was being freed from the hell of their lives. For her it was a choice between not being able to meet her happy daughter for the rest of her life versus being able to see her miserable daughter every day. What would a mother choose?

Under the spell of moving emotions, she recounted to Kasturi, "I beg you—please take extra care of my daughter. She is as simplehearted as a cow. The poor girl has hardly spoken since she was born."

"I can't produce proof now," Katori had continued, "but I can give you my word that she was very talkative while in my belly. No one else but a mother can make out those indications. Her activities in my belly were like a whisper to me which I could clearly understand. Now you yourself can decide and tell me if I can still be wrong with my judgments. You yourself are going through that splendid time awarded only to women by God, and unless you are unfeeling for emotions aroused by one's own child—which I am sure you are not—you will be more than happy to accept my point of view. Shimla moved extremely happily, and impatiently waited to see the outside world. Through those movements of hers, she once whispered to me very clearly, 'Mummy, when do I get to see you? I can't wait here any longer. It's getting so boring here.' She counted every passing minute in the excitement of meeting me in person."

Katori had moisture in her eyes by this time. She continued, "I didn't know how to make sure my reply reached her. So I touched my belly in order to appeal to her to have a little more patience. She understood this communication. From then on we talked in that manner and established a very strong bond of companionship."

Kasturi took a napkin from her purse and passed it to Katori.

"But destiny apparently did not have similar wishes," Katori said. "On the very day Shimla came out to the world, Adham had something come over his head. I had to receive Adham's idiotically timed fury on the day, thankfully only verbal, yet it seemed that the angelic bundle got an instant glimpse into her future. Her newborn face became devoid of smiles. Thereafter she hardly spoke and it seemed she wasn't excited anymore about our sacred bond of companionship."

Katori paused to wipe her tears. She looked around furtively, as if afraid that Adham might be listening, and continued again.

"Shimla had left all her joys inside before coming out to see the world. She only carried her shyness and forbearance. I want her to see and receive all the joys of the world because I could not offer her anything, not even protection from her father's evil treatment. I have died every day in my mind with disgust for not being able to protect my own children. I pray to the Maker to grant me at least so much control of my life that I can protect my own children. Give her so much love that she forgets about all the agonies of the past. I wouldn't even mind if your love makes her forget about us."

"She will never feel like she's not the daughter of my house," Kasturi promised Katori. "I have never wished a little harm even to my enemies, if I have any, but I wish Adham dies with no delay. I know you want him to live for your daughters to have the shadow of their father; but why would you want a shadow that only eats them alive?"

"Hope spoils our lives, more than anything," Katori replied. "I know too well that he is a Satan, but the hope that he would be fine springs from everywhere in my mind, completely conquering my wish to get rid of him."

When Kasturi was leaving, Katori gave a parting kiss on Shimla's forehead and promised to visit her at Kasturi's house.

After joining Kasturi's family serendipitously as a permanent member, Shimla started adding work to her responsibilities, all by herself. Despite Kasturi's affectionate opposition to it, Shimla actively looked for opportunities to take over all the humdrum work of the family. It made Kasturi cry, but she let Shimla follow her heart.

Shimla had complete freedom in the house to choose anything she wanted. Relatives often talked about how Daulat and Kasturi loved her like their own child.

Shimla's unassuming nature influenced her choices; she always chose things that she thought no one else would choose—so as to leave better things for others. No one stopped her from buying new clothes, for instance, but she chose to wear the old ones that were rejected by the other members of the house. Sometimes Kasturi forcibly ordered her to buy new clothes, unaware that Shimla's tacit goal wasn't to buy a good dress but to return as much money as possible. Hence her new clothes looked no better than the old ones.

Shimla's veil, as was now evident to the family, was an armor that had helped her hide from questions she might have faced from her friends if they were to see the marks given her by her father's stick. Apparently she had started covering herself at age ten. It was much easier to explain the veil than to answer questions about the wounds.

By the time she moved to Kasturi's house, the veil was almost like a part of her body, inseparable. When Kasturi initiated polite attempts to get her outside the veil, she finally realized the unification the veil had with the girl's soul. So Kasturi let Shimla be herself, forever in her veil.

Shimla had never imagined good people like Daulat and Kasturi existed in this world. Because of this, she prayed to God several times a day to bestow the best possible happiness on the family, even if it was at the expense of her own happiness.

Several years after Shimla's advent, when Coinman got married, Imli's anomalous passion for acting frequently invaded Shimla's personal space by making Imli disappear completely in her current role and making her exaggerate her behavior according to her role. But Shimla never realized it because her loyalty to the family had formed a layer of high tolerance around her body, her soul, and her mind.

8. The Seeds of Debacle

*H*ukum's promise to the victims of the coins cleverly camouflaged a personal clandestine agenda. He had waited patiently for the right opportunity—there couldn't be a better one.

Hukum's mind was unbearably defenseless at the sight of a lonely individual, and the susceptibility grew with the persistence of such a sight—a sticky condition he'd frequently had to abide during school days, too, at the sight of lonely children. Throughout his childhood, his sincere attempts to alleviate the situation by confronting the lonely children directly brought about gripes from teachers, students, and neighbors alike.

Over the years his mind developed extraordinary skills, such as identifying such kids without confusion, secretly shadowing them to cause fear, pushing them when they least anticipated it, spreading false rumors about them, leaving threats through anonymous notes, singing derogatory songs using their names, and whatnot. As a result, many a kid around him was afraid to come out to play with friends; kids skipped school for the fear of facing him. Some even felt depressed, for they considered themselves forever trapped, hopelessly, in Hukum's horrid den.

He was quite a nightmare to lonely kids. They tried to take cover in the company of an adult. For this reason the teachers were surrounded by such children, something that eventually played to Hukum's disadvantage, as numerous complaints started pouring in to his parents.

His parents consulted psychiatrists, one of whom, after a carefully distant but comprehensive examination, told them that hidden at the core of his bullying of the forlorn children was his feeling of insecurity. As the psychiatrist got into specific history, the parents revealed that they had a lonely child, Teju, among their relations who happened to be a psychopath and secretly hurt other kids his age very badly. The parents then revealed how they had discovered Teju's behavior, rather the hard way, only when they had come back from a month-long trip to pick up Hukum from Teju's place. Hukum's parents had planned a month's stay for him with Teju's parents, thinking he would enjoy spending part of the summer vacation with Teju, who was seven, as was Hukum. But it was everything but a vacation for Hukum. His parents heard the horror stories from their kid after they got home: how Teju, who never spoke a word, inserted a screwdriver in his right ear, threw him from the stairs once, pulled down his underwear once, locked him in the shoe closet once, pinched him with a sewing needle once, etc. Every time, the parents said, Hukum wanted to make Teju talk and explain why he would do that, but Teju wouldn't speak or even pay attention. This close encounter with Teju, and several other such kids that he came across thereafter (he had his luck written by the darkest of ink), led Hukum to believe that every lonely child was a psychopath. The psychiatrist concluded that since lonely people were hardwired as psychopaths in his brain, he felt that they had noxious hidden intentions.

The parents heaved a sigh of relief on finding the truth behind his behavior and took these findings to the school authorities. The school instated additional scrutiny around Hukum to help the other kids. It caused a constant trauma to Hukum: not only was he deprived of taking a protective measure regarding the psychopaths around him, but also it seemed that the authorities considered *him* a psychopath.

By the time he went to college, his instinct of insecurity had turned into the joy of bullying lonely and eccentric people. The change was so gradual and subtle over the years that he wasn't able to notice the transition point himself. But at the same time, when in college, he had to put more sanctions on his instinct, because adults are not pardoned as much for their mistakes as the kids are. So to bandage his craving instinct, he acquired another outlet, that of writing poems, lewd masterpieces. These poems of offensive content could be celebrated only in a limited circle of friends, sadly causing stillbirth of his writing talent.

Now, at the office, Coinman refreshed his old instinct. A dog that has lived without a bone for years, when presented with a bone again, couldn't be expected to control itself.

The stories of Coinman's lack of retaliation against bullying boosted Hukum's instincts even more. The one he remembered the most took place during Coinman's early days at the office and concerned a booze party arranged by the first-floor bachelors at a small apartment. Although Coinman wasn't into alcohol, he regarded it as important to be social with people at the office, so he went. As alcohol gave way to more alcohol, it took a very little time to travel to the attendees' brains.

It was a wild party, full of music, alcohol, smoke, and dirty talk. The partiers openly talked in lascivious ways, cracking graphic jokes, even commenting on anyone they could see from their balcony. After spending hours entertaining themselves that way, they got bored of it and started teasing each other by making up funny stuff on the spot. Even if the made-up stuff sucked, they still laughed loudly.

Then their jokes dried up and they needed a new catalyst; that was when they took Coinman to the small study room in the apartment and locked him in. They laughed, with their ears against the closed door, and then soon forgot about him. Coinman continued to gently knock on the door, but, heedlessly drenched in alcohol, his companions didn't care much. Coinman made himself busy with books in the room for a few minutes to allow the inebriated souls some time, then came back to knock again. By midnight the smashed company had crashed all over the place, yet, oblivious that his colleagues were all asleep, Coinman religiously repeated the knocking process till morning. Someone finally woke up around dawn and opened the door, half-asleep.

Coinman smiled at him and said, "That was a very nice party! I would've enjoyed it even more if I hadn't been mistakenly locked inside the room."

Thus Hukum knew how he'd find a way into Coinman's world: by pretending his interest was nothing more than sympathy for coin-stricken souls. He let himself float in Coinman's vicinity whenever an opportunity presented itself. Spending more time near Coinman meant more subjection to heartless coins. But Hukum was determined.

On noticing Hukum's increased presence around him, Coinman got suspicious, because he had already mentally labeled Hukum as someone he could never manage to feel comfortable with: daring, physically strong, arrogant, and stubborn. He thought that people with such traits always saw decent men as more vulnerable targets for the recreational ventures their extra power allowed them.

So whenever he saw Hukum approaching, Coinman engaged himself in something else: he'd adjust his wristwatch, or focus entirely on pulling a food fragment out of his teeth, or the like, till Hukum was past him. He noticed out of the corner of his eye that Hukum continuously stared at him, making every attempt to make eye contact with him. Hukum patiently overlooked Coinman's avoidance tactics initially, but over time they began to grate on him. Pissed off by the avoidance, he schemed to teach Coinman a lesson. He knew how; he'd done it for years.

One night it came to him, the perfect tactic. Sitting on his bed, he worked all night to write a poem on Coinman. Enthralled by his masterpiece, he ditched work the next day, citing a feverish condition—but called up his gang, one after the other, to recite his work. The next day, when the management was coincidentally out for an off-site seminar, the office workers took the poem from one desk to another cleverly, without kindling Coinman's suspicion, and praised his caricature in collective chorus. After everyone had had a good laugh, Hukum stuck the poem on the first-floor notice board.

From the **** of his own mother,
Came smiling this crazy ****er!
His father forgot to use a ****er,
But we are the ones who suffer.

Is it hard to guess for any soul?
Who the hell is this ***hole?
Nauseating us is his only goal,
For ringing coins he must pay a toll.

We could have been spared in whole,
If his father had only rested his *ole!
If on that evil night he wasn't on a roll,
Or had used a few coins on birth control.

The notice board endowed the poem with an official touch, making it even more enjoyable. Everyone wanted to read it again.

"Damn, the good words are all asterisked!" Hukum expressed his disappointment to his gang.

"I am not sure if they will understand it," Saarang said.

"The men only understand the asterisks. My worry is if they understand the rest." Panna killed everyone with laughter at that.

Coinman scoped out the entire activity from a distance until the notice board was lonely again. He then stopped by the notice board to have a look at the poem. He didn't believe it could come from his own colleagues. First disappointment, then turbulent anger overcame him in a matter of seconds. He wished he could shoot everyone on the spot. He tore the paper off in anger, ripped it into small pieces, and threw it in the trash bin.

Still angry, he found plenty of courage to walk straight to Hukum.

"You did it?" he demanded.

"Did what?"

"That shameful thing," Coinman pointed toward the notice board, "that you should not have done."

Hukum laughed slyly at this and said, "Oh, dear, dear! There's a mountain full of things that I have done which I shouldn't have done." He looked at the gang and passed a secret smile. "And of course, just as tall a mountain full of things I haven't done but I should have done; now tell me, what the heck are you talking about?"

"I know you did it," said Coinman. "Stop making fun of me now. As a social obligation, even a witch spares seven houses in her neighborhood." Coinman's entire body vibrated with rage, chin leading the pack.

Hukum barely resisted the urge to knock him off his feet. Instead he smiled, looking sideways at his gang. "What do you guys say? Shall we take him to our favorite place? The son of a constipated lizard is forcing us now. He surely could do with some mambo."

They burst into laughter. Coinman had hit the ceiling by now.

"I know the shamefully sleazy place that you talk about! Maybe you and your disgusting sidekicks here—and your respective families—along with your respectable mothers and sisters, all of you treat yourselves to a mambo binge there."

"Dude"—Panna couldn't stay quiet—"your pocket monster is getting out of your hands. Ding the bugger on the head before it's too late."

"Hey, don't cross the line here. Watch your rotten mouth. Do you really eat with that same mouth?" Coinman shouted.

"What the heck could you do?" Hukum brought himself forward, stooping over Coinman, his nose next to Coinman's. "And who crossed the line first, douchebag? It's clear that your ancestors have had a tradition of family mambo bingeing."

Both of them had had enough shots of adrenaline to get into a scuffle. Fortunately, the rest of the gang intervened to cut short the brawl by dragging them apart, but that didn't stop the two combatants from flailing at each other in the air.

"Too much for a day," Hukum said when the gang was back together in private. "The asshole has forgotten his place."

"Hukum, did you make a copy of your poem before the bugger trashed it?" Daya asked.

"That's a pure bummer." Hukum held his forehead in his palms.

"Don't worry about it," said Panna, "I remember it word for word."

"You deserve to get weighed in gold." Daya said.

"I need to go to the Unique Bar right now." Hukum wasn't in good spirits yet. "Who's with me?"

All hands went up.

9. The Standard Pain-Killer

*D*isappointment has quite a penchant for taking one by surprise. As the group arrived at the bar this evening, they found it closed. The bar had been as accessible to them as their pockets; and such was their rapport at the place that the bar staff often extended the closing hour to allow them to drink more. With such a mutual bond they had enjoyed with Unique Bar, they never considered other bars in the city. So they knew no other.

"That's a disaster. No worries, let's go to another place," Daya said, trying to uplift the mood.

"This shit sucks my soul." Panna was giving up already, "Now what next? I don't want to be an ass-can standing here."

"Take it easy, dear friends," Daya replied. "After a recent breakup with his psychonaut girlfriend, my flatmate has turned into an encyclopedia of the bars in the city. Let me give him a shout."

Daya buzzed his encyclopedic friend, and apprised the others after the call was over: "My buddy seems to have a fetish for this place called Apna Bar. He says if we don't go there tonight, he's not going to recommend anything again."

"Maybe he gets a cut," Sevak said, laughing. "Let's get rolling."

The gang arrived at Apna Bar half an hour later. The bar was very dimly lit inside. All the tables were separated by murk; that made them wonder how the waiters gauged which table needed their attention. A waiter steered them through the gloom to a table, the only source of light on it being a small candle in the middle. They needed to stoop toward the center of the table in order to see each other.

They ordered large glasses of their favorite locally made whisky with automatic refills and drank in silence before Hukum spoke.

"Fricking son of a popcorn pimp." he muttered, lighting a cigarette. "Motherfucker, the lover of his own sister, he had the balls to stand up to us in public. You tell me, Daya, why a worthless creature like him should be let off after pouncing upon the respect of an individual of honor, like me?"

Daya just laughed, which infuriated Hukum further.

"Why are you laughing? Did you hear me say a rib-tickler? Or has my face suddenly turned into a clown's? Maybe you are showing off your new toothpaste? But...no, I do not want to force a reason on you. Please tell me why are you splitting a gut at such a serious topic? Sevak, Panna, you tell me, did you think I was joking?"

"No, dear Hukum," said Daya humbly. He was scrambling for a story, because he had actually laughed at Hukum's self-flattery—the narcissism of calling himself an individual of honor. "I swear to God, I did not intend to poke fun at what you said. When you spoke about Coinman's mother and sister in that manner, and even as I understood that it was only figuratively, my mind flashed to many mothers and sisters I know; innocent women who don't have the slightest clue how frequently they appear in such conversations, through no fault of their own. I couldn't conceal my giggle on thinking of pious mothers and studious, homely sisters."

"If that's why you laughed, then I have to say that your sense of humor has been mis-calibrated. Assuming that's something recent, I am worried that your face is going to look like a retard's soon, because you will laugh at everything," said Sevak to Daya, and then looked at Hukum.

"I do not think that this guy's laugh was sufficiently justified."

"Why? Don't you see a point there?" Daya retorted, unaware of the teasing expression on Sevak's face. "Anyway, let's refocus on the booze."

"You've got a good point," Hukum said. Alcohol consumption always brought out the teacher in him. "But even under the influence of extreme feeling of any kind, one should behave as the situation demands. Imagine if you are reminded of such funny things at the funeral of a person whose life has been of great emotional importance; would you still laugh? You'd better not. So that's my point."

Panna exuberantly shook his head in agreement, as though Hukum were somehow reading straight from his mind. As soon as Hukum took a pause, Panna grabbed the opportunity.

"I cannot agree more," he said. "I am a firsthand witness of how my friend, Sandy, had his ass in a sling for laughing during a heart-to-heart conversation. It actually caused the end of his love affair."

"I am impatient to hear the story," Sevak said, after he'd done droplet drawings all over his sweating glass.

"Sandy, the most decent guy I have known in my entire life," continued Panna, "had a love affair with one of his childhood friends. They were neighbors since their early childhood. But due to the conservative atmosphere at the girl's house, Sandy couldn't meet with her as frequently as he would've liked to. Actually, forgive my drifting thoughts, they never met. She barely came out of the house. Her old man was such an animal."

"Where is the love in this story," Sevak put in, thumping the table with his right palm, "when they did not even meet?"

"Have patience and hold off your opinion until I finish," said Panna, without even looking at Sevak, as the waiter refilled his glass. "This is a real story, not the kind of story found in the books you read, I can't have this story start with tonsil hockey. Sorry, guys."

"All right, enough. Can you continue the story now?" Sevak said, looking surprised.

"Sandy had a mind as free of dirt as mankind had ever known. In fact, as a young teenager, I have to confess, I often thought of becoming a scientist to be able to research his mind to find out what kept it so virgin, despite pricks all around him."

As he said this, Panna couldn't avoid staring at Daya, whose fingers were gang-raping his two nostrils very earnestly. Several glasses of alcohol were greatly showing up in his "couldn't care less" disposition.

"There was no shit he ever seemed to be hiding," Panna continued. "No one ever suspected that his projection to the outside world was any different than his inner world. But despite him being awesomesauce, the dude was widely known as a nitwit."

Panna paused and took a cigarette from Hukum's cigarette box. Panna rarely smoked; only when he got extremely intoxicated and excited. "Give me a match? Yes, here," he said to the attendant, and continued with the story while lighting. "He was always laughed at by the people for not being able to grasp the most trifling matters, and no one really expected him to find a decent job. His father had some reputation in society—some kind of a prominent man, so he would not have allowed him a menial job. So that pretty much meant he was going to remain unemployed forever."

Daya was getting restless by now. "Enough of his background; come to the main story now. To hell with his job! How does it matter to us whether he had a good job or not, whether his stomach was full or if he remained hungry? I am still trying to digest the thought of these people being childhood friends when they didn't meet even once. Or did I hear it incorrectly?"

"Slow down, asshat." Panna's alcohol was making him more combative than usual. "You know jack shit about telling a story. Is there any fun in a story until what is necessary is told? Anyone bugs me once more, I am not continuing."

He paused for a few seconds, trying hard to look at the faces, wondering if it was low light or alcohol that caused his sight to dim.

"So, as I was saying, Sandy was not exactly the guy you could count on for getting a decent job to support his family, but he was a guy anyone could trust in all matters. In the matters of love, he would do anything for his lover, anything that was in his capability."

"How much of the story have we heard up to now?" Daya could not keep quiet.

"What do you mean?" Panna's eyes emitted embers.

"I mean have we hit at least ten percent completion of the story yet?"

"Why would you want to know that?"

"To know in advance how much more of this joyride is still left." A wide chuckle followed this, vexing Panna even more.

"I'm not going to complete the story. Not a word more. You guys simply don't deserve it."

"Complete surrender to the holy feet of Lord Panna. Forgive our dumbness," cried Daya, bowing his head toward the middle of the table in Panna's direction with both hands far stretched. "Please do not ruin us by leaving the wonderful story unfinished."

Everyone laughed madly.

In the history of their friendship, Panna's stories had never been able to escape a premature death. There was an unspoken agreement among the other three that, since Panna did not really have a full story to tell, it was their moral responsibility to cause him to digress before he had to face the embarrassment of not being able to finish the story.

They drank in silence again.

A small uproar occurred at the adjacent table. The group sitting at the table was preparing to leave after paying the check. Sevak almost fell to the side trying to defy the surrounding darkness to seize the last opportunity to have a look at the female whose charming voice had kept him guessing.

"O woman, thou art my imperfection," Sevak sighed to the gang, as the door closed behind the leaving group.

"Control thy libido, control thy libido," Hukum said, and laughed aloud.

Sevak saw an opportunity in this pause to put a thought across that he'd wanted to share with the gang for a long time.

"Here is an interesting thought that keeps crossing my mind," he said. "Let me supply the context first. Most of us have had single-gender education, a pre-birth death of the training to enhance our social skills. What was supposed to be a training ground for learning tricks of the love trade had turned into madness for test scores and greater academic orientation. I can never forgive the government for not thinking about this. Had these government people, whose stomachs get ballooned by some mysterious power, not experienced the same void in their young years? Then why did they not commiserate with us and change the system?"

"Sevak, do not let emotion manipulate the lovely tale that you are telling. You seem to have digressed from what you really wanted to tell us." Hukum spoke like a scholar again. "Many storytellers with possibly more potential than Shakespeare, even though I have not read much of him, could not hit much fame because they treated their stories like their wives. Rather than limiting the emotion only to flirting with their stories, they married them, thus limiting their chances of experimenting."

"Hukum, I get your point," Sevak said, "But don't you feel as pissed off as I do by single-gender schooling on the bogus grounds of social effect, moral education, and academic performance?"

"Sevak is opening up today," said Daya, smiling. "The disappointment caused by those million romantic hopes, hitherto hidden forcefully, has finally managed to leap from its grave."

"The sporadic parade of your intelligence really impresses me at times, pal," said Sevak teasingly, wanting to irk Daya. He gulped the rest of his drink as he spoke, and raised the empty glass in the air, hinting to the waiter for a refill.

This tested Daya's volatility, and proved that alcohol reduces the boiling point. "This surpasses the limit of ridicule I must allow from you, Sevak. You have to apologize to me."

"Apologize for what?"

"For your misbehavior."

"I was only praising your intelligence." Sevak was barely able to keep from laughing.

"One tight slap at your temple, and I am sure a 'sorry' would come out rushing from your mouth without a second's delay," Daya teased back.

"What are we arguing here?" asked Hukum, losing his patience.

As Panna was about to answer, his cell phone rang, and he picked up, said hello, and shouted after recognizing the voice, "Which tunnel of the world have you been putting up in? Are you still alive? Well, you must be, as you are talking to me. I need to kick your butt—" The other party hung up before Panna could complete the last sentence.

As Panna put his phone back in his pocket, Hukum turned to him. "What? Why do you look so perturbed? Has your sister eloped with her high-school sweetheart?"

Panna did not answer.

Hukum said, "That's why I say, never have an intellectual sort of conversation while drinking. That's not an economical business proposition. The elaborate application of mind drains the alcohol before it does its job."

"What about Coinman? We completely lost track. How do we teach him a lesson?" Sevak reminded everyone.

"Thank you for reminding us. I had completely forgotten about that. That topic needs some time. Please grant me five more minutes before starting on that topic." Hukum stood. "I need to go to the restroom as fast as I can."

"Hero," Hukum called to one of the waiters, "I need to offer a sacred water sacrifice at the porcelain altar. Can you guide me to the altar? Of course, only till the door."

"I am sorry, sir, the lavatory is undergoing renovation currently. It's not usable," The waiter said in single breath. He seemed to have had good practice saying it to many others that evening.

"Seriously! Have you had a look at yourself in the mirror recently? Wasn't it you who needed a renovation instead of the lavatory?" Hukum said angrily. "Go and check again. I am sure you are mistaken. No one can just play around with such an important place without establishing an alternative first." He then turned to his gang and said, "Absolutely ridiculous! Which planet are we on? Jokes apart, I think in general the lavatories in the bars have not claimed particular affection from the management. Some sort of a national reform movement is needed to improve their condition across the country. I would even suggest—"

The waiter interrupted, "I am very sure about it, sir. I work here and know every inch of this place. In fact, I myself have been going over to a place outside. To tell you the truth, I have even been consuming less water than usual, fearing frequent visits to that faraway place."

"Do you have any idea what I am going through right now?" Hukum cried. "The more I involve myself in your dumbass conversation, the worse I get. I need your manager. Right at this moment. Why are you still standing here confusedly? I haven't even mentioned your mother yet. Go, and bring your manager. I can't dare a move."

"Don't speak anymore, Hukum," advised Daya in a brotherly fashion, then cried to the waiter, "What will it take us, honorable sir, to make you run and get your manager here? Are we not speaking your language?"

"Daya, calm down. I will talk to him," said Sevak, tapping at Daya's shoulder, fearing Daya would get down to manhandling the waiter soon.

"Dumbbells addicted to forceful persuasions do not submit to the way of talking," said Daya, starting to roll up his sleeves.

"Someone save me. Oh, God, which earlier incarnation of my soul deserved this revenge that erroneously fell on this one?" cried Hukum in discomfort.

The waiter was back with the manager.

"What is it, fellas?" the manager asked.

"Don't you 'fellas' us. Our troubled friend needs to bless your restroom with holy water at this very moment. Are you helping? Yes or no?" Panna took the lead.

"No." The manager was curt.

"Why did you give him an option of 'no' in the first place?" Sevak muttered, irritated with Panna.

"Sevak, my condition is fast approaching Hukum's. I am trying to speak as little as possible. Can you take this conversation forward?"

"Yes, sure," said Sevak with pride; he wasn't generally given an opportunity to lead the pack. "Mr. Manager, can we know the reason behind that 'no' from your inhospitable mouth?"

"I am sure you are already informed, sir, there is renovation going on at this point," the manager said calmly.

"And why would you not think of an alternate place for the lavatory? Being in the business, you must be aware how impatient alcohol is to rush to the exit door as soon as it finishes its job on the mind and the heart?"

"That was a mistake, and I apologize in the most sincere manner."

"An apology isn't enough."

"What else can we do, sir?"

"Come to the point, bug-lovers," cried Panna, "or else we all will be in deep shit like me, and we all will need damn stretchers in the next five minutes."

"We don't have stretchers here, sir," the manager was quick to clarify.

"I know it's not a fucking hospital! Or, maybe it is. Look at us. Don't we all look like patients writhing in pain? Daya, where does your encyclopedic live? I am going to personally visit him first thing tomorrow morning to punch in his face for sending us to a hospital instead of a bar!" Panna was losing it.

"Speak of an alternate place." Sevak understood they couldn't afford a drift in conversation any longer.

"That's far away from here, some eight hundred meters."

"Arrange a cab for us, and two people to help us transfer Panna and Hukum to the car, and then from car to the restroom."

"A car is not even a distant possibility. We do not keep a car. In fact, none of us even has a personal car. These are bad times for the alcohol-serving industry. Margins are falling."

"Guys, we have professor of economics here. I was wasting my fucking time thinking he was the manager. Daya, please get this settled with him. I can't speak for long now," Sevak said, holding the lower part of his stomach.

Daya stood up immediately in excitement, but forgot in the next moment what to say or do. Just as a whale disappears in the sea after surfacing, the idea in his head had disappeared completely in less than a second. So in an attempt to do something, he went to the counter and brought back an empty bottle.

"How about this? Why fritter away the time when each second is so costly? Take this and go to some corner here. I can get one bottle for each one of you for the hygiene factor." Then he turned to the manager. "Sir, can you provide us a closed room?"

"Not for this."

"Only for five minutes."

"Not even for a second."

"Then suggest some place nearby."

"Go outside, take a left, take the first left, then take another left, bow down to the big teak tree, and release. You can keep the bottles, and please do not pick up anything again without asking us about it."

"Three lefts, one after other," Panna was calculating, "are you sure we are not going to go round this building to come back on the right-hand side?"

"That's another option. You can just take a right from the door and will hit the same place on the corner."

Hukum ground his teeth and flailed his fist in the air, pretending to punch the manager's face.

"We must not waste a second," said Daya, who was going to join the club any moment. He immediately paid for the drinks.

All of them slowly walked outside. "We will settle with him after we release," said Panna, grinding his teeth.

Several other tables had asked for checks after hearing the whole argument.

As the gang returned after emptying their bladders, they ensured that the manager remembered them for the rest of his life—for they swore at him like no one else could.

10. The Serendipitous Concert

"*T*he sun must have risen in the west this morning," thought Saarang, when he found a short note from Tulsi on his desk, beneath a file:

This Friday, 12:30 p.m., outside the office, at Barulay's Lunch Café…alone. Mum's the word.
—Tulsi Anand

Overjoyed that his attempts had finally worked, he couldn't contain himself for long. His triumph showed all over him in his conspicuous countenance of glee.

He read the note several times to ascertain his emotional fluctuations hadn't led him to miss a word. He shoved the note in his trouser pocket because it was dangerous, with wolves around, to put the note in his shirt's translucent pocket; someone might've snatched it and read it to the world!

A gift for the occasion is essential, he thought. Hukum's recent poem on Coinman had assured him about the success of his own writing, if he ever tried seriously. *If a muscleman like Hukum can write a poem, anyone can. Besides, there can't be a better romantic gift than a lovely handwritten poem.*

That evening, once home, he embarked on a rugged odyssey with his pen. Despite skipping dinner and working till the wee hours, he was annoyed with the results: his writing sounded so shallow. Quite a disappointment.

Frustrated and exhausted, he fell asleep in the morning to time-travel to William Wordsworth's house to learn how to write a perfect romantic poem. An old man of about seventy greeted him at the door, showed him his library located in the corner of the house, and inquired at length about Tulsi. Saarang made a mental note to let gossipmongers know that Tulsi's popularity had even made it to Wordsworth. Such was her glory!

The old man asked, "How long do you want the poem to be?"

Saarang thought hard and replied, "Neither too short nor too long."

At that the old man looked at one of his bookshelves, took out a dusty book with a completely faded cover, placed it on the study table, and asked Saarang to read the fifth chapter and determine which poem in that chapter came closest to his requirements.

To his shock, as Saarang turned the first page, the words slowly transformed into small cylinders, except for one-letter words, which preferred being spheres, and started rolling toward the vertical edges of the book. Black in color and bronze in texture, the words rolled off the sides to form a pile on the floor. That made these pages completely blank. It was not clear if it was the exposure to light or to his eyes that caused the words to desert the pages.

Saarang collected the cylinders and circles from the floor carefully and tried to put them back on the two pages, in desperate hope that they would resume their wordly state, but they rolled down again. He looked up to see that Mr. Wordsworth had shrugged in helplessness. Saarang turned the page, only to encounter the same situation again. So he asked Mr. Wordsworth if he could borrow a digital camera to trap the words quickly next time before they turned into spheres and circles. Mr. Wordsworth explained that digital cameras weren't in use yet.

Saarang ran outside Mr. Wordsworth's house and fetched a digital camera from his car. He got the writer to turn the page for him, so that he could snap a picture quickly. To his horror, as he looked at the picture, the words were captured in a half-transitioned state. He tried to take a picture several times, as the writer continued to help open a new page every time, but couldn't capture any legible text. At this his mind became so troubled that he woke up.

The dream, however, left him with an idea. That morning he skipped the office and searched the town library for the ten greatest Romantic poets of all time. There were, as he figured, several "top ten" lists available. He noticed that four poets, including Mr. Wordsworth, were featured on all the lists, and brought some of their work back home.

Discerning meanings in some of these, however, was difficult. *Why are the acclaimed romantic poems always so obscure to understand?*

Still he persevered, and read a couple of relatively simple poems several times before he came up with his own version:

O thy beauty,
The divine loveliness,
Sacred like a holy cow,
Fresh like a basil leaf,
It's only you
To whom the gods bow.

The thunderstruck we
Love dying,
When you execute us
With the knife of elegance,
And free us
From worldly woes.

A woman is art,

> An aesthetic creation,
> And you are the ruler
> Of such creations;
> You possess everything,
> The best they have.

Each time he read the poem, he became more satisfied with his work. He even pondered the possibility of leaving his mundane office job and developing a career as a poet.

But even as he considered himself done with the poem, he remembered that bad luck comes in threes.

Good heavens, I may have been digging my own grave! If I present her three stanzas, I am surely headed for disaster.

Quickly he sat down to write a fourth one:

> Although I should stop,
> I can't,
> Such is your beauty,
> That one can go on and on,
> And on and on and on,
> And on and on and on...

He copied the poem twice, on good paper in handsome green ink. Then he put one copy in his trouser pocket and the other one in his wallet as a backup.

On Friday his mind floated like a butterfly in anticipation of the event in the afternoon. Countless times he looked at the clock, at the mirror in the restroom, and at Tulsi. Every minute seemed an hour to wait; the last hour, eleven to twelve, was the toughest of all. To address his growing impatience, and pass the time without feeling every second, he decided to see if he could measure a minute successfully without looking at the watch. He looked at his watch, closed his eyes, and counted to sixty, then looked again. He wasn't good at it in the beginning, so he had to keep practicing—which helped him to keep his mind off Tulsi. By the time he got closer to sensing a minute exactly, it was about time. The trick had worked for him. He stood up from his desk and noticed that Tulsi's desk was unoccupied already.

Maybe she's equally impatient.

On that happy thought, he walked toward the café. Nervousness made his heart pound like a devil knocking at a huge tin door. His right hand constantly slipped into his trouser pocket to ensure the poem was still intact.

As he entered the restaurant, a porter with a vast mustard-oil-soaked handlebar mustache greeted him with a broad smile, clearly hoping his warmth would mean a better tip later. Barulay's was an inexpensive place with very modest furniture, arranged without much artistry. Saarang looked around for Tulsi before occupying a table.

A big occasion was only a moment away; a close encounter with the divine beauty! His heart pounded even harder, and the delay in Tulsi's arrival allowed him some time to compose himself.

Then she walked in, smiling, in her beautiful sunglasses; she located him in a blink and came straight to his table. The faded light-blue vinyl tablecloth hid every detail of the table other than the square shape. Pushing her sunglasses up in her hair, Tulsi sat on Saarang's immediate right and pulled her chair closer to his. Looking into his eyes, she spoke deliberately.

"So…Mr. Shameless, finally succeeded in making us talk, huh?"

She paused after saying this, maintaining an intimate smile on her face to make it appear a cordial conversation to the casual onlookers. She then took a quick around their table, turned back to Saarang, and asked, "So how can I help you stop being my tail at the office?"

Saarang was completely caught off guard by the sudden twist. Desperate for a response, he decided to feign that Tulsi was pulling his leg.

"Slow down, slow down, dear!" he said. "Take a breath or two. Do you want to order something to eat first? You will have ample time to pull my leg."

Tulsi turned her head around, feigning that Saarang was talking to someone else. "Whom did you just call 'dear'?"

"You, I thought. But if that's a big deal, I can just call you by your name. Maybe that's more appropriate for now. By our next meeting we may be more comfortable with each other."

"The next meeting? Who the heck decided there'd be a next meeting?"

"Well, doesn't a second meeting typically follow a first one? I would even go on to say that the second meeting is more important than the first one."

All he truly cared at the moment was planning his escape —he was thinking about it continuously in his mind.

"You know what?" A lovely smile still reigned on Tulsi's face. "Let's get to the point. What's your problem?"

"What's my problem? Weren't you the one who set this meeting up?"

"Well, because you shamelessly tailgate me, causing me a loss of reputation. What can I do to stop that?"

"For now, a friendly conversation would be highly helpful."

"Have you ever looked at yourself in a mirror? I'm not wasting my time on this meaningless conversation anymore. I only wanted to warn you to stop pestering me immediately."

Saarang was ready with a scheme for his graceful escape from the awkward situation.

"Tulsi, I implore you to not judge my behavior before giving me a sincere ear. I am here on a very serious purpose. Now, I am a person of jovial nature too—that's why I was trying to tease you a bit. Setting a lighter mood is always the best way to start on heavy topics. As of now I'll stop monkeying around and explain everything like it is."

The waiter had arrived for their order. Saarang ordered a cheeseburger with a soda, but Tulsi took a pass.

"Your observation is accurate," Saarang continued. "I have been trying to speak to you at the office. And I fully understand your perspective based on your side of the observations. But I was trying to strike up a conversation with you for a purpose."

"What was the purpose? And why in the weird world couldn't you tell me earlier—instead of just chasing me like a psycho?"

"The purpose was to discuss the coin problem that is plaguing everyone at the office. I have been seeking to make you an ally, as we can't do it unless everyone on the first floor is with us."

Finally Tulsi seemed interested. "So what are you planning to do about it?"

"The plan hasn't been finalized. We are working on bringing people together right now, so that we have the full support of everyone."

"So you were chasing me to gain my support on this?"

"Only if that's not too much to ask for."

"I need some time to think about it," she said as she got up to leave. "I'll let you know tomorrow."

She shook his hand formally before leaving.

A thousand good books have been written on man, woman, and love; but there is still so much that has remained unsaid on the topic. He tore both copies of the poem and sighed to himself, "Ahh, love, why is it so easy to let you in, but so difficult to let you out? Why couldn't you subsist only two-sided?"

11. The Dawn of the Heat Wave

When the world around is ready to back one unconditionally, one can become as unreasonable, unfair, and coldly sadistic as one likes.

The gang meticulously lined up the support before embarking on schooling Coinman. They also picked all the days when management was going to be away at off-site meetings.

One day at the first flush of morning, Hukum came to the office before anyone else. He went to Coinman's desk and rapidly worked through his shoulder bag to fetch numerous loose glossy pages from an adult magazine. He then arranged a few in a neat fashion on Coinman's desk and dropped a number of them all around his desk.

As the normal office hours started, people gathered around Coinman's desk like onlookers at a mass-casualty incident. When Coinman got in, he walked past the crowd, trying to stay away from the playful throng as usual, failing to realize at first that the epicenter of the quake was his desk. Then as he approached his desk, intrigued, he could see people chatting in loud voices, laughing, and even miming hysterical mocking gestures. On seeing Coinman, the loud discussions turned into a humming sound. They parted to clear a passage for him—much like a mob giving way to the cops at the site of an accident.

As Coinman reached his chair, he saw instantly what had occurred and simultaneously decided, astutely, to pay it no mind. He slipped off his shoes as usual after sitting on his chair and, without losing another minute, took some files out of a drawer and started peering into them. Let down by the lack of a reaction from him, the crowd slowly dispersed.

Coinman continued to pretend to be lost in the files for the next few minutes. When all appeared to be normal again, he looked around to ensure that no one was looking at him. He then slowly collected the blasphemy, piece by piece, from his table and threw it all in the trash can. A few minutes later, he slipped beneath his table and stretched his hands out to collect even more pieces from the floor. He had his head and body completely inside the table and arms close to the floor to keep others from noticing his activity. After successfully collecting all the smut, he slipped back into the chair, waited for a minute, and looked around one more time, just to make sure no one suspected anything.

Then, closing his eyes, Coinman started practicing deep breathing quietly to suppress his anger. He was very clear on who'd done this: who else but the most uncivilized man at the office, Hukum. A straight punch in the face would suit him the best for what he had done, thought Coinman, but a straight talk seemed more pragmatic.

So Coinman waited patiently for half an hour, until he saw Hukum heading outside for a smoke with his gang and followed after them. Once outside, he watched them from a distance until Hukum inhaled his first drag. Then he approached them.

"Hey, guys, do you mind a quick chitchat?"

No one paid any attention to him, as if he weren't visible and audible. So Coinman went on without wasting time.

"I know that was your lewd poop scattered all over my desk," Coinman said to Hukum directly.

Hukum rolled his eyes to his right, to Coinman's face, without turning his head. He didn't reply until the inhaled smoke had come out of his mouth as rings after concluding its stunt with his lungs. "Are you speaking to me, fella?"

"No one else is here, other than you and your sidekicks. Whom can I speak to other than you when I am standing next to you?"

"That's all right. Don't lose it, buddy. I just wanted to make sure before I decide if I want to answer." Hukum took a much deeper puff this time, held his breath, and again started making rings of smoke. Once the rings faded, he turned to Coinman. "Be a sport, young man! I could almost see your Max Johnson super-active over there—don't tell me you didn't enjoy it."

The gang broke out laughing.

Coinman began shivering with anger, his chin being the command post.

"Have your parents never taught you to behave decently? Don't you have any moral values, guys?" Coinman managed to keep his voice calm despite a storm passing through his head.

A sly smile played on Hukum's dark lips. "I do have moral values, but I wouldn't blow them on you. You know, I have a limited stock of them—so I save them for emergencies. It's hard to tell these days when one may confront an emergency—like the one you faced on your desk few minutes ago. I don't want to take a risk. It's better to play safe by saving for emergency situations. Wouldn't you agree?"

Coinman's chin could easily have measured more than six on a Richter scale. Unfortunately, an appropriate rebuttal, a *quid pro quo* for which he would have sacrificed anything, didn't occur to him. Frustrated, he merely turned and went back to his seat to save himself further mortification.

But the pranks had only begun.

The next day when Coinman wanted to pay a visit to the restroom, he realized that his shoes were missing. Someone had spirited them away very cleverly from below his chair. He looked for them everywhere possible—inside the drawer, beneath the chair, underneath the table, even on others' feet; to no avail.

He walked to Ratiram in the end. "You wouldn't believe this—I can't find my shoes. I was wondering if you have any ideas where to look for them?"

"Well, dear Coin, the only possibility lies with the mighty mice that are present aplenty here. I suggest you look at all the places that are normally hidden from view."

Though unconvinced by Ratiram's idea, Coinman went to each corner looking for his shoes, and came back to Ratiram to make a request. "Would you be able to help buy a new pair of shoes for me from the market outside our office?"

Ratiram shrugged and said, "Dear Coin, ask me for anything else within the office boundary, and I swear by you, I will deliver that. It's sad that my hands are tied a bit here. I cannot go outside the office during business hours. The management is increasing scrutiny on me, specifically on my disappearances during office hours."

It's not his hands that are tied but his heart, Coinman thought. Under the frustration of recent events and current madness, this was the first time Coinman ever thought of Ratiram that way. He knew for a fact that Ratiram had spent a great deal of time outside the office recently. *Even if that was for official business, can't he pretend this is business too—for the sake of friendship?*

"That's awful. Why would they do that to you? I hope all goes well with you regarding the scrutiny. In the meantime, I hope you don't mind me borrowing your slippers for a few minutes, so that I can buy a new pair," Coinman persisted, to test Ratiram's intent. "I will be back before you blink!"

Ratiram slyly smiled and slowly shook his head.

"Actually, I forgot to tell you about an internal swelling that I have in my feet today. Some kind of a bacterial infection that's in the beginning stage—can't be observed right now, can only be felt. Long story short, I cannot be without my footwear."

"Crazy liar!" Coinman barely kept himself from shouting back to Ratiram. *In this world, it is so difficult to judge who is on your side! Thanks, God, for revealing his true face to me today. It's strange how necessary it is to have problems to be able to prepare for avoiding future disasters.*

Coinman was happy to see Ratiram's true face sooner rather than later, yet was very sad to lose his best friend, especially when it happened so unexpectedly.

Now that he thought about it, Coinman realized that some of Ratiram's actions should have tipped him off about the guy's true self earlier. Coinman clearly remembered one instance when he had talked to Ratiram about his lack of companionship with Imli—his honest feelings about his married life at the time when Imli had gone to her parents' place. He'd extracted a promise from Ratiram to keep it only to himself. But what had happened? Only a few days later he had a colleague drop by his desk to talk about it and ask if he could help in any way. When he'd confronted Ratiram, he'd responded emotionally that Coinman's anguish had been too big a burden on him to bear alone. It was out of sympathy that he had shared with only a few colleagues.

It all became very clear to him now. Coinman rebuked himself for not knowing better. *I should have understood his true nature back then!*

Coinman called the admin department to find out if it could arrange for shoes; the person on the other side had the bright idea that Coinman could call his wife, who could then drive to the office with a new pair of shoes.

"If only that could happen," Coinman sighed, without revealing anything more. Instead he patiently waited till the last person had left the office, and then left barefoot.

Barefoot! It wasn't a matter of discomfort or money. It was a matter of pride. He was in no hurry to buy shoes now and drove to his house barefoot.

Thus, from that day forward, when Coinman arrived at the office, he took his shoes off and locked them in a drawer before commencing his work. Whenever he needed to walk, he opened the lock, took his shoes out, wore them, and went. When he came back, he again locked his shoes in the drawer. He did this religiously for a week before he got lazy about the endless locking, unlocking, and locking. So he started staying barefoot in the office. He wore shoes only while coming to or leaving work. He even recommended his barefoot enchantment to other colleagues.

"It's a heavenly feeling, when the foot, the powerhouse of reflexology, touches the cold marble floor," he said. "The collaboration sends a soul-fulfilling sensation through the whole body."

A few days later, when Coinman found that his lunchbox was missing from his bag, he didn't bother with Hukum or Ratiram, nor did he even search for the box. He remained hungry that day to demonstrate his protest. He brought a new lunchbox the next day. From then on, his lunchbox went into his locked drawer, right next to his shoes.

12. The Restroom Addiction

*S*ometimes two strangers are just waiting for a chance to discover each other to become best friends. This was true in the case of Daulat and Kasturi, who had found a soul mate in each other after the union arranged by their parents. In no time their afternoon siestas had emerged as a sublime platform for their soul-merging conversations, and were to remain so for the next thirty years, until Daulat's transformation into a schizoid personality began.

Their ongoing afternoon symposium had dealt with various hot topics while they idled around in their bedroom after lunch.

By the time their child, Kesar, had turned five years old, he had already won a spot in the symposium for not being able to commence his elementary education, despite their having tried all the schools in the area, because he was inconsolably upset in his parents' absence. It was déjà vu every time: they would leave him in school on his first day, he would become sick from crying the whole day, and the school administration would call Daulat and ask him to educate his child elsewhere.

It was a vicious cycle. The more the attempts to get him to a school, the more abandoned and insecure he felt.

"Next time you take me to a school," he often forewarned them, "I am going to flee to an unknown place and won't ever show up at home."

Then one day, on his sixth birthday, he actually disappeared from the house. His parents looked for him everywhere before calling the police, who then connected to the current "lost and found" reports to locate him quickly. Someone had already reported a kid crying alone in a strip mall at the city outskirts. The family was able to recover Kesar safely, but couldn't stop the issue from becoming explicitly visible to people outside the house.

Good neighbors always spy on you to make sure you are doing well. Cheela, being a good neighbor, had been constantly observing the challenge his neighbors had, and he couldn't resist volunteering his advice to the parents when he found an appropriate social opportunity for a conversation.

"We have been there with our son Bunty," Cheela said. "We asked around, looked into newspaper advertisements, and intercepted the parents of disciplined children, including ones we had no prior acquaintance with. Our attempts seemed unproductive and frustrating; we were ready to give up when we finally heard about this school that exclusively enrolled such children."

"Such children?" Daulat asked confusedly.

"I will not dawdle, Daulat. There is no point in housing troubles inside your underwear if you can't solve them by yourself. Put them right on your forehead for everyone to see. Besides implying your willingness to accept others' help, this will allow them to team up with you to help solve your problem."

"But there is nothing really wrong with Kesar."

"Then why is he not in a school yet like all other kids his age?" Cheela asked. "Daulat, I know it's tough for parents to see a problem in their child. But if you overlook it now, you may reach a point of no correction on this. You must admit your child's problem based on the facts and outcomes, instead of overapplying your heart's voice."

"How did Bunty do?"

"It took him only one year at that school to turn from the most introverted and shy kid I knew to the most extroverted kid in our family. The school has some sort of a magic wand."

"What's the name of the school?"

"TDMS—Tiny Devils Montessori School. All right, I get it, they probably don't have the best-sounding name! But look, it is what it is. That's their expertise—to help parents like you and me when nothing else seems to work."

"Cheela, I value your advice very highly. But I need to think more. It's not an easy decision. What would I tell him when he grows up and finds out that he was admitted into this school because we couldn't handle his ways that are a bit different from other kids', and for which no one else but us is responsible."

"He will love you more when he discovers as a grown-up that you acted in the best interest of his life."

"I am sure he will. I'd better get going—Kasturi must be waiting for me."

"It was great chatting with you. Keep me in the loop on how it goes, or if you need any help. And by the way," Cheela said before he left, "should you decide to admit your son in the school, make sure you don't get in the way of the school. They have devised fail-proof ways after years of research. Some parents find these ways different than anything they have seen in the past."

"What kind of ways?"

"You will find out. Just don't make it tough for them to follow their process by your undue intervention."

Daulat and Kasturi discussed the matter in detail throughout the week during their afternoon siestas, looking at it from every possible angle, before deciding to try out the school.

A tour of the school left them completely impressed. They couldn't wait to complete the admission formalities. Daulat couldn't check his enthusiasm, and called Cheela from the school itself to express the family's gratitude to him.

"Remember: no troubles go in the underwear ever in the future," Cheela reminded him, and laughed so hard that he had to put the phone down to cough.

The family had a memorable welcome on their child's first day of the school. The principal called the entire staff early for a meet-and-greet with the family. Despite the unexpectedly early disappearance of jumbo blueberry muffins, the complimentary breakfast buffet managed to enhance the occasion well.

After a grand welcome to the family, Ms. Ida was asked to take the child to her class. But Kesar held his spot on the floor, with his hands behind his waist, to prevent Ms. Ida from leading him with them. Every time she tried to get his hands off his back, he cried loudly. He then ran back toward his parents and grabbed Kasturi's right leg with both his hands.

Ms. Ida ran after him and dragged him from Kasturi. Then, to the parents' shock, she lifted him, holding his armpits, and heaved him in the air two feet above her head. She made it very quick and seemingly easy, lifting and heaving in one continuous motion. Then she released her hands when they reached her head's height, to bring Kesar as high as possible before starting the free fall.

Astonished, the parents watched as she made no move to catch him until he reached her waist height and looked almost certain to hit the floor. Kesar had abruptly stopped crying at that point and had shut his eyes in a nervous panic, bracing for the inevitable crash. Ms. Ida caught him then, by quickly lowering her arms at the speed of his fall and decelerating slowly to stop just an inch or two above the ground.

The terrifying fear of a crash had triggered the fight-or-flight response in the child, making him burn a mule, but only he knew about it—thanks to his tight and reliable underpants.

"Don't worry, Mr. and Mrs. Daulat." Ms. Ida tried to relieve the parents' state of shock. "We run complex software to make this a completely safe exercise. The software tells us the range of elevation and the point of catch accurately based on aspects like weight, height, and such. I myself have done this several thousand times, and no kid's even had a minor injury."

"But still, this was so dangerous. What if our kid was the unfortunate one to get hurt? The first one out of those thousands you talked about." Daulat didn't hold back his concern.

"Are you suspecting our process?" Ms. Ida challenged.

"No, that's not exactly what I meant."

"Then leave your son here," said Ms. Ida, looking toward the door without moving her head. "Please! He'll be fine. We will take good care of him."

The parents couldn't move. They were still frozen in awe of the unbelievable callousness they had just witnessed.

"Please get going now." Ms. Ida's tone became sterner as she put their child back on the floor. "Do you want your son to remain a sitting duck for rest of his life? You have ensured that a great deal already. We are trying to recover him from the damage you've done to him. Now leave him here, will you? At least you can avoid being the biggest reason behind him becoming a pinhead as an adult."

Daulat had a craving to snatch his boy from Ms. Ida and punch her in the face—with an apology to God later for having done so. But he resisted, considering the good intent and the school's success stories that he had heard from other parents. With a heavy heart, he decided to leave without Kesar to take some time later in the day reassessing the school, but his child broke his deep musing. With a quick move, Kesar grabbed Ms. Ida's right hand, raised himself to swing on her arm, and sank his teeth into her hand.

Ms. Ida shrieked in pain, shaking her hand vigorously to throw him on the ground. When everyone rushed to help her, the child seized the opportunity to turn and run toward his parents. Instead of caring for her desperately bleeding hand, Ms. Ida furiously ran after Kesar and grabbed him by the collar of his shirt before he could get to them. She sat on the ground next to him in a squatting position, and slapped him on both cheeks like a hurricane.

Before anyone could relay a protest, she lifted him in her arms and ran to the classroom at the end of the hall, threw the child inside, and locked the room. All other classrooms opened to a long corridor facing a lawn except this one: it was located at the end, facing the bathrooms, and hardly saw any daylight. It was used primarily as storage, although reluctantly, due to its nose-splitting smell of prolonged dampness.

Daulat and Kasturi demanded Ms. Ida unlock the door right away, under threat of complaint to the principal. When she didn't budge, they ran to the principal's office and told everything to her in a breath. Quite upset, the principal left what she was in the middle of and went straight to Ms. Ida.

"Are you guys not taking parents through all the conditions before obtaining their signatures?" she demanded of Ms. Ida. "We clearly state on the forms that the parents have no rights concerning their child while he is at school."

Before Ms. Ida could answer, the principal turned to the parents and said, "I sincerely apologize for our mistake. You can come back in my office, and I will again personally go over the conditions that you have signed on."

The parents were at a complete loss. Daulat made a few calls in desperation and assured Kasturi that he was getting support to get their kid out at any cost. He had to leave but asked Kasturi to stay near the room until he got the support with him.

"Don't make a court case out of it. This is normal here. Besides, no parents are allowed in the class area," the principal said.

"I need my son here"—Daulat spoke in anger, grinding his teeth—"right now. It's my fundamental right to have my child with me when I want him."

"We offer our best apologies," Ms. Ida said, "but that's not possible, sir. You've already signed documents to allow us to take full care of your son during school hours."

"Well, I don't get it. I am absolutely clueless as to why you have to keep him in a dark room! He is only six years old, dammit! You may do permanent harm to his mind—do you even care about that?" Daulat said, ignoring the fact that the situation left him little room for argument.

"We follow a time-tested process here. No one has ever been harmed here. Your kid is no different than other kids who have undergone the same process. He'll be just fine."

Kasturi was sobbing by now.

"All of you need a checkup from the neck up." Daulat shouted as he prepared to leave with Kasturi. He went on. "We will come back in a few minutes to get our child back from you monsters. And you will have a fun time soon, that's my promise."

"You aren't the first parent to try this. So don't feel bad about losing it on us when you come back in an hour apologizing for your behavior, like other parents have done in the past." The principal looked smug.

"We'll see soon who apologizes." Daulat started to go, stomping his feet in anger. Then he suddenly stopped, ran to the last classroom, and shouted through the door. "Be brave, Son. I am coming back in a jiffy to get you out of this lousy place. You need to help Papa and Mamma by not being scared for a few more minutes."

The child came to the door and thumped it, but his parents were gone by then. Nothing was visible inside because the door was the only source of light in the room.

Kesar wept for a few minutes, but when it seemed futile to continue, he stopped. Lying down on the floor, he thought about where his parents would be at the moment—wondering if they would get what they needed in order to take him back with them. Then he pondered the likelihood of his parents' method not working on the principal and whether, in that case, the school would release him at the end of the day. Lost in such thoughts, he fell asleep.

When he woke up, he found himself in bed, in his bedroom, with Daulat and Kasturi stooping over him.

"Hope you are fine, Son," Daulat said, his voice full of affection. Then, in a clear effort to wipe away his son's ghastly experience, he went on with a touch of mischief, "Show me your tongue. Let me make sure it's still the same one I left you at the school with. You haven't exchanged it with someone at school, have you?"

The son smiled. "That's not possible, Dad. You do not even know that much?" He turned to his mother. "Ma, Dad doesn't even know that tongues can't be exchanged."

Kasturi made suggestive eye contact with Daulat, and answered with a smile, "Ask your dad. He may have had some experience exchanging his tongue with someone."

"Really, Dad?"

Daulat laughed. "No, Son. Looks like your mommy still remembers it from her beautiful dreams. And you know, anything can happen in dreams and might seem entirely natural."

Seeing their son speak normally was enough to reassure them.

When Daulat and Kasturi had left their child at school earlier that day, they had at once visited their lawyer friend, Pappu, at his office. As it turned out, the school principal was a good friend of Pappu as well. Pappu assured the parents of a painless resolution and suggested that the best next step was to speak to the principal in person. The three of them then drove straight to the school. Such was Pappu's friendship with the principal that he didn't even need to knock on the door.

"Hello, there," Pappu greeted the principal as they entered her office. "How is it going, smart cookie?"

"Look who is here! Pappu, my friend, what a pleasant surprise." The principal got up from her chair and ran to hug him. "You've made my day."

"Likewise," Pappu said. "It's always so wonderful to meet you. I am not sure if we've seen each other since the wine-tasting trip."

"Wow. It seems you still have the same terabyte memory. How can you remember everything? Ha, ha—sorry, can't help laughing, your wife was completely legless and fell on the ground. And then, as we were coming back, she insisted on driving, and slapped you when you did not give her the keys."

"Ahem, well." Pappu looked away for a moment. "What a fun time, wasn't it? But, hey…the reason I am here and thought you could assist, is to help my friend Daulat. There seems to be some misunderstanding between him and your staff here."

"Allow me to explain," the principal interrupted. "After Mr. and Mrs. Daulat left their boy with us, the overall assessment of the staff was that he needed what we call a capsule course in discipline. For this we leave the students in a dark room for extended hours. The boy is completing the prescribed capsule course right now. He will need to be there for two more hours, and then he is all yours. Now, that seems very harsh, I understand, but it's a very normal thing for us. There is a science behind this which I want you to allow me to—"

Daulat stood up before the principal could complete her sentence. "Science, my eye! Are you saying that our son is still in the dark room? Tell me now, before I punch every single staff member of yours."

"Let me handle it, Daulat," Pappu interjected, and turned to the principal. "Hey, listen up. It's not legal to keep a boy hostage without consent from his parents. I demand you release him right now."

The principal understood that it was not about winning anymore but about handling the situation smartly. She didn't like that she had to release the boy but understood that she didn't have a case in Pappu's presence; Pappu could have easily presented a legal clause for maltreating a minor child, overruling the legal binding of the parents to the school's discipline. Debating with Pappu might even have landed her into a lost legal battle. So, resigned, she asked Ms. Ida to release the child without delay.

They followed after Ms. Ida and as she opened the door, Kasturi ran to pick up her son, who was in a deep slumber. Without waking him, she very carefully lifted him to put his head gently on her shoulders and her arms around his bottom.

As they were leaving, the principal couldn't resist a parting shot.

"You are making the blunder of your life! Your son is hopeless, and this was his last chance. You'll remember this every time your child fails."

"Wait till I see you in court," Daulat retorted quietly, careful to not wake his son up in Kasturi's safe embrace. He knew that he threatened only for the sake of it, because the school had influence over the city administration and nothing was going to happen even if he sued the school. But it made him feel better to at least tell her off.

They left the school without another word.

Mankind has relentlessly wished that everything in life was measurable but, alas, barring a tiny fraction, nothing really is. There's no way of knowing how much of an effect this event had on Coinman's life. Nevertheless, Coinman's parents were going to hold this particular event responsible, largely, for the singularities in his personality thereafter.

Following the event, his parents arranged a home tutor to see to his academics through age ten. While on one hand this could be considered successful because it allowed Kesar to be with his parents while getting his education, on the other hand it caused an economic misery for the family. Before he started school regularly at sixth grade, at age eleven, Kesar had already cost his parents a fortune without showing signs of genius. As a result of the teaching style of the home tutor, he had also acquired a peculiar academic quirk. During exams, he knew all the answers but wasn't able to successfully map his answers to the right questions. So as soon as an exam started, he simply started putting his answers in the order in which he remembered them. Every time he moved to a new class, his parents made the new teachers aware of this snag. The teachers acknowledged it and reassured the parents that they'd match his answers against the appropriate questions.

Thanks to his teachers' relentless efforts, he was able to fully overcome this mental handicap before he was in tenth grade; yet he still didn't do well in his subjects, despite studying hard. He attended all the classes, prepared notes with different-colored pens, and talked to the teachers after each class to clarify his doubts. When he got back home, he would sit in his study chair till late at night. His parents were at a complete loss as to why his hard work wasn't paying off. Had he been like other boys who did poorly because of their involvement in non-academic affairs, they could have handled it; but he was a very studious boy. They did not know what could be done.

"Just like a boxer can't win without a few punches on his face, a student can't be fully trained without ups and downs." Kasturi would say things like this to raise her son's spirits every time he had to repeat a course. And finally, his teachers' understanding about his limitation in academics, together with his hard work, gained him his bachelor's degree.

It was a time when a degree was expected but not much respected. To win a job one had to either be super smart or make up for it by having the right connections or the right amount of money to spare. Fortunately, Daulat's deterioration had only begun at the time of Coinman's graduation; he largely avoided social interactions but hadn't shut himself so much to the inward that he couldn't go back and open the social doors if he needed to. So he could still use all his connections and his remaining hard-earned money on getting Coinman a job. That's how he got Coinman a postman's job.

Coinman had completed one year at the post office, however, when Kasturi complained to Daulat about the job: "What kind of onerous job have you put my son into? Look at him, just look. He has lost almost half of his weight in one year! And I could swear his height is also getting worn down, inch by inch, because of walking on foot the entire day. Look here." She raised her right hand over her head, forming a letter C with her thumb and fingers, the thumb touching her head. "He was this much taller than me, before —this much, but now, he's just as tall as I am. Find him another job so that he can leave this miserable job now. Say, dear husband, what's the use of a job if it's a compromise of one's physical well-being?"

When Kasturi thought a topic deserved serious attention from the other party, as in the present case, she put her point across in a melodramatic way. Daulat's sharply declining emotional intelligence was constantly causing Kasturi sleepless nights—she at least wanted Daulat, before he was to lose his sanity completely, to use his contacts to land Coinman in a stable and more rewarding job. She knew that with the current trajectory of Daulat's condition, the family was running out of time.

Daulat had begun to be not quite himself already. But, when he was, for a small fraction of his time, he appreciated Kasturi's practicality about his condition. He found out that one of his own former colleagues was acquainted with the owner of a big firm. Daulat pursued the lead relentlessly until Coinman was offered employment as a clerk.

By the time Coinman had settled into his new job, Daulat had ventured further into his secret inward world. Additionally, he had had a sharp decline in his memory, and his social abilities had become very severely limited.

Daulat's world kept shrinking around himself—until it contained mainly him. He hardly spoke to anyone, unless he was made to, and hardly remembered anything unless reminded. He never asked for food, eating only when it was served. Kasturi tried to engage him in as much physical activity as possible; she even forced him out of the house for a walk around the neighborhood. Yet it was only a temporary interruption of his downward spiral. Doctors couldn't bring any ray of hope, either.

"What would you have for lunch?" Kasturi asked him on one occasion around this time, entering his room.

He did not answer. He was lost in the newspaper.

Kasturi walked to him and shook his shoulder. "Hey, listen, what do you want to have?"

"What?"

"Food, food. Do you want to eat rice or bread?"

Daulat stared at her face for a minute, looking lost. "Anything."

"Anything isn't available anymore. What would you like to eat other than anything?"

Daulat just stared at her again and said, "Maybe salads?"

Then he got up and walked out the door to go to the kitchen. He pulled out cucumber and kale from the refrigerator and started cutting them.

"At least wash them first," Kasturi shouted, then noticed that his hand was bleeding. He had cut himself but did not know it until she hurried to him with clean cotton and dabbed the cut.

"Look," Kasturi said, "you have hurt yourself so badly. That's why we tell you to ask us for what you want."

As such problems became more frequent, Kasturi was actually relieved when she saw Daulat develop a new fetish for reading the newspaper. He essentially started having another address within his house: he lived in the newspaper of the day. When someone wanted to locate him, the best advice was, "Look for today's newspaper."

As soon as he got up, he jumped off his bed and ran outside the house to fetch the paper for that day. The newspaper was delivered at six in the morning by the hawker, and Daulat set his clock to wake him up a minute before six. This had two purposes: first, to get him to the paper as early as it was delivered; second, to let him avoid having to spend any impatient waking moments without the newspaper of the day. In the rare event that he had to wait for a few minutes, he would get the previous day's newspaper from the shelf to kill time.

Daulat spent a large amount of time reading the newspaper in the bathroom, after accidentally discovering the joy of carrying out the two most important tasks of his existence together. What had started as a method to avoid a disruption to his avid reading by an unwanted call from nature soon turned into an addiction. Once he went in the restroom with his paper, he did not come out until someone knocked at the door.

If he found an exciting news heading, he immediately rushed to the restroom to savor it in the most enjoyable conditions possible. Once, during an increasingly rare moment of sanity, he even tried to convince Coinman of it.

"The joy of reading while simultaneously evacuating your bowels is second to none in the world," he enthusiastically declared. "You will have to experience it to really appreciate it. There are only a very few ways in this world to achieve utmost physical and mental satisfaction, both at the same time. The relief experienced by the execution of one activity helps in achieving a greater focus on the other. And as a result, each word that you read seems to be descending straight from heaven."

13. The Sublime Collusion

*S*ometimes fate just plays a strange game of Scrabble with you. Irrespective of your tiles, and your successful turns, fate always gets all the doubles, triples, and bingos. If you challenge a word, fate always has it in the dictionary. On the other hand, if fate challenges a word, the word stops being valid in the dictionary. You have no clue what words fate will create.

You are always in some game with fate. Sometimes, despite your impeccable position, all the right moves, and all the foresight, it's fate that dictates what happens at the end.

Given the hatred against the coins that had recently leaped from below the surface to the center stage, and Hukum's failed attempts to have a dialogue with Coinman, everyone knew that someone needed to spearhead a formal campaign, yet no one could have ever guessed it was going to be Saarang.

The unpredicted twist in Saarang's meeting with Tulsi had led him to organize, quite unexpectedly, the most historic event connected to this story. Call it Saarang's attempt to make his fabricated story to Tulsi more authentic, or whatever, it was happening.

It started when Saarang gathered the first floor in the cafeteria, to almost a full capacity, and addressed the gathering.

"Friends, brothers, wingmen," he said, adjusting his tie, "lend me your ears; I cometh to fury Coinman, not to hon'r him; woes that he causes hath become oppressive. Mine heart is with Coinman, but mine mind sayeth that he wilt be amerced. We wilt not mourneth f'r ourselves. We wilt outcast the lown."

"Mine broth'r from anoth'r moth'r," Panna said, "we all know your desperate attempts at literature. You aren't in the ivy halls of your miserable literature pursuit now. Without wasting more time, will thou cometh to the pointeth? Dost thou wanteth us to stayeth or leaveth?"

"Stayeth, stayeth...certes," Saarang hurried to say nervously. He wasn't known as the best public speaker—perhaps why he was taking cover under Shakespeare.

"Without much further ado," Saarang said after collecting himself, "I will kick off the session today by declaring that my undying persistence with Tulsi has finally borne fruit."

He purposefully paused to see the hearts leaping as high as a mountain before continuing, "Therefore, I have a very distinguished new member with us today. She is no stranger but our own golden girl, Tulsi."

Clapping is easily the best example of self-amplification in the world. It sprouts from a single wham to a wave of sound in no time. As soon as someone clapped on hearing Tulsi's name, an avalanche of applause followed.

Tulsi appeared from nowhere, smiling, effecting an addendum to the applause.

Some of them even pinched themselves to double-check it wasn't a dream that they were partners in the coup with the most divine of all beauties. Saarang probably hadn't received as much gratitude in his entire life as he did in those few minutes.

Tulsi was clad in a purple sari that artfully wrapped around her waist, skillfully showing her enchanting collarbones that were in perfect harmony with her modest neckline.

"That was some greeting! This is such an enchanting group," she said. "Firstly, big thanks to Saarang for all the efforts. Since he has already apprised me of the latest and greatest, I am not going to get into the background and all. Good use of time is the universal ingredient in cooking a palatable dish—doesn't matter if you are baking, boiling, frying, brewing, or grilling."

"Or even microwaving!" Saarang's enthused addition caused an abrupt end to the laughter Tulsi had managed to launch them into.

Tulsi continued, "I would say, though, that I can already see the future success of our endeavor on each face here. I am thankful to God for honoring me with such amazing colleagues." Then she laughed. "Well, except for one."

The group burst out laughing again.

"Before I go further, let's agree on our goal. I have to ask this. Don't raise your hands if Coinman has perturbed you beyond your tolerance limit. Please raise your right hand otherwise."

"Very good," Tulsi said after seeing that no one had raised a hand. "It's very important to make sure we all are into it with our hearts and souls. Our management has buried their heads in the sand, but I am glad to see that we are all willing to take matters into our own hands. We are, however, going to do it our own subtle way."

"Allow me a sec," said Ratiram, "to emphasize the importance of team spirit here. Like Tulsi has said, when something is being planned, nothing is more crucial than sticking together till the very end."

"You have hit the nail on the head." Tulsi addressed Ratiram. "Thank you for bringing this important element up. Adding to what Ratiram has said"—she turned to the crowd again—"there will be a need for great teamwork to carry out different parts—and no matter how dire a situation we land ourselves in, no one must reveal specifics of who did what to anyone outside this circle."

"I get it," Hukum said, "but are we only going to talk in the air here? Can someone help me understand what we are going to do?" Hukum, it must be said, was still sour deep within because Saarang had snatched his opportunity to lead the crowd on the matter.

"Wait," Saarang chimed in. "I request everyone to allow Tulsi to share her thoughts first."

"Mate," Panna interjected toward Saarang, "aren't you fully recovered yet from the damn diarrhea that made the poor janitor work twenty-four-seven like your sidekick? This isn't the restroom, buddy. You can't afford to have bigger accidents here while only attempting to let some gas out."

No one, except Tulsi and Saarang, could resist a laugh.

For his wit, Panna's popularity wasn't only confined within the gang; he had a much larger fan following on the first floor. It was said that he had learned this art from Ratiram, during the latter's early days at the office when he hadn't yet tempered expressing his raw thoughts to the sophistication level required to maintain his current reputation. People also believed that Panna had read every possible book that was worth reading.

Tulsi pretended she was in such deep thought that she couldn't pay attention to what Panna had said.

"Let's get back to the point." Ratiram brought everyone back to focus at once.

"Let's see what our two captains have come up with!" Hukum said sarcastically. "They must at least have discussed broadly what needs to be done—else why would everybody be called here for just wasting time?"

"Let us strip him of his coins," Tulsi declared abruptly, caught off guard by Hukum's direct attack. "Let's rob the filthy insect of its wings!" She shouted, "Let's snatch his happiness and share it equally among us." Then she dropped her voice to almost a whisper. "Let's do it in a way that lets us kill the snake without breaking the stick."

"But why the heck do we need to snatch the coins? We can always find other ways to get his coins," Sevak put in. Even though he knew the answer, he asked the question for two reasons: one, to win some quick brownie points from Hukum; two, for the benefit of many others in the room who, he thought, didn't have enough guts to speak their minds in public but were likely to confuse others later.

"Tulsi's approach seems very sound to me," said Ratiram calmly. "By symbolically robbing his coins together, we are going to make a statement that the entire office is united against his coins and won't stand them anymore. If all we do is steal coins, Coinman will bring another set in no time. There is no way out but to confront him openly, collectively, and prudently."

Saarang was desperate to speak, as he was feeling sidelined from the meeting he was supposed to be leading. He had been searching for something to say for the past few minutes to reestablish his lost authority.

"I am sure there were dark thunderclouds, tornadoes, tsunamis, earthquakes—everywhere—when he was born," Saarang said. "Nature must have demonstrated a giant disagreement on the event and, in this manner, must have warned the innocent people of an upcoming crisis. If it is up to us to free the world from his tyranny, we will rise to the occasion. We will teach him such a lesson that his fingers will tremble at the very thought of going near his pockets!"

"I have not heard anything that useless in a while," Panna said. "Although I'll give you that it sounded like something great. But it didn't mean shit."

"Let's wrap this meeting up here," said Tulsi, realizing that the discussion might go sideways. "Ratiram, Hukum, and I will catch up offline and meet everyone here tomorrow to update the details of our execution plan."

Saarang was clearly offended by not being included in Tulsi's invitation. "Hey guys," he said, "don't forget to include me as well in the discussion."

"Why not?" said Tulsi. "After all, you might be able to at least listen in." She laughed as she said this, and everyone else laughed as well.

Et tu, Tulsi? That was all Saarang could think.

14. The Grapes of Wrath

A clay pitcher that goes to the well too often is broken at last.

Thus the big event happened, on a day when management was out of the office for an off-site meeting. Coinman had barely settled at his desk that morning, after transferring coins from his desk drawers to his left pocket, when Hukum walked up to him and put a twenty-rupee bill next to his nose from behind. "Coinman, mate, I have gotten myself in a kind of a desperate situation and need your help very urgently."

Coinman's chin had sensed something fishy and had started to flutter worse than a trapped flycatcher bird.

"How can I help?" Coinman asked, pushing the bill away from his face using his right hand. Hukum walked to the front to face him.

"I need to buy cigarettes—but have run out of change. Can I get some change for this bill?" Hukum could not resist a smile that risked exposing the dubiousness of his request.

His colleagues' recent odious episodes had bred an extra vigilance in Coinman, equipping his nose to smell a malicious prank in the making. Thus his newly upgraded nose and notably precautious chin had formed a deadly alarm system that could sense and signal the minutest unfavorable activity to the brain.

"That doesn't explain why you need change. I have always seen a full pack with you. So why would you suddenly want to buy loose cigarettes?" Sufficiently alarmed, Coinman's brain was at work.

Hukum did not seem prepared for this question—he couldn't respond promptly. Then he thought fast.

"I have promised my wife that I am quitting smoking," he lied smoothly. "I am going to reduce the number of cigarettes I smoke every day. The only way I can do it is by continuously reducing over weeks. If I keep the pack, I can't achieve this. I have promised myself that I will go and buy a loose cigarette every time I want to smoke. You'd agree I have better chances with that. Now please—give me the change. I am dying with cravings here. I have had only one cigarette since I woke up."

"Well, these coins are a gift from a very dear friend," Coinman said, seeing that other colleagues were very attentively following their conversation. "I can't give them to you. My apologies. You can ask others. And if you think you might need some change tomorrow, I can happily bring it then."

"Actually, I need the coins right now," Hukum said, looking like a resolute lion detaining its prey. "And I really can't settle for any other coins but the ones that you are carrying in your pocket right now."

Coinman could see that a number of others had left their work and were gathering around them, keeping a safe distance.

"What kind of hooliganism is this? I have a right to decide about my own coins." Coinman could barely speak through gasps of anger and nervousness.

"You have only two options," Hukum declared. "Either gift your coins peacefully to us, or we are going to rescue the coins from your pocket without your consent."

"Us? We? Who else wants the change?" Saying this, Coinman looked around, and the entire picture flashed clearly in his mind.

It was a moment of truth. At a time when he really needed all the grit that could come his way, he instead felt like a deer detained by lions, and his heart bore the weight of the world. He felt he was sinking deeper every moment into a bottomless abyss. His chin had gone berserk—but it was more nuisance than help now, since he fully knew the danger he was in.

Hukum knew well that any imprudent move from him at this delicate point could make Coinman run zigzag in panic. So he inched closer to him in small arcs.

Terror-stricken, Coinman was frozen. Collecting all his courage, he slowly moved backward until he hit a pillar. Startled by this, he turned to his right and began to run toward the main entrance—only to find it blocked by Daya and Panna.

"What's the hurry, Your Majesty?" Panna said, and laughed. He was improvising his role in this. "Whence doth thou wanteth to goeth, leaving us hither?"

Coinman could see his colleagues were everywhere— blocking all the exits. And the worst: a number of them had started walking toward him in a circle.

Defeated, and sweating terribly, Coinman stopped and stood quietly in silent dread. No words could come out of his mouth, even though he wanted to shout. Worse, he knew that even if he'd been able to shout, no one would help— they were all in on this. He suddenly noticed, through blurring vision, that Ratiram was watching from a distance. Though Coinman had recently discovered the snake in him, this was the first time he saw Ratiram's open participation in his disgrace. It broke his heart again—somehow he hadn't given up fully on Ratiram until now. Until now he'd still hoped.

Caught in dejection, Coinman was distracted enough that Hukum had time to grip both his arms together in a handcuff position. Sevak slipped his hand in Coinman's left pocket, a place that had been more remote and confidential than a nuclear missile site, to grab all the coins. Amazingly, the coins seemed to have a mind of their own. They dodged his relentless fist every time. The imbalance in the united stance of the three men made every second challenging for Hukum and Sevak, trying to stay put until the coins were successfully retrieved. Daya and Panna rushed to bring in more stability and make it less difficult for Sevak to draw out the coins. Daya put a noose of his arms around Coinman's waist, while Panna dropped to his knees and held Coinman by his thighs pressed against his chest. Most of Coinman's energy was now focused on keeping him standing.

Help isn't always useful when complexities of mind are involved.

"Aaaaarrrrgh!"

Coinman screeched, a hysterical explosion in terror, and channeled force through his arms and legs to push everyone away from him as hard as he could. As a result, all five of them collapsed onto the floor. The coins were completely unprepared for this and were sadly deceived by their own inertia. As a result the coins sheepishly fell to the floor—old and new, outdated and in use, humiliated but still in the news.

Scrambling, Coinman made a frenzied attempt to collect the coins, but a dark mental jolt suddenly shook his whole body, entirely blinding him for a few moments.

His life so far hadn't prepared him to cope gracefully with this degree of embarrassment. In total humiliation, he lost control over his senses for a moment, lying helplessly on the floor. The overly colorful images of his colleagues appeared to pierce the dark that occupied most of his vision, to peek at him before disappearing quickly to merge back with the dark. Their faces had even begun to distort, exaggerating repulsive features normally hidden. Some of these faces even grew bigger in size and laughed before disappearing in the dark.

Coinman tried to speak but couldn't. He felt publicly stripped, as if his clothes had suddenly disappeared from his body. Bracing himself on his hands, he scrambled desperately for support to stand up again, but he couldn't seem to muster it alone. Of course no one came forward to help him. One by one everyone dispersed, leaving him and his coins looking like a tragic battlefield just after a war.

Coinman had no clue how to gather his dignity back, scattered in coins around him. It was few more minutes before he managed to get up and stumble away in silence.

15. The Qualm and ABC

*D*ead air ruled the first floor following the coin robbery —a perfect silence, much like the one that lingers after a storm.

The magnitude of the robbery had surpassed all their imaginations; they were worried now. There was only one possible sequel to this enormous incident—an ABC apocalypse. The engagement with ABC, the three most dreaded men at the office, was imminent. An incident of the magnitude they'd pulled off, they thought, was surely going to be reported to the administration.

They hadn't imagined it was going to turn out this way; all they had planned for was taking the coins out of Coinman's pocket, making a loud statement of their revolt against his tyranny. Now they knew that it had unquestionably gone too far. A breach of discipline of such magnitude had never escaped the ears of higher management, irrespective of where it happened, what it was, or who was involved in it.

On the other hand, the great mystery had always been *how* such things got reported to senior management. Some had even searched in vain for hidden cameras on the first floor.

The fear of the consequences made them radically reflective now. They felt their plan had been sloppy, impatient, and half-baked. Why would they plan in such a way, knowing of management's vulture eyes? Doubtless excitement had made them careless—excitement that came about from a synthesis of Tulsi's charisma, Saarang's want of attention, their desire to deep-six the coins, Ratiram's unconditional support, Hukum's steam, and, above all, a big opportunity to let loose.

In their excitement they had failed to understand that unlike their regular pranks, this one wasn't going to remain under the radar of the disciplinary process that had been enforced at the office for years. Realizing that only now was a humongous source of shame.

No one could blame them for a collective cold sweat.

Discipline at the office had long been enforced by the use of three methods: the meeting of the first kind, the meeting of the second kind, and the meeting of the third kind. These easy-to-remember methods were comprehensively documented in the employee handbook to help managers enforce superlative discipline at the workplace. The new associates were told about them as part of their onboarding process.

In a nutshell, when a discipline infringement occurred, its scale determined the method. A bigger offense warranted a meeting of a higher kind. It was technically possible, as was well documented in the handbook, to upgrade a meeting to the next kind on the spot if the need and circumstances left no other option. However, this was roundly discouraged to ensure the right application the first time; one of the things people did best at the office was to use flexibility to its last atom. It was not permitted, however, to upgrade a meeting of the first kind directly to a meeting of the third kind; it had to then go through the two-level process—an upgrade to the second kind, and then, if proceedings of the second kind warranted, another upgrade to the third kind.

The meeting of the first kind, simply referred to as "first kind," was the most sparing of the three. It was a meeting with one's own supervisor, and could come about for practically anything. The meeting of the first kind was purposefully kept fluid to allow a universe of possible topics. The handbook had left it fully to the discretion of the supervisor to determine what a good-enough cause for the first kind was, citing some examples such as missing timelines repeatedly, humming lousy songs during office hours, getting caught shopping during a sick day off, dancing when others worked, keeping a skin flick at the office, wearing revealing clothes, using Ratiram for personal work, complaining openly about management, or dispensing soundless air biscuits deadly enough to knock an elephant to the ground.

For this reason "first kinds" were taken so lightly that it was almost customary for the suspect to receive verbal tickling and even compliments for having been invited. The only thing that could go wrong with this kind, a negligible possibility, was an upgrade to a second kind.

The handbook clearly stated, however, that if an employee was referred to a meeting of the first kind for a fifth time, it automatically upgraded him to the second kind. These meetings were very carefully tracked by the administration in a centralized system that proactively spotted automatic upgrades.

"Small crimes multiply," the handbook stated philosophically, "to consolidate into a bigger crime. Bigger crimes need bigger probes. The automatic upgrade to the next kind covers the risk from inevitable inconsistency in decision-making by individual managers, thereby taking our vision of a hassle-free workspace to an unforeseen level."

The serious business started with the second kind: a meeting with the unit head, Jay, a most polite man who could hold his calm composure even while delivering the most unfavorable message to the other party. During a second kind, the suspect was consistently roasted with tough questions until the matter was resolved, or until the meeting was upgraded to the third kind. If the suspect was determined guilty, Jay not only determined the penalty, but also warned that the next offense of the second kind within six months would automatically qualify the offender for the third kind. Even though people knew that no one had lost a job during a meeting of the second kind, the suspect lost sleep until the verdict came out—because a second kind brought the suspect very close to a third kind. For this reason, someone subjected to a second kind received a vanilla wish from everyone of, "Hope the meeting remains true to its kind!"

The last one, the third kind, was the gravest of the lot. It was also known informally by many other names: "third degree," "date with ABC," "summons," "gold letter," or "deathbed." All the third kinds in the history of the firm had ended with a termination of the suspect's employment with the firm. The meeting was a form of abysmal trial conducted by ABC, Andar, Bandar, and Chandar. Their exact positions with the firm could never be confirmed, yet it was common knowledge that they possessed the highest authority in matters of utmost importance to the firm. The only way to see or meet ABC was through meetings of the third kind. It was a catch-22 situation for anyone who wanted to meet them because that meant the last day at the firm for that person. So no one wished to meet them. A mere mention of their names was enough to bring a cold chill up the spine.

Ratiram had famously described it once to the gossipmongers: "It's our version of a black hole. Just like amply compact mass can distort space and time to cause a black hole, a sufficiently dense breach of discipline in our office causes a black hole that sucks the offender away for eternity, never to spit him back."

Since an offender of the third kind slipped directly into abysmal oblivion at the culmination of the trial, no one could ever witness the debris from a third kind. Yet rumor had it that the offender's cerebral state after this trial was in such an indescribable mess that if asked, the person would probably need a few minutes to recall his father's name.

The last time a third kind had happened was around two years back when the accountant Ramta, who found it difficult to remain non-abusive during a meeting of the second kind, was referred by Jay to a third kind. Despite this decision's being a no-brainer, Jay had taken two months before upgrading Ramta to a meeting of the third kind—such was the prudence exercised by the management, because a third kind had to be well covered from a legal perspective.

It was said that Ramta had received an invitation to a third kind via a golden envelope in his drawer at the office. The rumors said that Ramta couldn't open the gold letter immediately because the strength in his shaking hands had failed him completely. That was the last time anyone had seen him. His disappearance had been no surprise, but confirmed that the sanctity of the process was still fully intact. The rumors had added that Ramta had held ABC's feet to plead for mercy as the only source of bread and butter for his family of seven, but ABC couldn't tarnish a success story that had spanned decades.

Why were the workers here, with a discipline so hard to bear?

It was a mixed bundle of reasons: First, a group denial carried people through the days: bad things happen only to others. No one ever believed that it could be him…until it really was. Second, the third kind was very unlikely in most cases; per the records, there had been only five third kinds in the last twenty years—probably fewer than the number of people who'd kicked the bucket during that same time period. Third, the workers knew of no one else who had as much fun at work as they did. It was said that no one had ever left the firm voluntarily.

"If you ask me," Ratiram had once said, "it's the daily kick of the place more than anything else. No superior fun like this comes without taking a chance. Acceptance of the danger is of the essence for playing a quality sport."

Panna had once told Daya that golf was no longer the most popular sport among the corporate czars because they found playing with natural balls much more satisfying.

"In the case of ABC," he had added, "the enjoyment is even more fulfilling because they get to dispose of the balls after each game."

16. Connubial Fluctuations

*D*espite progress witnessed elsewhere in matters of the heart, parents in this part of the world haven't quite come around to letting their adult offspring choose their lovers.

Coinman's parents were certainly different from the majority. Kasturi had very open-mindedly allowed Coinman a decent amount of time to find a partner for himself. But after observing the lack of acquaintance his mind had with romantic possibilities, and considering Daulat's complete descent into the newspaper, she began selling marriage to Coinman.

"A man is a scattered energy until he is married." She started saying this kind of thing around the time when Coinman had been in his job for about five years. "A marriage helps him to accumulate this energy at one place and direct it to the best possible use. Look at the enviably successful married life your father and I had before he was shrunk to a glass bead by his sickness. After finding an outlet of his most secret worries in me, your father was able to keep negative energies from getting stuck within him."

She was very concerned about her son's lack of a social life. At times when Coinman was away from the house, she even searched his bookshelf and computer for any graphic evidence of her son's romantic involvement; all in vain. What made things even worse was that she couldn't share the concern with her best companion of the past, now lost to nothingness. She missed her afternoon chats as never before.

But Kasturi wasn't one to sit quietly. She thought Coinman just needed help in approaching girls, so she increased her participation in community events, and volunteered him frequently, along with her, for events more relevant to young women. She played a bridge in introducing him to girls, sometimes even disappearing abruptly from conversations to let the chemistry work all by itself.

Sadly, though, word soon got around the community, advising people to avoid the mother and son.

"Maybe God is earnestly planning on him becoming a priest," one of her close relatives sighed to her once. Kasturi couldn't appreciate such careless speculation, yet it raised panic in her about the situation.

So she decided to take the matter entirely into her hands, resolving to seek an arranged alliance for Coinman within one year.

She lost no further time, embarking on extensive travel with Coinman to visit prospective families for an alliance. Coinman's reserved nature toward women hindered him from starting an interesting conversation with any of the girls he met. Coinman lost his patience when the eleventh girl they had met declined to take the matter further with him.

"It's kind of derogatory," Coinman finally said to Kasturi in frustration, "to continue offering myself this way. I feel like oversized trousers on sale, not even made of good material, that no one wants to buy. They just hang in there hoping that someone someday will compromise for their low cost."

Coinman's candid sketch of his current distress doubled Kasturi's grief; she was already heartbroken about her son's recent bad luck.

"Don't overanalyze this, Son." She tried her best to uplift him. "You are a perfect gem, one of the very best men I have known in my life. Matters of the heart are so incalculable! I am sad that none of these girls could permeate through the layers of your outer personality to find the gem that's at the core. In a way it's good it did not work out with them, because if they failed to see the gem in you, they wouldn't have appreciated your qualities later."

"Well, even if I consider for a minute that I am a gem waiting to get discovered, I still have no patience left to put myself on sale to get discovered."

"But Son, one has to get married. The world turns into an unbelievably lonely place without a partner. People around you may often seem to be good stand-ins, but they can never fill the void a lack of a partner creates."

"I understand. But it looks like we have a deadlock situation here. Honestly, I couldn't care less about getting married. But I can't bear to see you sad, so I will marry whomever you find for me."

"God bless you, my son. Your openness to getting married is all I need."

Having secured carte blanche from Coinman, Kasturi went back into the game. She wanted to go over things this time with a fine-tooth comb.

"It's Mr. Rout's daughter," she announced to him after accomplishing her mission in less than a month. "Her name is Imli. A beautiful name, like her beautiful heart. I am told that she is one of the best artists in the town. Son, I won't keep you in the dark—there are things that people say about her, not all positive at times. Her parents have provided me with a full disclosure."

"Tell me more about them," Coinman said without expression.

"They are a family of cows—so humble and honest. Apparently she is more talented than anyone else among their relations or in their neighborhood. Pissed off by this, some people badmouth her behind her family's back. That's what I mean when I talk about not keeping you in the dark. That's no concern to us because, as history tells us, talented minds have always been stealthily targeted by mediocre ones."

"What kind of artist is she?"

"She has worked onstage in numerous plays. Also, unlike many other girls of her age, she does not engage in idiotically wasting her time. Given she has acute focus on her acting career that allows her no time for other stuff, who would be surprised if her neighbors think that she isn't very social! Everything can be interpreted a hundred ways. So what do you think, Son?"

"Why would she marry someone she hasn't even seen?" Coinman asked.

"Because she is a gem just like you that hasn't been discovered yet." Kasturi replied.

"Is it a hassle to arrange a meeting with her?"

"Not at all, dear." Kasturi said. "Actually, Imli's parents also asked if you two could meet—they are an open-minded family and would love their girl to see her husband before marriage. That said, I am so excited because I think it's a done deal. Let's prepare the guest list. We haven't had a feast for years—actually, not since Uncle Sukhi arranged your third birthday party."

Thereafter, when a meeting was arranged between Coinman and Imli, for some reasons that no one cared to understand later, they waited for each other at two different coffeehouses with the same name. At that time cell phones weren't yet accessible to many common people. As a result they couldn't do anything immediately to fix the goof. Later, the prerequisite of a meeting was withdrawn by both parties as, they thought, the effort could instead be put toward marriage preparations.

For the dual reasons of the family's economic state and Daulat's societal detachment, the marriage was held at Kasturi's house itself.

The newlyweds' first night did not seem to go well. On the following morning, when their close cousins knocked at their door—part of a family tradition, to get them ready for the follow-up rituals—they were taken aback by Imli's ghastly red and swollen eyes. It appeared that she had cried the entire night. The fragility of the occasion led Kasturi to immediately take charge and lock herself with the couple in their room to have a dialogue with them, but neither of the two opened up to her.

The episode somehow made it to the gossip sessions at office, and as always, the gossipmongers stretched their minds to promote several rumors about the story behind it all. The most reliable rumor speculated that on her first night, Imli discovered that it was Coinman's second marriage: he was already married to coins. And when she asked him to divorce that first wife, he pledged instead to being helpless in both of them.

Thereafter, for a long time to come, Imli generally remained upset. A trifling matter was enough to make her eyebrows shrink toward the center of her forehead, and her mouth spew venom. And each evening, after everyone had had supper, she would go to her room, sit on the bed, and weep heartily. This weeping was like a fire drill in the beginning, drawing the rest of the family to gather around her bed immediately. It quickly lost its place in the spotlight, however, as its prolonged tedium eventually reached a point where the family attended her tearful requiems only to avoid an abrupt end to their consoling presence while she cried.

The attendance for her howling enterprise dropped off, eventually, to a point when no one would join her for the first few minutes, hoping another family member would. Then came a point when no one joined her at all, and she cried alone.

Finding no attention to her weeping, Imli was in a fix. She didn't wish to continue the stunt, either, but needed justification to stop it. She did not have to wait long; the family soon received an invitation to her cousin's wedding. They gathered around her the night before the function, for the first time in several months, to console her and remind her that she would want to look her best at her cousin's wedding. Daulat, completely a lunatic by this time, unfortunately slipped into the room.

"Daulat," Kasturi shouted, "go to your room. Right now."

But Daulat did not listen. Instead he came to Imli's bed and spoke.

"Leave her alone. She'll be fine," he said, speaking with a voice that had been lost for years. Even Imli lowered her voice in surprise. "This is a natural phenomenon about women," he continued. "Just like a beard comes naturally to men, weeping comes by nature to them—to satisfy some secret oath made to God on their behalf."

Then he turned to Coinman and said, "Most of a husband's life is spent in doing research on his wife. I do not want you to fall into the same trap, so let this be a warning to you." He smiled slyly, looking up at the ceiling—as though making a universal statement, but also to avoid looking at Kasturi. "A man wants too many things before marriage, but only peace after it."

Kasturi couldn't believe her ears; Daulat had never been such a jerk, and she was embarrassed to her core—because she had spoken very highly of her relations with Daulat prior to his lunacy. She took Daulat back to his room.

This gave Imli the opportunity she'd waited for. She wiped her tears, got down from her bed, and started looking at her wardrobe for dresses for the wedding.

On that day Imli started to get her acts together. She made a grand list of items to address immediately to bring back order in her life. The top five, out of fifty-four items in her list, read as below:

1) Keep the house free of coins, whatever the consequences.
2) Get back to theater. Break a leg.
3) Transition more household work to Shimla to create availability for theater.

4) Find another doctor for father-in-law; he has gone from being nuts to being dangerous.
5) Research if there are rehabs that treat non-substance addiction (maybe behavior disorder is the term?)

She started from the top. She permitted Coinman a week's time to clean the house of all coins.

Coinman removed coins from the house fully, except for keeping some in a secret hiding place to allow him to have brief gigs with the coins at times when Imli was lost in daily chores. Any meager chance would make Coinman jump to the secret place to quench the thirst of his mind.

However, one day, due not to his carelessness but to Imli's random break from her cooking, he was caught red-handed and lost even this vestigial privilege at home.

A breach in trust brings mistrust, followed by a multitude of troubles. Imli bought a high-range metal detector that she ran over random places on random days every week to expose any secret places where he might house coins.

The curtains on his trysts with coins at home caused an additional pressure on the coins at the office—the latter needed to do overtime every day to consume the mental stress their master accumulated at home. Coinman didn't waste a second, after reaching the office, in unlocking the drawer and putting the coins in his left pocket. Each evening, as he prepared to leave the office, his heart sank over the rift until the next morning. Friday evenings were the worst.

Meanwhile, happy with her progress on the first item on the list, Imli focused on the next. She visited her previous manager, who couldn't have been more excited to see her back. "I was expecting your call. How long could an artist of your caliber have her soul suffocated by the smoke of mundane affairs? It's not been an ideal run here, either—no one has been able to fill your shoes, so huge they were." He literally hugged her for minutes.

If I weren't connected to all of this, Imli thought, *my existence might have shrunk to the futile affairs of the house. I might have excelled at cooking to win laurels from family and friends for temporarily gratifying their taste buds, yet would surely have remained devoid of satisfaction.*

Imli felt as if she had never left the theater. She was at her best on day one—picking up where she had left off. Then, on one occasion, when a background actor fell ill just two days before opening night, and the group had no one else, Imli promised her group she was going to bring someone to fill the role. She was confident that Coinman could easily manage it, as it was a very small appearance where the character had only this brief line to say: "If you really want to talk to the big boss now, make sure you leave your balls here with me, for he likes no balls on people he is talking to."

That evening she came home early and eagerly waited for Coinman to come back from the office.

"Hey, how was work today?" Imli struck up a conversation as soon as Coinman had entered the house.

"Same old same old. How about you?" he asked, taking off his shoes.

"It's been exciting. We are working on a new play. We have a show in two days."

"Wow! That's great. I am so glad that you could go back to your real passion."

"I couldn't be happier, actually. Things are working out so well. How have your days been at work—any fun?"

"Well, my job is not quite like yours…we do a lot of boring work. You guys are plain lucky! I wish I had some creative genes in me to do something like you do."

"Hey, why don't you try out something—some sort of a hobby or interest?" As she spoke, she busied her hands putting her wardrobe in order. "One needs to pursue some sort of a creative interest in order to keep life from eating us alive."

Coinman looked at her silently for a few minutes. She clearly was conducting herself very differently from usual.

"But at this age?" he replied, "No, I am done."

Imli smiled to herself. "Oh, trust me on this, honey, the only thing required is a little willpower. The only thing God is afraid of is a strong-willed human."

"Maybe I can start reading fiction? That may be a good hobby."

"Or maybe you can start learning keyboard…or even start with background work at the theater."

Coinman looked puzzled. "Look, I have wasted half of my life without having anything to do with art."

"But history is full of great artists who started very late in their lives."

"They probably had it in them, and did not get an opportunity until late. I don't have it in me."

"I think many late bloomers felt exactly that way in the beginning. But then their hearts took control and couldn't care less about failures, as long as they loved what they did."

"Listen, I am open for something I can do. I just don't think I can pick up just anything now. My learning capabilities may be dried up."

"Oh, I doubt that." Imli turned to him with a smile. "I have something in mind—my current play has a very small role, and I am sure my troupe would love to have you. You don't have to do anything, just stand on the stage and say one short sentence."

"But isn't your show in, like, two days from now?"

"Yes, it is. But you will be just fine."

"Why do you think so—that a new person who has never acted will be fine with two days' preparation?"

"Because you just have to stand on the stage, and say just one sentence. You have enough time to practice that sentence a thousand times between now and the show. Besides, we have a final stage rehearsal, too."

"I can try it," Coinman said, "but I have a condition."

"I accept any condition you want to have."

"Then you must allow me coins in my pocket at home for one year."

"That's blackmail. I can't stand you with coins for a second. As you know, I have already been looking at ways to get you fully out of this habit. Allowing you this will make us go back to square one."

"Well, I should get rewarded for my theatrical efforts."

"Ask for something else."

"This is the only reward that would make me happy."

"Well, all right. But only for two days; as soon as the play is over, you are out of coins again."

"How about one month?"

"Three days."

"Three weeks?"

"Four days."

"Two weeks?"

"One week, my final offer."

"One week and one day."

"Fine. But, of course, only with the condition that you leave your coins behind when you are with the troupe. We can't afford a coin rhapsody on the stage."

There was not much of an option for either party!

Coinman at once jumped out of the house and came back with a pocketful of coins in a flash.

For next two days the monster of acting gobbled up Coinman's freedom and made him rehearse his dialogue an uncountable number of times.

On the eve of the show, during the stage rehearsal, he had great difficulty in delivering his dialogue at the right time, with the right voice and the right emotions. He attempted several times, but something was always missing. He had seen several plays in the past, but this was the first time he understood the internal hurricane actors experience while onstage. If he remembered the timing well, he forgot his dialogue, or he forgot how it was to be said. If he remembered the dialogue by repeating it in his mind, he forgot about all other elements, because the dialogue became a heavy burden that he wanted to dispose of as early as possible. When that happened he said his dialogue even before the preceding dialogue was completed, something that irritated the actor he was addressing. But eventually, after numerous rehearsals, Coinman was finally able to do it right consistently four times in a row. That was it—Coinman was ready for the final show.

On the night before the performance, Coinman couldn't sleep until midnight, and got up several times before he was wide awake at four o'clock. He was extremely nervous about being able to deliver the dialogue correctly. He had been practicing his dialogue the entire night—whether awake or asleep. Unfortunately, in his dreams he hadn't gotten it right once.

He thought brief physical exercise would make him feel fitter, so he brought out his old yoga book and performed all the asanas. He skipped breakfast, as his nerves made him feel sick looking at the food. He repeated numerous questions that Imli had already answered—about the stage, the audience, the curtains, the seating arrangements, the acoustics, the sound system, and whatnot. Imli told him that these things would be clear when the company did the final rehearsal onstage, just two hours prior to the show. She told him that she could not give him an exact idea of the audience, but she expected there would be a few hundred, as the show had been well advertised and was a performance of one of the most popular plays in the area.

Coinman acted well during the final rehearsal—everyone in the group praised him backstage. But each of the pats on the back they gave him seemed to turn into an additional expectation to meet, making him even more anxious.

Backstage, Coinman was still very much a stranger among the group and did not know what he should engage himself in while others were busy. He tried to give a hand a couple of times, but seemed more of a hindrance than a help. He found a corner that suited him and started rehearsing his dialogue. Imli visited him after a while, asking him if he wanted to accompany other members to lunch. He said he wasn't hungry.

As the rows started to get filled in the evening, Coinman sank into a deep nervousness about his performance. He suddenly felt very hungry, too, as he had hardly eaten anything during lunch in his anxiety. There was no food in sight. He prayed hard to God and promised that he was never going to try acting again. His whole body seemed to float like a balloon, and he made frequent trips to the washroom to splash water at his face, trying to feel normal. How can an outer treatment help with an inner condition?

The applause on the opening of the first scene seemed to put even more of a burden on Coinman's shoulders as he waited, rehearsing his line ceaselessly, in the right wing. Then the testing moment arrived. Coinman made an impressive entry on the stage, head held high and with a confident walk up to the place he was to say his dialogue from. He turned in the right direction, facing the audience, to say his line— but, alas, the right words would not come to his mind. What repeatedly popped into his head instead was a line from his favorite movie: "Over my dead body!" Clearly it wasn't prudent to say that one instead.

Each second that went by made it even more difficult for him to remember what to say. Everyone onstage looked at him, and the crowd fell silent in nervous anticipation. Those onstage initially thought that it was only a small glitch and hoped that Coinman was soon going to recover, but seeing Coinman turning into a statue, they lost more hope with each second.

Sensing a growing impatience within the troupe about the situation, specifically a panicked look on Coinman's partner in the dialogue, the crowd started to wonder if the unanticipated dramatic pause was truly a part of the script. It wouldn't be surprising if they thought that Coinman had dropped the ball. One whistle somewhere from the back rows in the auditorium was enough to start a chain reaction of whistles from all directions.

And then Coinman delivered.

"Over my dead body or surrender your balls with me before you enter."

The preceding long silence, the serendipitous merit of the dialogue, and the pompous effect in the delivery caused by desperation filled the dialogue with such an immense volume of power that the audience erupted in several rounds of crazed applause. It was clearly the best applause the group had ever witnessed—they had to wait for a minute to let the ovation die before saying the next line.

As soon as the play was over, a few influential members of the audience showed up backstage to shake hands with Coinman.

Yet the group was done with Coinman. Not that Coinman was surprised by that. Imli never even brought up the incident with him.

It was definitely a rare situation, in which a career had started and ended simultaneously on a very high note.

On the other hand, Imli's star rose higher and farther, day after day. Her hard work paid off, as she went on to become a popular performer, frequently covered by the newspapers. Like all great actors, in order to live the characters in the most impressive manner on the stage, she practiced at home all the time. The moment she was assigned a role in a play, she could visualize her name being announced as that of the best actor in the play—and most of the time it wasn't a flight of fancy. She won, and won often.

This absorption in her craft, however, wasn't necessarily what other members of the family would have wished for. Her talent, in fact, was a big menace to the family.

Once, when playing a ghost, Imli started living the character completely in all facets of her existence. She perfected her ghost demeanor by responding in what she imagined was a ghostly way, even in the most trivial matters of day-to-day life. She pretended to be invisible at all times, always dressed in white, maintained a depressed outlook, conversed only through moaning, and slept during the day, to be active during the night.

A benign spectator of her drama, Coinman received the byproducts of her obsession more than other members of the family. At midnight she would rush upon him, mouth wide open, screaming, "Boo!" She hounded Coinman in all corners of the house, waiting for him, hiding in the most unexpected places—in the wardrobe, or under his bed—to pounce upon him like a wildcat.

Not surprisingly, when that show went on, she was named the best actor again. She had even bettered her own past records of artistic folly by descending into the audience to boo a few random individuals.

Then, when she played a lady devoted solely to her husband, in order to perfect herself in that role, she became an extremely good wife to Coinman. The chemistry between the couple transformed overnight. She waited at the door when Coinman came back from the office, took his jacket, and rushed to prepare tea for him. She relieved Shimla of many of her responsibilities and insisted on cooking herself for her husband. In bed at night, she shared every detail of how her day had been, discussed her worries for the future, and became intimate beyond precedent.

This newborn happiness did not last too long, however. From this role Imli progressed to the role of a wife who suspected that her husband was having an affair with the maid.

But at least Coinman had company now, in Shimla, in facing the torch from the Broadway monster.

17. The Grandpa Epics

*D*uring their children's early years, parents often get so habitual in foreseeing and ensuring a great future for their offspring that they fail to realize the lesser degree of control they must exercise when the children are grown up and married. That's most true for mothers, because the fathers move on easily with changing times, understanding the degree of independence kids demand with every year of growth. But mothers never seem to give up. Kasturi wasn't going to give up, either, on her attempts to become a grandmother—to get an heir for the family.

During the first three years of Coinman's married life, Kasturi patiently hid her impatient anticipation of signs of Imli's impregnation. Whenever Imli had nausea, or felt fatigued, or had a craving for a particular food, or did not feel like eating a certain dish, Kasturi got excited, prayed to God, and took additional care of her daughter-in-law. Then, when she saw no progress, the compressed impatience of years gained enough strength to leak out in the form of small hints to the couple. This leakage, with time, became increasingly barefaced.

She would engineer ways to keep company with Imli several times a week, to let out the reminders. "You both have a big responsibility on your shoulders," she told Imli on one occasion, "to further keep our name alive. Sweetie, there is no feeling in the world that compares with your child growing in you. Also, this is the best age to ensure a healthy baby."

Imli would nod as if listening, but in fact she was too engaged in her acting trance to recall these reminders once the discussion was over. Therefore Kasturi bade adieu to a mother's hesitation in taking the matter up directly with her adult son.

"There is nothing in the world," she would say, "that belongs more to you than your own child. Besides, one needs a child to support oneself during those cruel days of life when one's own body, under the influence of old age, can no longer act fully on one's own commands."

When the generic line of reasoning didn't seem to work, she devised a strategy she thought was faultless.

"When your dad was three years old," she told Coinman, "he fully remembered his past life, that of his grandfather."

"What do you mean?" Coinman looked at her in disbelief.

"I never talked to you about certain family secrets. For several generations every birth in our family has actually been a rebirth of an ancestor. Your great-grandfather, for example, had returned from heaven to take birth as your father."

"Do you believe in that?" Coinman's rejection of the notion was visible on his face.

Kasturi excused herself to rush to her bedroom. Coinman could hear her open Daulat's old steel safe.

"See here, this diary? Your grandfather started making a journal when your father, at age three, spoke spontaneously of intimate and accurate details from your great-grandfather's life." She handed the diary to Coinman and continued, "You can read it in your spare time, but let me tell you the gist: by age four he knew all about your great-grandfather's life: names of his close friends, his dog's name, and his weakness in mathematics. He insisted that the locked wardrobe that belonged to your deceased great-grandfather was his—he could describe all the clothes in it without ever seeing them. This was when your grandparents took him seriously and had no doubt that your father was actually his grandfather's reincarnation.

"Your father specifically had an infatuation with an unused room in his grandparents' house—as it turned out, this was your great-grandparents' bedroom, and it was where your great-grandmother, his wife in a previous life, had died."

Kasturi paused to see how Coinman received all this.

"So what's the point you are trying to make?" Coinman asked flatly.

"Dear Son, the point is that our ancestors typically wait long in heaven above for the right moment to reincarnate in the same family. I know for a fact that your grandfather is patiently looking to come back as your child. It's not an easy pursuit. First, he has to display a whole portfolio of good deeds performed during the prior life in order to come back to this world as a human; most people come back as ants, rats, and snakes. Second, he has to furnish good enough justification for wanting to come back to the same family."

"Now, is this knowledge well documented somewhere?" Coinman asked, flipping through the journal Kasturi had given him.

"There are things in life that science will never be able to see. We have to rely on what has been passed from our ancestors, generation to generation."

"All right," said Coinman, smiling. "So how do you know that my grandfather has done everything needed and is cleared to come back to this family?"

"That's not something we have to bother about. He has to do what he has to do to come this way. Our duty is to allow him a full chance to make it after he has done his bit."

"Everything seems so puzzling and counterintuitive. But something you just said a few moments ago makes me very curious. How in the world can you say with certainty that my grandfather is waiting to come back as my son?" Coinman asked his question with such honesty that it made Kasturi smile.

"When on his deathbed"—Kasturi orated from her memory—"your grandfather promised Daulat that he would come back to the family as your son. Interestingly, you had not even been conceived at that point, but, out of the wisdom he had gathered all his life, he somehow knew about your future birth. Just a couple of minutes before he died, he whispered his last words in your father's ears: 'Son, it's time for me. I have got to go now to visit the other side, and I have already started to get a glimpse of it. But before I fully leave here, I have a promise to make. I have loved this family more than anything else and would do everything possible to come back. Please do all that is needful to receive me, just like your mother and I did, to receive your grandfather through your birth. Don't neglect to see your son get a good wife. I can already see him in the world where I am going. As much as I can see, he is supposed to leave there in about two years to make Kasturi eat for two. I will be indebted to God if your son keeps his door open for me.'

"These were his last words. You must have heard from us that he spoke very loudly. So all of us present there could hear what he whispered in Daulat's ear, although for some reason, Daulat never mentioned it to anyone. Not even to me. So if it had not been for your grandfather's strong voice, we would not have known his wish. It's very hard to investigate into your father's motive behind that, but all this is beside the point. Not receiving a request through the expected route is no excuse for not fulfilling it.

"So, my son, you should understand now how restless the soul of your grandfather must be. It's only you—of course, in agreement with Imli—who can help him. Moreover, Son, just consider this: only when you bring an offspring to this world will it be possible for us—your own mother and father—to come back to this family again. Wouldn't you want us back again?"

"Let me think about it," Coinman said. "You know, Mother, how busy Imli and I are right now. But I hear you. I will do whatever I can."

Despite his promise, Kasturi didn't let it go. She continued her efforts; she spied outside Coinman's bedroom every night, after Imli locked the room from inside, with her right ear pressed hard on the door, trying to detect evidence of their consideration of her requests.

Kasturi kept the "grandpa topic" alive. She would narrate stories to Coinman about his grandpa's heroics whenever it seemed appropriate.

"For a long time during his prime youth, your grandpa had resolved to stay in the village," Kasturi once said, during one of her many story sessions. "He only moved to a city much later to ensure a better educational opportunity for your father. He said that though there was more money in cities to lay your hands on, good-hearted people were scarce in cities. Your grandma supported him wholeheartedly. She was a doctor herself, and a very down-to-earth lady—she hardly cared about the impact of living in the village on her career. Such was her dedication to her husband's wish.

"You have a fair idea by now how progressive your grandpa was; let me tell you about one episode in particular. Your grandpa was once transferred to a city full of drunkards. The social order of the city was on the verge of decline as the residents just drank and abused. They robbed people from other cities to have money for their alcohol consumption. Because your grandpa had a very successful history of sorting out such matters in past, he was posted to this city after many prior administrators had failed.

"Although your grandpa had been the most successful administrative officer in the past, this particular task was so challenging that even the best of his friends and well-wishers believed that he was going to taste failure for the first time in his life. That kind of spotlight only made your grandfather more resolute about achieving success.

"On the very first day of his arrival in the city, all the alcohol—every drop of it that existed in the city on that very day—was disposed of down the open sewer lines. It was then announced throughout the city that any person in possession of any amount of alcohol would be fined a large sum of money per drop. No one could dare to bring any alcohol to the city. Most drunkards quit drinking for the inconvenience of having to travel to other cities to satiate their desire; the rest, only a small fraction of the total, migrated to other cities.

"There was a funny side of this that I can't resist telling you. All the donkeys, pigs, and stray dogs—the most common living beings in the city, even more prevalent than their human counterparts—were found drooling over the alcohol flowing through the open drains for about a week. Then they could sense that the newly acquired taste was for naught in the city, as what they'd gotten a taste of accidentally was all the city had to offer. So to increase their chances to ever taste it again, they found it prudent to migrate to other cities.

"So this was a positive by-product of your grandpa's action: driving away unwanted stray animals and thereby beautifying the city. Many believe that even this was a premeditated outcome, and that your grandpa had planned to kill two birds with one stone: getting rid of filthy animals and drunkards, both at the same time. Some had even said that your grandpa did not actually distinguish between the two. So maybe it was indeed a single goal in his mind.

"This way of handling the case later went into several textbooks related to management and administration, and the case study is still part of the curriculum at a number of universities. The point they stress is, the prior approach focused on drunkards, incurring huge expenses without achieving a partial solution—but your grandpa's alcohol-focused approach made the solution seem like a cakewalk!

"No great soul, as they say, lives for very long. Because God desperately wants all the great people near him. It was no different in your grandpa's case. He was perfectly built and could have defeated five men simultaneously in wrestling—but he suddenly took to his bed. Some people thought that one of his friends, jealous of your grandpa's capabilities, mixed something in his food, a sort of clever poison, which even doctors could not trace in the reports later. And, my dear son, what I am going to tell you now is based on my own experience: people who are constantly in poor health seem to live longer than healthy people. I have seen, over and over again, that healthy people, who never saw a doctor in their entire lives, pass suddenly, while people living on medicines carry on. To me it looks as though medicines are mandatory for the maintenance of a human being."

Sadly for Kasturi, though, in the end none of these tactics ever worked: she waited in vain for her grandchild.

18. The Lethal Complaint

*T*he duel may go on for a long time, but self-defense often wins over self-reproach.

On the day following the coin robbery, the chief robbers convened to rapidly form a foolproof strategy against the anticipated complaint from Coinman, and thereby defend themselves from an ABC apocalypse.

Tulsi was there, but not to boost their morale. Looking at an imminent involvement from ABC, she admitted freely to harboring nervousness.

"This was an outrageous demonstration of our shameful intelligence," she declared, voluntarily assuming the soapbox. "Had we not decided to perform this as gracefully as a dancer's leap? But we turned it into a dinosaur's dance party! For heaven's sake, tell me if anyone disagrees with me on what is going to happen now. Many of us will be gone. No one knows where! Some of us who are deemed less useful, and whom management has been waiting for an excuse to get rid of, may be thrown out as well. The job market is down the toilet—so we might land ourselves in the worst misery of our lives."

Tulsi's discourse turned Hukum's mind into a volcano. *As though everyone here except her is a fool!* To avoid an eruption in his mind, and hence prevent innocent casualties, he started walking toward the exit door. "If all we're going to get is an insult, I'm out of here."

"Wait," cried Ratiram, rushing in Hukum's direction with his right hand outstretched, gesturing to him to halt. "We are not here to fight with each other."

"I mean, seriously?" Hukum turned back. "Do you see how snobbishly Tulsi is blaming all of us for this? Wasn't she as much a part of the whole thing as anyone else? As a matter of fact, when push came to shove, she was standing in a corner, completely dissociated, while we robbed the coins. If she really was the smartest of us all, why didn't she lead us all in the right direction? Anyone can lecture from the butt; only very few can act." Then his anger faded to disappointment. "I understand it very well now. She is only blaming me because she is trying to set me up here as the designer of the robbery." He then turned to Tulsi with a grim smile. "If I drown, I assure you that you will drown, too."

Hukum looked around, gauging his support, but found mostly dumbfounded faces.

"Well, all right." Hukum went on. "If you people still believe in her good intentions, you can continue to do so, but I am not going to compromise my respect here. If you thought with your minds and not your roosters, you would get the point."

Tulsi gasped, with her right hand on her mouth and her eyes getting watery, and left the room in anger and humiliation before anyone could react to Hukum's last statement. Silence filled the room for the next few minutes, everyone looking at one another in disbelief.

Finally Ratiram spoke up.

"Hukum, everyone present here understands your point. Even Tulsi does, too, I am sure. These are testing times. If we blame each other and don't work on this problem as a single entity, we are surely going to land ourselves in an enormous tragedy." He looked at the door, as if hoping to see Tulsi come back. "We can't do anything successfully without politeness, respect to fellows, and trust in everyone's abilities. If we lose sight of these, we are headed for a catastrophe. These are times for tuning our individual instruments to compose a song together, not for singling out others' instruments as messy."

Many of them nodded in respectful submission to Ratiram's thought.

"Let me apologize on behalf of anyone who might have hurt another team member's feelings," Ratiram went on slowly. "What's done is done. So I appeal to each one of you to help us as a team to brainstorm a solution. I will separately reach out to Tulsi and keep her in the loop."

Everyone sank in deep thought, some bracing their chins on their hands as if that additional stability enabled the mind to focus on thought better.

Several minutes passed without anyone volunteering an idea. Indeed, they all seemed to think Ratiram would save them. So Ratiram stood up at last and spoke again.

"I admit, I've been thinking about a plan since the time we robbed him. First and foremost, we need to accept the fact that this is not an easy situation to get past without taking a few hits. Let's be mentally prepared for some damage. The damage is inevitable—we can only minimize it."

"That's damn straight," said Panna. "We are up shit's creek."

"Second, if each one of us takes responsibility for what has happened, we may achieve a greater moral satisfaction, but I can assure you, we'll land ourselves in deep trouble, too. We are not part of a world where honest confessions are rewarded by forgiveness. It is a world where the loud conquers the soft, and a friendly attitude is taken for a weakness. A quiet and nervous person may be perceived as a thief while a self-assured thief comes across as a cop. So if we want to end up on the winning side, we must think of going on the offensive at once."

Everyone quickly nodded.

"What are we going to do?" Daya was certain that Ratiram would have made a thorough plan already.

Ratiram answered, "Let's file a complaint to Jay before Coinman does. Let's tell him how Coinman has been the biggest impediment to all of us at the workplace."

Everyone keenly agreed. They promptly drafted a letter, signed it, and handed it over to Jay's administrative assistant, who made no delays in passing the letter to Jay.

Jay opened the letter silently but very eagerly:

To
Mr. Jay Tripathi
Unit Head

Dearest Sir:

We would like to bring an important matter to your kind notice. A great many sacrifices have gone into making this firm an enviably great place to work. However, there has been a recent development that has a big potential to jeopardize the culture of the firm.

We would like to draw your attention to the highly disquieting demeanor that Mr. Coinman has been exhibiting. It has been causing a grave concern to everyone at the office, and lately it seems like he has been trying to cook up something against the office. We would request you take appropriate action before it goes on to cause irreparable damage to our firm. An early response to the situation will be greatly appreciated.

Yours sincerely,
The workforce at this unit
(Please refer to the attachment for names and signatures)

19. The Meeting of the Second Kind

*K*nown as a good man and a sincere leader by his staff, Jay preached that attaining more knowledge constantly was central to earning a respectable living. To set a good example, he had resolved to learn at least one significant new thing every month, subsequently noting each in a personal notebook for future reference.

His style had recently made a complete U-turn when he learned that over the thirty-five years of his working life, he had very rarely referred to past notes. He acknowledged that time ran much faster than he'd previously thought, another one of his recent useful learnings, and that such inefficiencies as making notes for later were only going to make life even shorter. As a result, he duly stopped taking notes for the future and began to address everything on the spot instead.

On receiving the complaint, Jay first met secretly with Coinman's supervisor, who gave an oblivious shrug.

"Then why did you sign the complaint?" Jay asked.

"Because everyone had already signed it before it came for my signature. Did I have any other option?" Coinman's boss asked.

"Well, you could have taken some time to understand what was happening."

"If I hadn't signed it then, I would've lost my place in the association."

"So there is an association now?"

"No, I am just referring to the group on the first floor that periodically correlates and connects for working together smoothly."

"Why would discussing an issue about your own associate with them cause a strain in your relationship with them?"

"I don't know. It was more like a feeling in my bones."

"All right, then. I need a separate discussion with you on this topic—can you have an hour blocked with me later this week?"

"I will do that. May I ask out of curiosity if that would be a general meeting or of the first kind?"

"This is the first kind, happening right here, right now. Based on our discussion, I have decided to upgrade it to a second kind."

"I am very sorry for my lapse," Coinman's manager said. "Is there any way I can get the second kind converted into yet another first kind?"

"Unfortunately, no. The process must be followed."

"I will do as you say, sir."

"Also, it's urgent that I meet with Coinman. Can you have him see me at the earliest possible time today?"

"I will ask him to come by. Would you need me in the discussion?"

"I don't think so."

"What is a good time?"

"Anytime is a good time, as long as it works for him. My day is very light today," Jay said, concluding the meeting.

Late in the day, on his entry to Jay's office, Coinman couldn't help noticing dirt on the green plastic lid that covered the glass of water on his table. This was one thing Coinman had never understood since his early childhood. It seemed that these plastic lids were never washed, which defeated the very purpose of having them in the first place.

Seeing him completely lost in the glass of water, Jay asked him, "Do you want me to order some water for you?"

"What? Oh, no, I am fine. I am sorry for the lapse."

Jay stood up to shake hands with him. "No problem at all. That happens to me all the time. Once, during a certain class in high school, my eyes were so constantly stuck on a stain on the ceiling formed by rainwater leakage that I failed to pay attention for periods after periods. The beautiful patch certainly deserved to be a painting. There is indeed an immense amount of beauty around us, in the most ordinary things, that we fail to notice most of the time. We pay a high price to go to painting exhibitions, but fail to notice the weathered wall of our open public offices; some of the best sketches I have ever witnessed have been on those walls. In short, I don't blame you for getting a momentary fixation on that glass. Come, have a seat, now, please."

"Thank you, sir."

"I don't think we have ever had an opportunity to meet in person earlier."

"Actually, we have met once, sir."

"Have we? Can you please jog my memory?"

"It was when I joined this firm. You asked me if I was doing well."

"Oh, yes, yes…I remember now. Time flies."

Coinman laughed, as if Jay had cracked a joke.

"So." Jay came to the point. "I want to speak to you about a few things. This may take a few minutes—if that's OK with you?"

"You need not ask, sir." Coinman coughed slightly, clearing his throat. "My time is all yours."

"Tell me briefly about how things are with you. What's working well and what may not be working adequately."

"I am enjoying work. It's been hectic, but that's always good. Everyone's very supportive. So that's working very well. I can't think of anything that's not working well." As he said this, Coinman's left hand impatiently slipped into his pocket, without his permission, despite the strict instructions from him to defer gratification during the meeting with Jay.

"Tell me something about the support you are receiving from your colleagues."

"They are very kind with their help when I need it."

"Has anyone ever complained to you about something?"

"Not really. What do you mean by that, though?"

"Have you been aware of any issues that your colleagues have been facing?"

"Well, no, none that I know of."

"You may want to think more about it." Jay's manner indicated his seriousness about something.

"Maybe the elevator—it takes forever to go from the first floor to the second floor—but almost has a free fall the other way around."

Jay ran out of patience at that. Briskly he went on. "Coinman, I will be candid with you. I have received reports that your conduct has not been appropriate lately. Now I need to understand from you what that means."

"I haven't done anything that's outside the office decorum."

"Coinman, I have had a formal complaint from your colleagues on the first floor that you have not been carrying yourself professionally. They have said that they are finding it very challenging to continue their jobs."

"Do you have any details of my unprofessional behavior?"

"Actually, I don't. I have spoken to your manager briefly and couldn't get more details. I wanted to speak to you before I speak with other people who have complained."

"May I know who has complained?"

"Almost everyone from the first floor."

"If there was at all a need for a complaint, it should have come from me." Coinman was growing angry.

"Please explain."

"They conspired to attack me and threw me on the ground while trying to rob me of my coins."

"When was that?"

"Two days ago."

"Before you get into more details, may I ask why you have been going in circles until now? You could have told me this right at the beginning. And why would you not complain about such an outrageous event?"

"I did not want my colleagues to get into trouble."

"May I ask why?"

"Yes, sir. Individuals at times become helpless against a group's combined stupor. I am sure no one was at a fault individually. I didn't think twice about it—I don't blame anyone. I have no concerns."

"It's much bigger than your problem, Coinman. What they have done is beyond my imagination. I can surely expect a third kind on this."

"This was a rare incident, I am sure, that will never be repeated by them," Coinman said humbly. "I can talk to them and let them know that I won't press any charges. Maybe they would take back their complaint? It would be very sad if this matter reaches ABC's ears."

"We will follow the right process and ensure the right course is taken," Jay said. "At this point I have what I need from you. I won't keep you longer now—I will call you again if I need more information. I truly appreciate your flexibility."

"Anytime, sir," Coinman said as he clumsily prepared to leave, almost falling to the ground, as his right leg had entangled itself in an empty chair.

So much has been happening in the office right under my nose, Jay thought after Coinman had left. *Ratiram is definitely going straight to ABC. The real question is—who else besides him?*

20. The Involuntary Compromise

*A*ll the progress in science can't be used to build a smell receptor as capable as the one that a true leader possesses— to smell trouble or just something fishy. As a bear can smell food from several miles away, a true leader can smell a problem that's wrapped in several layers of delusion. Jay belonged to that class. Also, even though he was a very humble man, he was hardly about conducting a group hug session when he needed to have a tough dialogue with his staff. The meeting with Coinman had left him thinking that there was much more to the affair than met the eye. So he had individual discussions with five randomly chosen members of his staff from the first floor.

These discussions helped him crystallize the reality; all five of them were united in their accounts. Try as Jay might to approach each discussion from different angles, the responses were abnormally homogeneous. It was as if he heard one voice, over and over again, repeating the same story, with no variations at all.

A widespread meticulous consistency causes a bigger suspicion than the most obvious inconsistency does, Jay thought as he walked to the parking garage after a long day, through a pouring rain, feeling completely exhausted. He was so lost in thought that he realized he was trying to open someone else's car only when his car key didn't work.

Tossing in his bed that night, he pondered possible interpretations of his observations; what had in fact really happened? He knew that only Coinman had spoken the

truth. *A man in pain is more likely to take refuge in telling the truth.*
So where did that leave him? Draining a coffeepot over the
course of thinking it through, he made up his mind that a
quick fix was immediately needed to relieve the tension
among his staff. He would have time to think about a more
holistic solution after people relaxed, after their initial fears
were calmed and they felt a bit of solace.

"Often a baby step takes you much farther than you'd
imagine." His father's advice came back to him often, and
was as useful now as it had ever been.

The next day he called Coinman's supervisor first, and
pursued the matter until he understood that the real cause
behind the coin incident was the tyranny of the jingling
coins.

Jay then called Coinman to his office and came to the
point right away, skipping over small talk.

"Coinman," he said, "it looks like I have a fair
understanding of the matter. I wanted to set an expectation
that there is no easy way out of this. It may take a while
before I am able to make my final recommendations. The
good news is, I have a quick fix till then. All I need is your
cooperation in enforcing it."

"I will do anything that's in my control," Coinman said.

"Thank you for your cooperation. Just as I expected." Jay
went on, "May I ask that you not bring any coins in the
office for a short period of time until I have a better idea of
how to proceed?"

Coinman's chin began to move vigorously. He wanted to
react quickly, but the emotional rush had temporarily
blocked his access to words. He gazed on the table between
them in anger.

"And if you get coins in change from a purchase," Jay
persisted, "like buying lunch at the office, please feel free to
leave those coins as a tip at the counter. I'll reimburse you in
paper currency later, once every month."

The chin very aptly signaled Coinman's misery. "That's
an off-the-wall compromise to ask!" he said. "If it has come

to intolerance to personal habits in the workplace, then how are the others able to get away scot-free? Are you also going to tell Daya to stop digging gold in his nose? Or are you going to send Ratiram for voice therapy to treat his loud voice? Hukum's entire body smells of nicotine—are you planning to ask him to quit smoking, or are you planning to install air fresheners on the first floor? Panna is a swearing machine—how are you going to stop him?"

Jay had been thinking over those very things.

"Look, Coinman, I completely understand your frustration and I want to assure you of two things: First, the inquiry into the matter will continue to find the next steps in the matter so that nothing like this is conspired against anyone in the future. Second, we will take a holistic look at it. We can't address everything at once. We need to take things one by one. So while the inquiry is in progress on this matter, it would be in the best interest of the firm to have you drop your coins before entering the office. And I am very positive, given your great track record in the past, that you will comply with the interest of your employer."

For a moment Coinman's face looked like a two-year-old's when he sees his mother embrace another child. It would have taken only a hint of empathy to make him cry; someone to just say, "I am sorry for what happened to you."

"If leaving my coins at home makes everyone happy, I will do it." As Coinman said this, his own eyes betrayed him by letting a teardrop fall onto Jay's table. Jay passed him a paper napkin, got up, and walked behind his chair. He slowly put his right hand on Coinman's right shoulder to comfort him. "This will pass very soon. I am with you in this difficult time. We need to stay strong to be able to do the right thing."

Coinman put his hand over Jay's, in a gesture of appreciation for his support. He couldn't tell Jay, for reasons that he couldn't fully understand, that the coins were already outlawed at his house; Jay's forbidding them at the office had slammed the last door on him.

"I know, Coinman, this is not the best time to talk about it, because you need some private time right now, and I don't want to get in the way. But I wanted to let you know that, for the sacrifice you are making, I am open to discuss how we can work on some sort of a reward, one-time or enduring, to offset your malaise."

Coinman glared at him. "If I get this right, are you hinting at financial gains in return for giving up my soul?"

"Don't get it wrong. Maybe I didn't word this right. What I meant was…"

Coinman didn't wait around to find out, but instead sprang up from the chair and left the room before Jay could finish.

21. The Addict's Dilemma

*H*ope meets a dead end when the only chance in sight comes to naught. It had taken Coinman several years to fully acclimate to the new coin timetable after Imli had swept the coins from the house. It wasn't easy for his mind and his hands to adjust to the sanctions at home—but time had eased his desperation, slowly but steadily, and eventually cured him of the agony of his loss. But nothing was more hopeless now than losing his coin rights at the office, too.

To make it worse, this new catastrophe had come at a time when the situation at home was quite out of hand—Imli's theatrical fever was at its worst. In her portrayal of a stranger, she feigned no acquaintance with the members of her family.

One charade inevitably hatches another. To develop her stranger demeanor to perfection, she kept herself disengaged from anything that could slightly indicate an association with the other occupants. To legitimize her stay at the house, she imagined that her house was suddenly populated by four strangers—the only way to perfect a notion of unfamiliarity with her family without having to leave the house. And how could someone allow strangers in her house? Therefore she confronted family members frequently and asked them to leave.

After his discussion with Jay, Coinman had collected all the coins from his drawer before he left the office. He had taken the coins home, hoping to plead mercy from Imli and ask her to allow the coins at home until the situation at work was normal.

But as soon as he entered the house, the coins were detected by Imli's sonar ears, and like a flash she rushed toward Coinman to grab the coins away from him.

Then she suddenly stopped. She realized her dilemma. *I am a stranger!*

She instantly dropped herself on the floor to position herself like a street beggar, arrested Coinman by grabbing the crease of his trouser in her left hand, and gestured with her right hand for him to empty his pockets into her hands. Instead Coinman backed away.

"For God's sake," he cried aloud, "can you please leave me alone for a few minutes?"

Imli started Rudra Tandava, a vigorous dance expressing the pinnacle of rage, slowly floating up, her fully stretched arms sideways, her palms vibrating passionately. She danced, burning in this anger, for about two minutes.

Then she paused and lurched at Coinman again. "Who might you be?" she demanded. "A wretched lord of cacophony and sheer decibels? Or a ruthless assassin of harmony?"

Before Coinman could answer, she spoke again. "And what's that in your pocket, causing every cell in my body to flutter? I must unburden you from the mire of the metal!"

Before Coinman could respond, she slipped her hand into his pocket and got all the coins! She then dashed outside the house and reappeared a few minutes later without them.

That began Coinman's real trials. A life without coins was no fun!

He spent the night thinking about strategies to win the coins back. In the morning he craved coins as soon as he reached the office. His feet darted outside into the market— all by themselves. He scooted to the first shop that he could set his eyes on and, without delaying a second, reached to the shopkeeper and thrust a ten-rupee bill in his left hand.

He then quickly scanned the shop for the lowest-priced item, and decided on a pen that cost just one rupee. Then he demanded nine rupees back in coins.

The shopkeeper patiently counted all the change and handed it over to Coinman. The change went into his left pocket in less than a second. Having found the lost privilege suddenly, his mind spread itself across the entire cosmos, leaving a very sparse presence at any given locus. In such absent-mindedness, he left the shop without the pen.

The shopkeeper ran after him.

"Buddy, you left your pen," he called.

"Please keep it," Coinman requested. "I can't express enough gratitude in accommodating my bizarre request for half a pound of change."

The shopkeeper smiled, nodded his head, and returned without a word. He was probably too busy to spend any more time on this oddity.

Coinman continued his stroll around the market, pondering ways to alleviate his situation. His mind seemed completely empty—or full of some sort of sticky paste, making it hard for any ideas to enter it without getting caught at its surface. He deferred deep consideration for a future day, when the sticky stuff would be gone. In the meantime he figured as long as he could find a permanent hiding place for his coins, he at least wouldn't have the burden of getting new change every day. Moreover, Daulat had taught him since childhood that money loves only those who wisely spend it—that was another reason he didn't want to dispose of the coins after each use.

So he walked into the only public restroom in the area and went straight into one of the stalls, which had an overhead tank and a pull-chain flush system. Climbing up on the toilet bowl, he lifted his hand above his head toward the overhead tank and ran it over the top surface to ensure it was clear of any objects. He then took the coins out of his pocket and placed them at the top.

No one will ever find these, he thought. *The municipality's inattention to sanitation has some benefit after all!*

A smile finally found his lips.

When he came back to the office, however, it was only a few minutes before he had a desperate craving again. It was as if someone had stripped him of the most useful part of his being. His now-underprivileged left hand constantly slipped into the pocket out of habit, but encountered only dull fabric instead of coins. The same fabric that had once enhanced the joy of playing with the coins had now become bitter to his hand—just like wandering alone at the venue of past trysts after your lover has deserted you.

His hands could directly feel the void created in his life.

On that day he also noticed that Jay passed by him two times. This was very unusual—it hadn't happened in the past several years of his work history. He had never seen Jay on the first floor two times in a day; this made him suspect that Jay was personally keeping an eye on him. So, despite his terrible craving, he changed his mind about rushing outside to the public toilet.

The next morning Coinman went directly to pick up his hidden coins, then walked and walked the streets. He just couldn't make up his mind to go to the office. So he ended up spending his entire day outside: on the footpaths, in parks, at shops, on local buses, and in the movie theaters. He preferred noisier places so he could continuously play with his coins.

He consumed all his vacation time for the year wandering this way. His supervisor had a letter sent to his house asking him to report to the office immediately.

When Coinman came back to work, he was asked to see Jay in his office for a brief discussion.

"I only have a minute before another meeting," Jay said, "but needed to tell you that I was speaking with your boss yesterday and became aware that you couldn't use coins at home. I take the blame for getting you into this painful situation and apologize for not being thorough."

"It's not your fault, sir."

"Coinman, I will see to it personally that this issue is fixed in no time. Your anguish is going to be very short-lived." With that, Jay smiled and left his office for the meeting.

22. The Manager's Illusion

*I*n troubled times one wishes for a sound sleep more than usual, but, realizing its amplified importance, sleep smugly impedes all attempts to woo it.

Jay had trouble sleeping that night. He turned and tossed in bed. Being an early riser, he knew that sleeping late would spoil his day. So he tried even harder, inadvertently thwarting sleep even more.

Finally he got up to search the Internet for suggestions on securing a sound sleep. He tried three recommendations that figured frequently in the articles: he made his room colder, blocked out the traffic noise fully by shutting all the windows, and got a warm glass of milk.

None worked.

By midnight his head had started pounding as if a bunch of rhinos were trapped inside his mind and were desperately trying to escape. He started to feel weightlessness and attempted to overcome the strange experience by taking a hot bath. That did not help, either. When his disquiet rose to a level he could no longer handle, he climbed the stairs to the roof of his single-story house, where he was the sole resident. The moon was bigger than usual and looked excessively bright to his eyes. He noticed that a large, circular dark cloud surrounded the moon, as if vainly trying to trap it; the moon effortlessly moved out of the loose noose.

Jay stood there for a long time, looking at the sky, as though making up for not having looked at it well enough for numerous years. He remembered how, during his childhood, he and his siblings used to look at the mystifying sky together for hours from their roof to spot the shapes of the clouds.

Peaceful as they were, however, his thoughts were broken by a chain of bites from a swarm of unfeeling mosquitoes.

Back in his room, with sleep still away, he lay back down in his bed and tried to read a short story, massaging his head at the same time. Soon he realized that despite having attempted three times, he couldn't make sense of the opening paragraph in the first chapter. He tried the same paragraph again, and again, and again…but to no avail. He wasn't able to focus—so he put the book away and tried to go back in time, to his childhood, remembering as many people he could from his elementary school days.

Strangely, that worked instantly, launching him into dreamland.

After several bizarre dreams, he dreamed that his boss visited him at his house to discuss the Coinman issue. They talked at length, until a gust of heavy wind appeared from nowhere to blow away almost everything around them. His boss stood up from his chair with a jerk and stretched both hands in Jay's direction, palms facing down. The boss then chanted mantras loudly, making black cobras emerge from his sleeves to float in Jay's direction.

Jay couldn't run. To his horror he was completely frozen and couldn't move a limb. He screamed for help, but words did not come out. He was in a soundless world! He could feel his pulse through his entire body. The snakes had formed an aerial queue to bite him on the face, turn by turn, until Jay fell into an infinite pit, completely weightless.

Jay woke up screaming at this point, and was much relieved to realize that it had been only a dream.

His heart was still beating fast, and he noticed that his hands were resting over his chest. He remembered his mother's warning to him during his childhood. "Never sleep with hands over your chest," she would say. "It turns you into a mute and gets you into ghastly nightmares without being able to call for help."

He looked at the clock, pleased to see it was only four o'clock in the morning; he could still sleep for two more hours. He slipped back into bed and was back to dreamland within a minute.

Unfortunately, the nightmares weren't through with him yet. This time Jay was mysteriously trapped in his office. As he was coming out of his office door, he noticed another door, and then another…and soon he was passing through door after door, endlessly, until he completely lost his sense of direction to the exit. The office was glaring with white neon lights. He did not recall ever having allowed those to be installed. There were no people; he found himself thinking that others might have left well ahead of time, being aware of the spooky metamorphosis of the office after hours.

Every door he passed through was situated in such a way that he could see only one room at a time. He couldn't see the next room without leaving the previous one, at which point the door would close automatically behind him. Every time he passed through a door, he landed in an identical room. It seemed he was stuck in the labyrinth of infinite identical rooms. Each room had four doors and the same objects in exactly the same states. No matter which door he tried, the situation remained the same. Once he jumped back into the previous room—trying to dodge the maze. But to his surprise, it was a new room. He'd figured this out by dropping his watch in the previous room; the watch was gone when he had jumped back through the same door.

"This means," he told himself, "it isn't possible to enter the same room again after exiting."

Intrigued, he continued dropping his stuff to study more. *Maybe there are just ten of these identical rooms with four doors*, he thought, *all somehow connected*. His thought, however, proved false once he'd dropped more than ten objects, each all by itself, and still did not see any of them anywhere in other rooms. When he was out of watch, pens, coins, shirt, shoes, and socks, he hopelessly started taking off the rest of his clothes to help map his location in the maze. He stopped throwing his possessions when he had only boxer briefs on —and had the horrible thought, *What if I meet someone from the office in one of these rooms?*

He completed a full circle of thinking and re-postulated to himself that there was only one room, which he was entering and exiting at the same time through one of the four doors—but that somehow, by the design of this maze, the objects he dropped disappeared during a transitional point so infinitesimal that it was not observable with the naked eye.

In frustration he broke the chair in the current room and exited through one of the doors. The next room, too, had a broken chair. Next he scratched some paint from the current room and entered the next one. The next room had scratched paint as well.

"Wow," he murmured to himself, "there is only one room here."

He took the curtains down from the four doors and meticulously tore them into thin, long strips to make a rope. He then tied one end of the rope to the broken chair and entered the next room with the other end, carefully getting the rope through the space between the door and the floor. The broken chair in the next room had the same rope tied to it—exactly the same way he had left it in the other room. The other end was going out from another door.

"It could be this end that I am holding?" he asked himself. "God! Where am I?"

He went through the door and in the next room saw that there was a rope coming from the chair going into the door he had just left.

Confused and lost, he now followed the end he was holding and went through the door from which he had entered. There was a chair in a similar condition, with the other end of the rope disappearing through another door.

"So this doesn't work, either," he murmured, and then screamed, "Anyone here?"

Surprisingly, even though he was in an enclosed room, the sound echoed multiple times, as though it went through each room he had been to so far and somehow channeled back into the room he was in currently. Completely exhausted from hopelessness, he gave up and sat down on the floor.

He thanked the sun when its morning rays fell directly on his face, waking him up from his nightmare. The fitted sheet was completely crumpled to one side, exposing most of the mattress, indicating how violently he'd moved during sleep.

In the bath, a good solution to his dilemmas suddenly flashed into his mind. Next thing he knew, he was talking to Coinman in his office.

"Mr. Coinman," Jay said, making his tone as friendly as possible. "How have you been?"

"I have been living." Coinman's tone, on the contrary, was devoid of any cheer.

"Well, I wanted to provide you with a quick update. I am still working on the right solution, yet I may have found a way to bring some temporary relief to you."

"I am eager to find out," Coinman said, although he didn't seem very excited.

"As a temporary solution, I propose to get rubber coins made for you."

"I am sure that wouldn't work."

"Have you tried them in the past?"

"No, I have not."

"Let's at least try. What do you say? I will make sure the rubber coins feel the same as the metal coins do. Your hands won't even realize that they have been dodged. Besides, I have completed a good study on this—and found that there is a way to make rubber that has a similar density and feel as metal."

"How about the sound?"

"What do you mean? Isn't that what we are avoiding here?"

Coinman nodded. A drowning man counts heavily on the smallest speck of hope, and Coinman was no different. Even as he very much doubted the solution would work, he wanted to try it.

"We will sail through this together," Jay assured him. "Consider me your comrade in the trouble you're going through. We'll find the best places to make the rubber coins to our specifications, so that your hands get the same experience they once had."

The highly customized rubber coins were ordered and delivered to Jay the following week.

Before handing them over to Coinman, Jay put them into his right pocket and, to compare, put some metal coins in the left one. He slipped the coins through the fingers in both pockets, trying to see if they felt the same. Then he swapped pockets and repeated the exercise. He then closed his eyes, to focus even more on what his hands were experiencing. He was gratified to realize both types of coins felt the same to him.

Jay got the coins gift-wrapped and personally handed them to Coinman at his desk.

Coinman tore open the envelope impatiently and emptied the coins into his left pocket. But his left hand's instant disappointment traveled to Coinman's mind in less than a second.

The rubber coins were completely bogus.

I should still try to get adjusted to the new coins, Coinman thought. *Who knows if after a few weeks these coins may be helpful?*

So he gave them a chance, and a few weeks passed, but the rubber coins did not solve anything—they were instead a sort of burden on him and had even started to irritate him. One day he threw them in the trash, then went to Jay's office and knocked at his door.

"Come in, Coinman. Please have a seat."

"Thank you, sir."

"May I help you with something? How are we doing with the rubber coins?"

"First, my apologies for barging in uninvited like this," Coinman said.

"No, you are good."

"I appreciate what you're doing, sir," Coinman continued. "I know how important your time is. So I would talk straight without much huddle-muddle. The rubber coins suck! I also want to tell you that, going forward, I don't want you to share my burden."

Coinman had said this in one breath. He paused to let Jay have time to digest it.

"Keep talking. I'm listening," Jay said.

"If for a few minutes I take myself out of this situation, to look objectively at it as an outsider, I can't help but think that no one else but me needs to deal with it. If I cannot come to grips with my own sufferings, and find a resolution, I do not deserve to be a man."

Coinman acknowledged to himself that the sudden rush in his blood wasn't going to be very useful. So he paused to take a few breaths.

"It's my pain and I must fix it," he said again, with such determination that Jay did not want to offer any views.

"So be it," Jay said. "I respect your confidence and determination to solve this on your own. I want to tell you that I am always here to help, should you need it. Good luck, Coinman! Keep me posted on how it goes."

Jay saw a ray of hope in Coinman, a spark that hadn't been evident in the past, a determination to possess his future by assuming captainship of his present. That, in his opinion, was all to the good.

23. The Fundamental Cornerstone

The loss of a reliance on others often helpfully forces a more sophisticated rumination that enables the opening of previously unknown avenues.

Taking the responsibility into his own hands, Coinman scrutinized the issue at an unprecedented level. He was able to get down to a list of potential workable solutions: leaving home forever to live alone, and changing his job; or, alternatively, asking Jay for a separate office, putting a wireless sound capture and transmitter system in his left pocket to transmit the jingling sound to his ears without releasing it to the surroundings, asking permission to work from home, or even doing a presentation to the entire office on the joys of coin jingling. Then he drilled each one of these solutions down to the minutest details and listed the pros and cons of each. He thought he was drawing very close to determining the best solution and wondered if a second opinion would still be worth it, given the importance of the matter.

He thought of running his list past Jay first, but then, considering his last discussion with Jay, he thought it best if he could get someone else to weigh in—someone who had enough intellectual capital to not only understand the complexity of the situation, but also discern the precise nature of the interest each party had in the matter. He knew only two such people, other than Jay: Ratiram, and his childhood friend Funda. The robbery had exposed Ratiram's real face to him. So Funda was the only option.

There was a reason Coinman considered Funda in this esteemed group. Funda had been considered the best in their college circle for his knowledge about almost anything on earth. His friends had nicknamed him Funda because they had believed he could get down to the most *fundamental* aspects of any topic. If he started explaining something, people became quiet and listened, spellbound, until he finished. The most significant thing, they said, that put Funda in a different league from his competition was his practical approach. Despite knowing theoretical aspects and ideal-world scenarios to perfection, he didn't get bogged down by theory alone and invariably cut through complexities to deliver the most pragmatic blueprint.

During their youthful days, they had never needed to ask before visiting each other's houses. Their families did not have phones during the early years of their friendship, so they just used to pop in at will. And by the time their families got phones, the affectionate practice of uninvited and unannounced visits had firmly established itself.

Coinman didn't have Funda's phone number—they hadn't been in touch for years. Even if he had known it, he didn't want to depreciate the amicability of the historic practice.

He felt lucky that it was already Friday and he did not have to wait before visiting Funda's house. Without wasting any time, he called home to inform Kasturi about his plans to stay overnight at Funda's house. Kasturi reminded him that the family needed to attend an important wedding ceremony.

"I need to miss it," he replied. "Apologize to them on my behalf and tell them that I had an unavoidable business matter pop up at the last minute."

"Is everything OK, Son?"

"Yes, nothing to worry about. It's just that I need to speak with Funda on an urgent business matter."

"OK. Work is always first. I won't delve any further."

"Will Father be OK alone? I assume Imli and Shimla are coming along with you?" Coinman asked.

"Yes. We are going to lock the house from outside—he wouldn't be able to leave."

"You have it well covered. We don't want him to get lost."

"I have to say, though," Kasturi added, "you may have noticed, too, he seems a bit happier lately and has even looked impatient. Maybe he is getting better? We should arrange a doctor visit this week to get a read on his current state. I am very hopeful this time."

"Sure, let me call the doctor tomorrow morning."

"Take care, then."

"You too. Also, keep an eye on Imli." Coinman laughed as he said this. "I am glad that her play is over and she's no more a stranger. But her transition into a doctor hasn't been any less painful—I wasn't too worried until yesterday, when she gave me a shot. I hope she remembers at all times that she is at a social event, not in her dispensary."

Kasturi couldn't help laughing. "Don't worry about her. She is in a very good spirits right now. Knock on wood, it seems good days have started to show up for us. You should be very happy to know that Imli did my hair today!"

"That's nice. Very well, then. Good night, Mother."

Coinman purposely didn't pursue the line of conversation about Daulat much; he knew talking about his deteriorating condition depressed Kasturi. He also knew very well that Daulat's condition was on a downward spiral —and could only become worse. He did not want to prematurely slay Kasturi's hopes, which were destined to be short-lived.

As he started driving to Funda's house, Coinman tried to reassure himself that an unannounced visit wouldn't be a problem with Funda's family.

It was an hour's drive to Funda's house, long enough to allow more memories from their childhood to surge into his mind. He remembered how they had met for the first time on a bus, traveling with their parents to attend a two-day wedding function. Once they discovered that they lived in the same community, they returned from the wedding as close friends. Thereafter their families also benefited from their friendship and spent considerable time at each other's house.

Coinman remembered how he'd loved the large collection of comic books at Funda's house. Often he brought comic books home and hid them inside his schoolbooks while reading—typically inside the science books, with their large size—because his parents hated comic books and thought that they derailed kids' minds from academics. A smile appeared on his face when he remembered how this had led his parents to surmise that he had a passion for science! And how they remained clueless, throughout most of his childhood, about his failure to do well in exams despite "studying" for long hours!

Comics weren't to blame, Coinman thought, *it was the control. If I had been allowed to bring comic books home openly, like other kids my age, I am sure I wouldn't have spent so much time on them. Easy accessibility gradually tapers engrossment.*

Still smiling, Coinman arrived at Funda's bungalow. He noticed that the giant ashoka tree in the front yard had been replaced by a modest lemon tree. When he stepped inside the metal gate without knocking, exactly as he had years ago, he immediately noticed enthusiastic housecleaning going on. He caught sight of Funda's elder brother, Raju, instructing the housemaids in a loud voice. The lawn was fully occupied with household items: utensils, beds, couches, dining table, table fans, bookshelves, and much more. The grass on the lawn was doing its best to survive the abuse from these items.

Then he realized that Raju had been staring at him and had just seemed to recognize him.

"Coinman?" Raju asked, his voice full of excitement. Even though it had been years since he last met the family, they had remembered him by his new name.

"Yes, it's me, brother." Coinman reciprocated the excitement.

"Wow! It's so nice to see you after such a long time," Raju said, hugging him. "Come this way to the drawing room."

"How have you been, brother?" Coinman asked.

"Can't complain," Raju said, smiling. "Wait to see how happy Funda and Mother will be when they see you."

Funda was on the phone as they entered the drawing room. He cut short his conversation at once, ran to Coinman to hug him tight, and lifted him enthusiastically, just as he had several years ago.

"You look great. Exactly the same," Funda yelled in excitement.

"And you've got some real meat on your bones now. Do you remember how we used to tease you by calling you 'shirt on a hanger'?" Coinman said, laughing mischievously.

"Ahem!" Funda cleared his throat. "Why don't you make yourself comfortable on the couch? Let me get you some water. I'll be back in a jiffy."

Coinman could hear overlapping human voices from other parts of the house, occasionally mixed with sounds of moving furniture, pouring water, sweeping, and hammering. It made him curious what it was all about.

In the meantime Funda's mother entered the drawing room and came straight to him.

"Look who is here today!" she exclaimed with excitement, and then teased Coinman, "Maybe I am dreaming. Let me pinch myself."

She took Coinman's hands in hers and kissed them with motherly affection.

"It's been a while since we saw you last," Raju said, as Funda served Coinman a glass of water.

"That's right," added Coinman, "we met last at Funda's wedding."

"That was exactly two years after your marriage," added Funda. "And that reminds me—how are Imli and everyone else doing?"

"They are all doing very well," Coinman said, and turned to Funda's mother.

"How has life been with you, Auntie?"

"What life?" Mother complained in her signature melodramatic way. "A life without sweets is not much worth living."

"Mother, don't get started on this again. He is visiting us after years—he certainly deserves a better topic." Funda only provoked his mother by saying this.

"You tell me, Son," she said to Coinman. "I'm only fifty-three. Should I be subjected to these miserable restrictions at such a young age when much older people, some even with one leg hanging in a coffin, feast on a ton of sweets every day?"

"That surely is a senseless discrimination." Coinman said, as the conversation started flowing just as in the olden days. "Who dared to sweep sweets from your life? This heinous injustice needs to be disputed at once."

"These cursed doctors declared me diabetic when I fell on the sidewalk in the market one day. And the worst part was, it turned every member of my family into a spy camera. I had to hide sweets in the bathroom at first, but then they started securing the sweets with a lock."

That made everyone burst into laughter.

"What is this cleaning all about?" Coinman finally found an opportunity to kill the question that was troubling him.

"We are having some guests tomorrow afternoon—a family that's seeking an alliance with our daughter Kirti."

"That's great news! Where is Kirti, by the way?" Coinman had completely forgotten about her.

"She has a sleepover with her best friend tonight," Funda's mother replied.

"But isn't that an early marriage? She is like, what—maybe twenty years old?"

"You know better, Son," the mother responded. "This new generation is so keen to have a love match. We don't want to take a chance. We want her to be married good and early. You're very close—she just turned nineteen this year."

"I fully understand," Coinman said. "Who is the lucky boy?"

"His name is Neel. He's studied computers in America and operates computers in a big company. Raju, what's the name of the company? It's just on tip of my tongue."

"Mother, I have told you at least thirty-seven times," Raju grumbled. "Equanimity Technology Services."

"It's not my fault, Mr. Smart! Who can remember such a name? Nevertheless, it's a very big company; that's all that matters." She turned back to Coinman. "Take something, Son," she said, pointing to the variety of sweet and salty snacks that were now available on the table in the middle. Then she went on.

"So, as I was saying, the boy works for a big company in America and definitely, he would expect cleanliness in the house. We don't want to take any chances."

"That sounds like very good preparation," Coinman said.

"That's nothing. We have had a paid trainer to train her on Western formalities. Sadly, she couldn't learn to cook because of her studies, and the boy is very particular about home-cooked Indian food. But we've got that covered, too —we have hired a very good cook for tomorrow. And once this is through, we are going to ensure that Kirti learns to cook well before her marriage."

"Ma—is it really needed? Like lying in a relationship before it has even been established?" Raju said.

"Raju and Funda—these boys were definitely my moral science teachers in our previous birth." She turned to Coinman. "Wouldn't you agree that a lie for a good reason is better than a truth that destroys? I know you would."

"I can't agree more. That's a flawless plan." With her appeased, Coinman changed the subject deliberately. "How is our Junior Brother?"

Everything came to a rest for a moment.

"Junior Brother," as they affectionately called him, was Funda's youngest brother, bedridden since early childhood because of a 'rare wasting illness called Batten disease', as Funda's mother would refer to it. She would often say, "There is no God for sure, else how could one justify terminal diseases in small kids?"

"He is no more," Funda broke the silence.

"When? How? Oh, my God! May his soul rest in peace! I am very sorry for the loss. And so sorry I asked."

"That's all right." Raju tapped Coinman's right shoulder. "He has a very special place in our hearts."

"What happened to him?" Coinman asked hesitatingly.

"You know he was deeply depressed about being confined to his room," Funda explained. "And you also saw him having fits often. Well, his condition kept declining to a point where it was impossible to keep him happy at all. We all loved him, but the situation had taken such an awful turn that we started praying for freedom of his splendid soul from the rotten dungeon of his body. It was a tough prayer, yet necessary, for none of us could stand his agony and painful screams.

"Junior was summoned by the Ultimate Soul on the very day he had turned eighteen. I remember clearly that he was singularly quiet on that day. There was a certain gaiety on his face, and his behavior had the confidence of someone who could see beyond the obvious. He eagerly wore the new shirt and trousers that Mother had bought for the birthday party. He cut the cake, set the party into full swing, and managed to slip into his room alone at some point. Later on, realizing his absence from the party, we looked for him and found him dead in his bed."

Reminiscences of Junior filled Coinman's mind. He could clearly remember that the first thing he always did at Funda's house was to go to Junior's room to greet him in his bed. Junior was very fond of surreal fiction and was invariably reading a thick book.

"Don't feel bad," said Funda, putting his left hand on Coinman's right hand. "Mother even believes that he makes secret visits to her once in a while and asks her about all of us. She thinks that he has even become stronger."

"Yes, I am sure he is fine with God," she said quietly.

Noticing small tears forming in Funda's mother's eyes, Coinman hastened to switch topics again.

"How's your teaching going, Funda?"

"Ask us about it." Mother jumped in, wiping her tears. He is becoming a weirdo teacher of the kind students talk about all the time."

"Auntie, don't worry. Funda couldn't become a weirdo. I know him." Coinman laughed, and winked at Funda.

"I do not see how teachers are any more weirdos than people in other professions," said Funda sincerely. "Are some of those tellers at the bank any lesser weirdos, when they keep sipping their tea, ignoring the queue in front? Do you think that street hawkers are any lesser weirdos, when they ring the doorbell a second time at your door only two seconds after the first? Or cab drivers, who start to drive fast to scare you if they don't like a comment from you—even if you're talking to someone else? Or do you think that those big honchos sitting at the top of the corporate ladder are lesser weirdos? No. Weirdos are in uniform circulation in society."

Funda paused to eat a sweet from the table, then spoke again.

"It's just my personal observation, of course, but I am pretty sure on that. It seems to me that around five percent of people are weirdos in one way or the other, and that doesn't include situational or occasional weirdos. Everyone is a situational weirdo. So the point here is we have been overly critical of teachers, while other professions like doctors, engineers, post office employees, clerks, accountants, politicians, and whatnot, have just as many weirdos."

There was a silence of a few seconds—it seemed that Funda had stretched it too far.

"How ridiculous I am!" Funda said with a laugh. "We get together after such a long time, and I'm boring you with all this nonsense! Come, Coinman, I want to show you something."

Funda got up and grabbed Coinman's right hand, dragging him to another room. Alone in a quieter place, Funda turned to him with an all-business look and said, "You look distressed to me. Is everything all right?"

"I don't know where to start. Things haven't been quite hunky-dory for me lately. It seems God has been practicing shooting troubles at me. I have come here to seek some guidance from you."

"Coinman, before you tell me more, I would like to share my outlook on life," Funda said thoughtfully. "People say we have thousands of options in life. I say we have only two: we can either be happy or be unhappy."

He paused to look deeper at Coinman's face. "Every individual has the power to choose between the two. The world around has enough happiness if one chooses to happy, and it has only sadness if one chooses to be unhappy."

Saying this, Funda realized that Coinman's attention was starting to scatter. So he said, laughing, "OK, enough of a lecture on happiness. This is an endless dialogue. Sometimes I do doubt myself and think my mother is actually right on my becoming a weirdo. Pardon my chattering habit and expand on what your trouble is."

"I am very depressed these days. That's one of the selfish reasons I've come by your house today after such a long time. You are a winner in life—someone I feel is never out of control, and someone who could see black and white even when it's all a colorful illusion. I am here to seek your guidance on my issues."

"Before you go further down that path," Funda jumped in, "do you really think that intelligent people, or people who are winners in life, do not get depressed? As a matter of fact, they get just as depressed as you and I do. To tell you the truth, they are typically more depressed than an average person. And the reason is twofold. First, by being winners, they bring about great expectations from others, and living up to those expectations constantly isn't easy. There is lurking fear of a failure. And when there is a failure, the people around, most of whom are good for nothing themselves, will not let any opportunity go by to debase them."

Funda paused to appraise Coinman's engagement, and, noticing hints of impatience, summarized his thought. "The reason I am telling you this is to let you know that everyone gets depressed. So never think for a moment that winners are not depressed, and stop thinking negatively about it. Depression is a reality with everyone. What's important is the ability to move on. Sorry for digressing again, let's go back to your story."

"I actually want to discuss two issues. Both of them are very personal, so I request you keep them confidential even from your family."

"Most definitely."

Coinman's chin started to wiggle. "I don't think I ever told you about Imli's highly unpredictable nature. You can never know what she will do from one moment to the next."

"I don't recall. Tell me more about it. It would be good if you can cite some examples of her behavior."

"She is insanely in love with acting. Critics consider her one of the best actors around, but no one knows how difficult her blind immersion makes it for everyone at home. She lives at home in the same character that she portrays on the stage. At times she doesn't seem to realize that she is actually physically hurting us."

Coinman gulped water and spoke again.

"She is currently playing a doctor's role. She bought a first-aid kit that she carries in her left hand all the time. She treats me as if I'm her patient these days—she takes my pulse and checks my ears and eyes every day as soon as I get back from the office. But the worst of it happened yesterday: when I was in bed trying to sleep, she rolled me on my stomach and gave me a shot in my butt. I panicked, for I didn't know what in the world she'd injected me with. Turns out it was harmless, but…"

Funda just shook his head in disbelief.

"I don't get a minute's peace at home because of this. She spares my mother and is almost well behaved to her, but she doesn't always behave nicely to my father and Shimla. You mightn't know that my father is in a downward spiral with mental decay, and Shimla is uncomplaining as ever— that makes it even more painful. I don't understand how to handle this situation."

"Hasn't she seen a psychiatrist yet?"

"I asked her once; unfortunately, she was playing a police officer then. She tied me to a chair with a thick rope and had my trial going for the next two hours. Can you imagine that everyone in my family allows that kind of stuff?"

Funda looked at Coinman in awe. "I am shocked. First, this is so much to digest. Second, I am awfully nervous about how complex the second issue is going to be!"

Coinman said grimly, "I won't keep you in suspense. The staff robbed me of my coins in the office." Coinman was barely able to speak, for an uncomfortable lump had formed in his throat.

"What do you mean? They robbed you, like real robbing?"

"Yes. They forcefully detained me and took all the coins from my pocket."

"But you can't live without those coins. I know that very well."

"Management has now intervened as well. Long story short, I am not allowed to carry coins in my pocket at the office. And what makes it worse—Imli had already wiped our house of coins earlier."

"Dinner is ready," Funda's mother said, knocking at the door. "Come have food first. You have the whole night to talk about the old days."

After dinner they went for a walk outside the house to continue the discussion.

"Tell me now." Funda was very keen to know more.

"So, fast-forwarding a bit," Coinman said, "I have brainstormed a few potential solutions to the issue. I wanted to discuss them with you, kind of a second opinion."

"What are the solutions?"

"Maybe I can leave home forever to live separately from everyone. Or change my job. I thought of asking Jay for an enclosed office. I thought about a transmitter to bring the sound from my pocket to an earphone, or I could work from home. Or I could get people on my side, and present to the entire office the joys of coin jingling!"

"Coinman, without much pretense, I would tell you that other than a couple, none of these is practical. Getting a separate enclosure, and working from home—both of these will work very well, but only if Jay allows you these. To be fully candid with you, though, giving you such a privilege might make the problem worse for him. If your boss is a sensible man, he wouldn't accept either of these two."

"That means none of these will work?"

"I am afraid not."

"Before I came here, I was very happy. I thought I had a bunch of solutions—but it seems like none of those may work. So I am back to square one!"

"No, you are not. I have a very good solution."

"That's my friend Funda I know. You create solutions like this." Coinman snapped his middle finger and thumb. "I can't wait."

"Do you remember when we were talking about Junior Brother earlier today?"

"Certainly."

"We bypassed a few important details in the story."

"Well, not that I understand the connection, but I am burning with curiosity now."

"One of our relatives happens to be an influential aristocrat in the ministry. You know—one of those high-connections kinds. He had a very singular attachment to Junior. He went out of his way to find new medicines, research, doctors, et cetera, to help Junior's condition in any way. Just six months prior to Junior's departure, he took us to a certain Sage Mangal. He had expressed extremely high opinion of him and told us that the sage did not serve just anyone and everyone; he only accepted people through recommendations from the most influential people."

"Was there a reason for that? A service like that should be equally available to everyone."

"Well, our relative told us that Sage Mangal had a divine spiritual power that could solve the toughest problems in the world—but he could bless only a limited number of people each year."

"And you trusted him?"

"We did not. But then our relative introduced us to a person who had completed the curriculum with the sage. In fact, he had the same disease as our Junior had, and he was completely healed."

"How did the sage heal him?"

"No one knows the details. And the students, as he calls them, are made to take an oath not to share any details of the process with the outside world. I have heard that the sage applies some sort of psychic capabilities that target the soul of the subject instead of the body—and they say that when the soul heals, the issues of the body disappear like they never happened."

"So what happened to Junior, then?"

"There, I digressed again." Funda smiled, and then sobered. "We were late."

"What do you mean?"

"It usually takes the sage about eleven months to work on a soul to bring about its transformation and have it reflected well on the physical body. He told us that Junior did not have that much time—that his condition was beyond recall."

"Surely he could have at least tried?"

"He was very sure that wasn't going to help. He clearly told us that Junior had about six months to live from there and suggested we just be with him and enjoy his company for the last six months of his life."

"That's very sad, indeed. I wish you had known about the sage earlier."

"You are spot-on. You can very well imagine how we felt coming back from the visit. We had firsthand witnessed the ethereal evil of crushing hope just when it had peaked—like an open door, visible to you as you approach it from miles away, just closing on you when you have only two more yards to go. Everything we felt was just beyond our senses —as though someone was knowingly waiting till the very last second before turning the tables on us."

"So you believed the sage when he said Junior only had six more months?"

"We actually did not fully believe it. In this way, hope is the best and the worst thing at the same time. It kept our spirits from going low, yet it made us find ways to disprove the sage's prediction."

"Were you able to?"

"Unfortunately, no; we worked tirelessly to meet a few more patients that had successfully completed their time with the sage. Everyone had a grand success story. Then we happened to meet a family to whom the sage had given the same message about their son as he did to us. The family said his prediction was spot-on."

"So you knew his prediction was going to be right about Junior?"

"Not until very late. We exhausted all six months in doing follow-ups and research. We lost him within days of knowing there was no reason to believe we wouldn't."

"I am very sorry for the loss, again."

Funda nodded in acknowledgement, without making a sound. Then he went on.

"So let's go back to your situation. Given the state of things, Sage Mangal seems to be the only recourse for you. Please don't think that I consider you sick, by any means. But the holistic experience with the sage will guarantee your rescue from the current situation."

"Putting aside several other things that pop into my mind right now, the biggest doubt I have is about Jay. There is no way in the world that he would agree to a yearlong absence for me."

"He will. Just try it out."

"What makes you think he will?"

"If nothing else, he gets a year free from the issue, and enough time for a plan B, should your endeavor with the sage fail."

"And would he spend the firm's money on this?"

"He sure will. By the way, your spouse gets free entry. Jay needs to pay only for you."

"If you are confident about everything you have said, what issues can I have? I will speak to Jay."

"Don't hesitate to discuss it further with me if you have a doubt," Funda told him. Then he looked at his watch. "One of the biggest disadvantages of being grown up is seeing the time rush by faster. I did not realize it was already midnight. Let's go get some sleep before you leave in the morning."

Coinman couldn't sleep for the next three hours. His thoughts wouldn't let him. He could catch only a two-hour doze before leaving in the morning.

He drove to his house in almost a half-asleep condition, relying so heavily on his muscle memory that he didn't completely realize he was home until he had turned the ignition off in front of his house.

But then, from the car, he saw that Kasturi was waiting at the door, tears continuously falling from her eyes.

"Mother! What's happened?" Frantic, he ran for the door. As soon as he reached her, she fell into his embrace.

"The most terrible thing has just happened!" she cried. "Your father is no more, Son. We are completely devastated."

24. The Untimely Grief

"When it rains, it pours horrible shit."

Panna's unique saying popped, unsolicited, into Coinman's mind, and he realized yet again that everyone's mind has sort of a slum division—a flirtatious spot that doesn't give a hoot about how grave a situation is but constantly endeavors to derail more earnest thoughts, almost like a death-wish backseat driver.

But now wasn't the time to entertain such musings, either.

Coinman darted inside the house, straight into the old man's room. To his horror he saw Daulat lying motionless in his chair, his head rolled to the side and his eyes open, wearing a blissful smile on his face.

Grief follows no rules, and Coinman's first thoughts wandered toward the mortality of humans instead of lingering in the pain of the unfathomable loss that lay in front of him. At that moment it all felt like a dream to him, a dream where events of paramount impact happen without drawing much reaction, making the dreamer feel he's walking in the dark in an unknown place. *Death can happen to anyone, anywhere*, he thought, *but the widespread low acceptance of its inevitability and lack of adherence to a schedule is disturbing.*

Kasturi broke his thoughts by embracing him tightly, for she suspected he had suddenly gone quiet because of a mental trauma. He noticed that the three women around him were constantly sniffling.

"Why would the Lord summon him so early?" Kasturi sobbed. "I am so sad for all his sufferings. He did not even see his full life. He will miss so much."

"Mother," Coinman said, gently guiding her out of the embrace, "I am very sad, too. But my sadness is not for Father, but for us. He has died, and is free of any sufferings, memories, or even thinking what he will miss by departing early. So, please, let's not feel sorry for him. Feel sad for us, because we have forever lost this opportunity to be in his interesting company."

Kasturi seemed a bit stupefied by this; she sobbed less intensely now.

"Tell me what happened," Coinman said quietly. "There are no clear signs of a cause here."

"He committed suicide," said Kasturi, sniffling again as she spoke.

"What? How? And how are you so sure about it?"

"The old man poisoned himself using Imli's first-aid box."

"But there was no poison in the box. Was there, Imli?"

"No, there was not." Imli intensified her weeping.

"Did we have poison anywhere in the house, Mother?" Coinman inquired.

"We didn't...unless Daulat bought it himself and hid it somewhere in the house."

"I am responsible for this," Imli said, barely audibly. "I feel such a heavy burden on my heart right now that I can't even think."

"You aren't responsible for this," Coinman said, trying to console her. "None of us is, actually. Think about death being inevitable, and unpredictable, exempt from the law of averages. Everyone has a turn, and no one knows when. Don't feel sad for Father for future joys that he could have experienced—there is no future in that sense. His future never existed in the first place beyond the point when we lost him."

As he spoke, he pressed Imli's head against his chest.

"It's our own selfish reasons for wanting him to live longer that we should truly be sad about. And once you understand them as selfish reasons, the sadness is not hard to conquer."

"I don't concur." Kasturi could no longer have Coinman going on philosophically. "I understand most of your argument, but not the part about sadness being a selfish thing. What do you think about the memories from the lovely past that now sting my heart: all the moments we cherished together, his funny jokes, his always being there? Countless memories are now flowing in my heart, one after other, just waves of pain. Can pure matters of the heart, like such, be termed as selfish?"

"Mother, I am sorry, it seems I hurt your feelings. I am feeling very sad myself. Our loss is incomparable to anything else. I get this painful feeling right now that I always took his time for granted, almost a commodity that we could avail ourselves of at the push of a button. Now that we have lost him, I feel that there was so much that was left unsaid between him and me just because of losing the sight of life's fragility."

"Shimla," said Kasturi abruptly, "can you call and inform the police?"

"Yes, I will do that now." Shimla was ready to flee at the first opportunity; she'd been clearly agitated listening to the arguing between Coinman and his mother.

"Wait a minute," Kasturi added then. "Inform the doctor and the transportation office, too—we need to get the body released for cremation and then transport it. Also, on the way back, please inform Uncle Raghav's family. I will give a list of other names to Coinman shortly so he can call them all to inform them."

Shimla nodded and left.

Kasturi took hold of Coinman's upper arm then. "We have a problem, Son."

"A different problem than this one?"

"You can decide yourself; I am not sure if I can answer yes or no."

"My heart is sinking now." He sat so abruptly on the floor it felt as if he dropped there.

"When we came back to the house, Imli and I came directly to my bedroom to change, and Shimla went directly to Daulat's room to check on him. Seeing the old man dead, it seemed that she trembled all over. Then she saw Imli's kit next to the old man, and, with a momentary lapse of reason, considered the possibility that Imli might have poisoned the old man under the spell of her doctor's character. She remembered how Imli had given you a shot a day ago."

"And?"

"So Shimla became very concerned for the family. She told me she couldn't imagine the sadness that Imli's imprisonment would cause this family, on top of Daulat's departure."

"What does this mean?"

"The poor girl picked up the syringe and the small bottle of poison—to deliberately leave her fingerprints on them. She couldn't imagine, as she told me, that Daulat might have killed himself."

"Oh, Lord, this is so unbelievable!" Coinman buried his face in his palms.

"You must only consider how big a sacrifice she was willing to make for this family."

"Where are the syringe and the box right now?"

"I have carefully preserved them in a clean cloth."

At that, Imli reentered the room.

"Mother," she said, "the house needs cleaning before we have visitors. I am going to start on that."

Kasturi signaled agreement, and Imli left the room.

"Tell me more about it," Coinman said. "I hope you haven't rubbed off the fingerprints?"

"I was thinking about rubbing them off. But my mind wasn't fully working. So I wanted to discuss it with you."

"That's great. If you had rubbed them off, we would have had one option less."

"I don't quite get that."

"If you had rubbed off Shimla's fingerprints, we couldn't have surrendered the syringe as it is."

"Why not?"

"Because it's clear that an injection of poison caused the death. So having no prints on the syringe would have caused a bigger issue of tampering with evidence."

"I get it. But we can't submit the syringe with her fingerprints on it, either."

"Why not?"

"I would rather ask you how we could."

"I am sure there is a way to prove the truth. In fact, if you had removed her prints, we would be in a worse mess. We would then need either to get Daulat's fingerprints again, or ask Shimla to do hers again; in either case it would have been a moral ordeal."

"I see your point now."

Coinman swam in deep thoughts, thinking about any possible arguments that would prove Shimla's innocence. Seeing Shimla coming back after fulfilling Kasturi's instructions, he made haste to the drawing room.

"Everyone, come here, please, at once."

The three women of the house followed him immediately.

"I understand that there is a lot we need to complete before visitors start coming—but first things first. Nothing is more important right now than for all of us to understand exactly what happened in every detail and account for every bit of the time, right from when you guys left for the party till now."

Everyone was in agreement.

"Could one of you tell me from the beginning," Coinman asked, "the exact sequence of the events of yesterday night?"

"It was around six thirty when I served him dinner," Shimla volunteered, "and half an hour later, we left for the wedding."

"We locked the house from outside, as usual, so he wouldn't be able to open the house for strangers or just walk outside," Kasturi added.

"Do you remember," Coinman asked, "what happened between six thirty and seven?"

"Nothing much. After serving him dinner in his room at six thirty, we continued to get ready in Imli's room. We left the house at seven."

"Did you check on him at all between serving him dinner at six thirty and leaving the house at seven?"

"No. We were running late already."

"What happened after you left?"

"We were at the wedding till very late," Shimla said. "We left there around three o'clock in the morning, and got home around four. As we came in, I went straight to check on him. I saw him lying motionless with the syringe still stuck in his arm. There was also a small bottle of poison on the floor."

"What happened after that?"

"In my stupor I pulled the syringe out of his arm and had a good look at it."

"Do you think you left your fingerprints on the syringe?"

"I am sure I did. Such a fool I was to do it."

"What happened after that?"

"I started wailing, and Imli and Mother came rushing in. We all started to cry."

"Did any of you try to reach me?"

"How could we?" Imli intervened this time. "You don't carry a cell, and we did not have Funda's number."

"That's fine," Coinman said. "I am just ensuring we ask all possible questions and have all the answers consistently understood among the three of us."

"That's very important. We don't have Daulat's fingerprints on the syringe. We are likely going to face a deep inquiry," Kasturi added.

"What happened after that?"

"After hearing from Shimla about her fingerprints," Kasturi said, "I picked up the syringe and the first-aid box in a clean cloth and carefully moved them to another location."

"What happened between then and when I came back?"

"Nothing much. We have mostly been crying."

"All right. So first, we need to bring the syringe and the box back to his room and leave it on the floor.

"Do we leave Shimla's prints on it?" Imli asked.

"Yes, we will have to leave them as is," Coinman responded.

"Shimla should not get in any trouble," Kasturi protested.

"She will not," Coinman said reassuringly. "With all that you have said, it's very clear that the old man killed himself between six thirty in the evening and four o'clock in the morning. I am sure a postmortem report will be able to provide an accurate time when he consumed the poison. And we have alibis for that time—the folks at the wedding for you, and Funda's family for me. So we can prove that when the old man was poisoned, none of us was in the house."

Kasturi was very proud of Coinman.

"We have a small issue, though," he said.

"What's that?" Imli asked.

"The only shady part is the period between six thirty and seven o'clock. I am doubtful this will be a problem—but just for the sake of argument, if the postmortem report shows that poison was consumed during that half hour, it would mean that you three were still in the house, and that would completely make our argument futile."

"So what do we do then?" Kasturi asked.

"Sometimes life plans unbelievable coincidences," Coinman said, like a philosopher. "In some context, Funda's mother said yesterday night that a lie for a good reason is better than a truth that destroys. I couldn't have imagined then that she was giving a way out of this strenuous situation."

"Don't puzzle around, Son. My heart can't take it," Kasturi said.

"Yes, exactly, what do you mean by that?" Imli put in.

"It means that we will tell a lie. You need to forget that you had left the house at seven o'clock. You need to tell yourselves that you served him dinner at six o'clock and left at six thirty, without checking on him."

"And this is because there is a possibility he may have consumed the poison before we left?" Shimla wanted to confirm.

"That's exactly why we need to do this." Coinman took a deep breath. "Are there any other questions?"

"I think we are good," Kasturi replied.

"Then let's all get back to work again," Coinman said. "There is so much to be done today. Damn those dark clouds gathering above us—I sincerely hope it doesn't rain."

The cops arrived later in the day and, looking at the conditions present at the time of death, ordered a post mortem on the body. The family spent most of the day on mourning with the visitors.

The family could go to bed only around midnight. At their bed, Coinman almost whispered to Imli, "Do you remember my dreams where I have been chasing a black cobra to every corner in the house for the past year? I can probably interpret those dreams now. It seems it was nothing but a symbol of death hovering over our family."

"We would know. You have had that dream every night."

"I would say about three times a week. You're right. We would know."

"How are you holding up?" Imli asked.

"I am doing all right. I just can't get him out of my eyes. Moments spent with him that I thought I did not remember have suddenly become alive. The times when he took care of me as a small kid while Mother was away from the house flash more often than any other times."

"You'll be fine. I hope you get some sleep. With the body coming back from post mortem, tomorrow is going to be a big day. We have to finish the rest of the planning for cremation." Saying this, Imli kissed him on his forehead and turned to the right side of the bed to turn off the bedside lamp.

25. The Investigation

*I*n the first days after Daulat's death, without his existence, the house felt like a pair of ice jaws.

They had figured it out. It was a case where the idea of an existence was more important than the existence itself.

The existence wasn't acknowledged much until it perished, and its absence received an acute emotional reception, as though the world would have sacrificed anything to have it back again.

On a lazy Sunday afternoon, a week after Daulat's passing, when the family was sitting in the drawing room together, a visitor rang the doorbell.

"I've got it," Coinman said, running to the door.

"Is this Mr. Coinman's house?" a stout man wearing a sky-blue shirt and black pants asked, as soon as Coinman unbolted the door.

"Who are you?" Coinman demanded.

"I asked my question before you did. Isn't that a good enough reason to get an answer first?"

"How can I help you?"

"That's your question number two, quite ridiculously, that you have asked with a perfect disregard to not only my question but also to your own previous question!" The visitor was speaking louder now. "For your convenience I'll repeat my question again. Is this Mr. Coinman's house?"

"May I ask you keep your voice low, mister? My family is trying to unwind a bit—we have had a kind of a bumpy ride recently."

"Humble soul that I am, I give up on my right. I am here to salute Mr. Coinman, even touch his feet to offer my respect, if he allows me to do that," the visitor said sarcastically. "Do I now deserve to meet His Majesty, Mr. Coinman?"

"I am he."

"Phew!" The visitor feigned relief. "Do you always twist your arm behind your neck in order to touch your nose?"

"Let's focus on why you are here."

"Mind if I am honest with you?"

"I don't think so."

"It was not my goal to come here."

"Someone else sent you here?"

"No, that's not what I mean. And please, give me time to breathe next time before you contemplate jumping in." The visitor continued, "I was actually chasing a terrible trouble for days before it led its way to your house. Trailing behind her, I had to knock at your door."

"I would highly appreciate if you could rein in your failed attempts at wit. You are not sounding funny at all. At least not to me, with what I have gone through recently."

"Let's cut to the chase." The visitor seemed slightly insulted. "I am Patil. Police Inspector K. C. Patil."

"Mr. Patil, I apologize for the confusion. I was making sure that a tramp wasn't trying to burgle us. Why are you still standing here? Please come inside." Coinman guided Patil to the drawing room and ushered him to the couch, but Patil chose not to sit. The three women abruptly left the room after exchanging a greeting nod with Patil.

"What can I do for you, sir?" Coinman asked.

"I am investigating Daulat's murder case."

"It wasn't a murder."

"Let's not hurry to any conclusions. That's my job, anyway, not yours, to decide if it was a murder or not."

"I am only telling you the truth. We told it to the vigilant officers as well when they took Daulat's body for postmortem. They thoroughly recorded our statements about the poison and the syringe. Have you had any chance to look at the report?"

"Are you suggesting to me how I should go about my business?" Patil was vexed by this.

"Not at all, sir. I am only trying to save your important time."

"How exactly are you trying to save my time?"

"By reminding you to consider our earlier statements to save you from asking too many questions."

"Are you assuming now that I don't prefer asking too many questions?"

"No. I may, however, have assumed that you may not like to ask the same question twice."

"I love asking the same question over and over again a thousand times. I had a murderer in the trial room yesterday, and I don't even remember how many times I asked him, 'How did you kill the dumbass?'"

"Look, I apologize. It's not easy to win with you."

"You need to be my wife to win with me," Patil said, and laughed uproariously at his own sense of humor. He then slipped his right hand in his shirt pocket and took out a receipt. "Do you recognize the purchase of a first-aid kit last week, Coinman?"

"Yes, I do. But let me first call the three women here. You may need them as well."

"OK. Let's call them."

Coinman introduced them once they were in the drawing room. "This is my mother, Kasturi; my wife, Imli; and Shimla."

"Who did you say Shimla was?"

"She is our distant relative."

"And she is the one who had fingerprints on the syringe that vigilant officers had collected?"

"That's right. But she did not kill my father. We have it all detailed in the report that I talked about earlier."

"Let's get this straight." Patil's whole body vibrated in sudden anger. "You mention that freaking report one more time, and I am taking all three of you into overnight custody. Am I here to play 'pass the parcel' with my balls? I might as well have rolled the report in a thin tube and shoved it up my ass!"

The faces of Coinman and the three women turned red in embarrassment.

"That's the last time you are swearing here." Coinman found his courage. "If you do it again, I will forget that you are a police officer."

"What will you do if I swear again?"

"Not much. I will just make a call to our relatives in the ministry." Coinman had just in time remembered Funda's mention of his relative working there.

"That wouldn't help. We get these calls all the time."

"Well, it's up to you. At least I know what I am doing if you swear one more time."

"Let's go back to the Shimla conversation," Patil suggested. "I am going to fast-forward a bit now because you have wasted quite a bit of my time here. Because of the time crunch, I am going to be going by the story in the rotten report. I do have few questions on that."

"We are ready for your questions."

Patil now sat on the couch.

"Do you know what was uncovered in the postmortem report?"

"No."

"How could you still maintain that the old man killed himself without even knowing the time of his death?"

"He was alive when the ladies here left, but was found dead when they came back."

"Where were you during all this time?"

"I was at my friend's house the whole night. I went there directly from my office."

"How many days a month do you guys all remain outside your house? And what's your friend's name?"

"His name is Funda."

"How often do you visit him?"

"I hadn't visited him for several years."

"Why would you suddenly decide to visit a friend on the night your father was getting killed?"

"I didn't know about that when I decided to visit Funda."

"Give me Funda's address and phone number."

Coinman wrote it quickly on a piece of paper and handed it over. "Here."

"Thank you!" Patil nodded. "Now listen carefully. The postmortem report suggested that the poison was consumed around eight o'clock in the evening, and death occurred within five minutes."

"The ladies left at half past six," Coinman said. "That should lead you to conclude that my father killed himself."

"We don't have any evidence yet to prove that you all were elsewhere at eight o'clock. Specifically, I would need an alibi for Shimla."

"Let me write the names and numbers of the people we were with during the wedding at that time," Kasturi said. "You can talk to them. These names are also in the report we talked about earlier."

"That would be helpful. I will go talk to these people tomorrow."

"Is there anything else we can do to help you?" Imli asked Patil.

"No. I have all I need. I will get going."

"What should we expect as the next steps?" Kasturi asked.

"I will speak to these people you have mentioned, and based on that, I will prepare my report. On the basis of the report, my department will make a decision whether the case can be dropped here without further processing or if a trial will be needed."

"What could possibly lead to a trial?"

"I can't say."

"Any rough guesses?"

"If your alibis' accounts of the events don't match, we would go a more rigorous route, that of a trial, to get the investigation going."

"That explanation helps," Coinman said.

"Is there no way to avoid a trial? Whatever it takes, we can talk about it right now," Kasturi almost implored.

"Are you hinting at bribing me?" Patil said.

"I can't even do that in my dreams," Kasturi said.

"And that's why you want to do it in reality? Well, bad joke, I was trying to raise your spirits a bit. On a serious note, I think you guys don't have to worry if you have told me the truth, because you all had other people with you elsewhere at the time of the crime. However, the process has to take its course. If everyone is innocent, I have faith in the judiciary system that everyone will come out as innocent. Unfortunately, there is no way to avoid the pain you might go through as part of the process."

"That's understood." Kasturi nodded.

"Look, I really need to get going. I have to visit another family before my day is over." Patil turned to Coinman with a half smile. "I understand I can't swear here, but can I call you later today and let out on you what I had to suppress?"

Both of them laughed.

Patil shook hands with everyone and left. He'd barely gone when the family jumped on the phone and called those who could corroborate their alibis, one after another. Everyone took a deep breath after they had briefed all their relatives on what had happened and explained what was expected from them all.

"How many times can one have a heart attack within a week?" Coinman asked a question that had no better response than silence. And everyone responded perfectly.

26. The Unsought Date

"*I* am not sure if I can survive this deep sea of anxiety in the pit of my stomach any longer," Tulsi muttered to herself, biting her lip, while coming down in the elevator of her apartment building. "No one knows what I am up against today."

She realized that in her mental turbulence she had come down a little early to wait for the company cab. She walked to a bench by the side of the road and sat down, but she just couldn't take her mind off the meeting with ABC that she had to attend in an hour. Her palms became sweaty, her heart raced faster, and her ears filled with white noise.

The office cab showed up on time.

"Hi! It's probably too early for you?" Tulsi greeted the driver as he got out of the car to open the door for her.

She did not receive a response.

"So you work with our company? I don't think I have ever seen you." She had another question for the driver as they drove to the office. It seemed that her anxiety was making her unusually talkative.

"No."

The short answer wasn't enough to tamp down the effects of her anxiety.

"So they hire you for every pickup?"

He did not respond. Tulsi hummed a song to herself, continuously drying her palms with her handkerchief and dabbing her forehead.

"I wonder what time these shops open." Tulsi said, looking at the market shops from her window. It was another desperate attempt by her anxiety about the meeting that was moving up the neurotic ladder very visibly by making her nervously more talkative.

"Madam…"

"Yes?" Tulsi was so excited on hearing him speak that she jumped in before he could say another word.

"I am not a jerk, as you may think," the driver said, looking in her eyes via the rearview mirror. "I have very strict instructions to say no words, answer no questions, and not fiddle around when I am on duty."

"It's OK, you can talk," said Tulsi. "No one would ever know."

"I don't talk to anyone while on duty, madam. This is the first time I have spoken to someone."

"What is your name?"

"Chela Ramani, madam."

"Chela," Tulsi asked, "how many people have you driven for ABC meetings before now?" Tulsi finally seemed to have found someone who might have more information about the adventure she was going to embark on shortly.

"You are the second one. I have one more tomorrow."

"Who is the lucky one tomorrow?" Both of them had a quick laugh at Tulsi's question.

"That I can't reveal, madam."

"Why not?"

"Professional discretion and ethics, madam."

"All right." Tulsi was a bit disappointed by this. "Can you tell me who was the first one?"

"Ramta, madam."

"Tell me more about him."

"I picked him up from his house. His family came to see him off as he boarded my car—they gave him hugs and farewells as though he was going to war on another continent. I drove him to the office without saying a word, even when he was talking the whole time. I think he was more scared than you, madam."

"What? I am not scared."

"Then I was asked to drop him at the airport." Chela did not respond to Tulsi's claim. "He was badly sweating, and it seemed it would have taken him only a second to break down if someone just asked him what had happened."

"What had happened to him?"

"No one knows," he said. "Madam, we will reach the office in two minutes. Can I remind you please not to tell anyone that we talked?"

"I will not. I mean…I won't tell. I promise."

"Here you go. Good-bye, madam, if we don't meet again," Chela said, putting the car in park. He got out and opened the door.

"Why? You are the one who is taking me back home after the meeting, right?"

"I don't know, madam. I don't have any instructions as of now."

"All right, hope to see you around."

"All the best."

Tulsi came up to the second floor at seven o'clock, two hours before normal business hours began. A twentysomething girl greeted her and ushered her to ABC's office.

She had longed in the past to find out how ABC's office looked from inside; its eternally locked state had captured her imagination. Now, when she had the opportunity, she would have given anything to escape it.

Fate has this weird way of making your wish come true by supplementing it with ten other spiteful things, she thought, sitting down on one side of the large rectangular wooden table. Her chair seemed to be the target of figurative daggers from the three chairs on the other side of the table, as if the three chairs shared the same chemistry with the one chair on the other side that ABC did with the suspect being questioned.

Alone in the room, she forced herself to look around and was startled to notice that there was another door at the back. It was impossible to discern from the outside that there could be any space behind ABC's office. Tulsi became very curious about where that door went.

"Maybe this is where ABC enter from," she told herself, "and that's why no one ever sees them at the office."

"Care for some tea?" the twentysomething girl asked, after knocking at the door.

"That would be very nice."

"You got it," the girl replied. "By the way, I'm also supposed to apprise you that the three big bosses are running about ten minutes late because of a prior engagement. So please feel free to ask me if you need anything else, too."

"I won't hesitate. I appreciate the kind offer of help."

"You are very welcome. Let me get the tea for you."

The girl left and locked the room from outside, and Tulsi nervously let her gaze wander around her. The decor was stunning, comprised of artful antiques and expensive paintings. She would have loved to walk around and explore, but her fear had an upper hand at the moment.

The young lady was back in minutes with the tea.

"How much sugar and cream would you like?" she asked Tulsi.

"Please don't trouble yourself. You can leave it here and I will make it myself."

"Very well, then; good luck!"

"Thank you."

Tulsi did not have to wait much longer. There was a knock at the mysterious door at the back, followed by a ten-second wait before the three most dreaded gentlemen of the firm appeared through the door, one by one.

ABC paused after closing the door behind them to look at Tulsi from a distance, exchanged a quick glance among them, and nodded to each other before approaching the three imperial chairs on the other side.

They sat on the three chairs and gestured to Tulsi to sit down; she had stood up from her chair on seeing them.

They were of light-brown complexion, stout, and somewhere between fifty and sixty years of age. They wore identical white beards, and the same "uniform": black suits with broad mono-color ties—green, brown, and blue, respectively.

The first one was smoking the most beautiful pipe Tulsi had ever seen. The polished bowl of the pipe was made of hand-carved wood that merged smoothly with the shining black stem. The second one smoked a cigarette. The third one kept his hands busy with a pack of cards on the table.

Tulsi hated passive smoke. She just couldn't stand the smell. In public places she usually held her breath and walked fast to go past a smoker quickly. She always felt as if the smell of cigarettes clung to her for a long time if she allowed it inside her nose. So she held her breath as long as she could—almost to a point of choking at times. But she had no choice here other than to try to breathe less than normal to minimize her discomfort.

"Tulsi, first of all, a big thank-you for your flexibility in making this meeting on short notice," said the man with the pipe. "I am Andar; the gentleman on my left is Bandar; and to his left is Chandar." He took a puff from his pipe.

"I will come to the point without further ado," said Bandar. "Tulsi, things haven't been working very well. We have bad news for you."

"We are here to relieve you from your responsibilities, effective immediately." Chandar wasted no time.

"What do you mean?" That was all Tulsi could manage to say.

"As you know, the whole Coinman thing was the most disreputable matter that has ever come to our table, and a disciplinary action has been determined on the key engineers of the incident," Andar explained.

"Being one of the chief architects of the debacle"— Bandar took it forward from Andar—"you are impacted by the decision, and it is our duty to let you know that your employment with the firm ends as of today."

It was almost as if Tulsi's ears had stopped working; she could only feel voices hum, not hear them. Her vision blurred as well. Her world seemed to crumble before her. She imagined how it would feel to go home and tell her mother, who had leisure travel planned, that she had been fired. All her monthly financial obligations flashed in front of her eyes. She didn't even have any savings.

Chandar broke the silence. "Are you all right, Tulsi? Can I get you some water? Please understand…we follow our disciplinary process very religiously here. High productivity and a healthy environment are two unconditionally entwined buddies. Our process allows us to abort any attempts toward crucifying either of the two—because as soon as one of them dies, the other follows suit."

Having said this, Chandar divided the deck of cards in three equal piles and placed one each in front of Andar and Bandar.

Andar took a draw off his pipe. "We don't necessarily claim that our process is perfect, even as we always strive to make it the best, but at least it works. Core to our process is our proactive monitoring of undesired events. We try to assess these events on a scale that we have developed over a period of time and accordingly apply our disciplinary measures."

"Do you have any questions so far?" Bandar asked Tulsi.

"I am trying to absorb this, sir." Tulsi paused to collect herself fully. "My initial reaction is a disagreement; I haven't breached any discipline here."

"Why do you think so?" Chandar asked, abruptly stopping his shuffling.

"I wasn't one of the key architects. Everyone contributed to the plan and helped execute it. How can one determine if something isn't right when everyone you know is advocating it?"

"While a democratic process is morally desirable for arriving at a decision, it doesn't necessarily produce the best outcomes." Andar had quickly taken his pipe out of his mouth to respond before his two partners could.

"I am not saying it was the best outcome," Tulsi retorted quickly.

"It was the worst, probably," Bandar replied, "and that's precisely the point."

"Honestly, I was disappointed myself in the event. In fact, I dissociated myself from the group after the event," Tulsi said.

"Tulsi, you can rest assured that this team knows every single detail of what happened and has done elaborate research on the case. We are no longer looking to ascertain who the architects were. We know that factually." Bandar lit another cigarette as he finished saying this.

"Well, in that case, since I have no option to contest, I'm completely at your service. Let's move forward with the next step. I may need one favor, if possible."

"Shoot," Chandar said.

"Can I have a month here before termination? That way I will have a chance to find a job and may not ever have to tell my family about getting fired."

"Who else do you have in your family?" Andar asked.

"It's just my mother. My parents got divorced when I was eight years old. I was their only child. She teaches in a community school because she enjoys her time with the kids."

"Tulsi," Bandar said, "one of the biggest ironies in this world is that we all know the right solution to a problem— but we don't often pursue it. Sometimes we want shortcuts. Other times we extend ourselves outside the boundary of the problem and want to achieve more than just addressing the problem. And that rarely works. Bottom line: we are not going to be helpful on this."

"We are past the second step." Chandar seemed to be the timekeeper among the three. "The next step is negotiation.

The way it works, we provide you with a proposal with two options. You choose one of those two options, and then sign the respective contract. And we wrap this meeting up."

Tulsi was sweating again. "What options are you talking about? Should I get a lawyer?"

ABC looked at each other before Andar spoke.

"Well, Tulsi, in addition to terminating your employment with us, we strive to enforce an 'extinct relationship' policy."

"Extinct relationship policy?" Tulsi was clueless.

"In layman's terms," Bandar said, "it means that once you are gone from here, you remain gone. No one at the office should ever be able to get in touch with you. Most people facing this in the past have actually moved to a different city—they change their phone numbers, addresses, social website handles, and such."

Chandar wanted to be done quickly. He said, "The options we offer you are these. Option one: we terminate you and, as per our firm's rule, pay you six months' worth of severance. That's a normal termination. Option two: you resign and we give you a bonus equivalent to two years of your salary."

"Who would even take option one?" Tulsi asked.

"People whose ego blinds them beyond belief," Andar said, and laughed. Then he resumed a sober demeanor. "That's a topic for another conversation. I am glad you are not one of them."

"Why is the second package so lucrative? Is this real?"

"That's an excellent question," Bandar replied, "First, a separation with this package ends the matter in a win-win; and second, the contract clearly states that the person will need to return all the funds should he or she get in touch with anyone from this office—a big incentive for not doing so. Makes our job easy."

"I will go for the second option."

Chandar rang the table bell immediately and the twentysomething girl appeared again.

"Deena," said Chandar, "please prepare a 'graceful exile' package for Tulsi. Make sure her mother is not inconvenienced in the process. You should have received all the information already this morning—but if you need anything else, let me know."

Deena nodded and left.

"Do I have permission to ask a question, sir?" Tulsi said.

"As long as you know that the permission to ask does not include the right to get an answer," Andar responded.

"Who else have you called for this meeting?"

"That's classified information," Andar said.

"Even if I ask about a specific person for a yes-or-no answer?"

"That's right. So that wraps it up."

Tulsi got up from her chair, ready to leave.

"Adios," said Chandar, as all three of them rose to shake her hand. "We wish you all the best for your future endeavors."

Tulsi paused barely long enough to shake hands with them all, then darted from the room.

27. The Unsought Fate

"**I**s this what you get for decades of service to the firm?" said a disgruntled Ratiram to himself, as he prepared at home for an early-morning meeting with ABC. "I am not going to give up easy. This firm has my blood and sweat in its foundation."

His brain was troubled by an unbearable sound at the moment, similar to the one made by a train on squeaking wheels, a dial-up modem, or a thousand females all talking at once. He rushed to his study room, searched for ABC's invitation, and shredded it within a second.

The office cab was on time, now waiting outside his single-family home. Ratiram could see it, yet knowingly made it wait until the driver honked.

"Your impatience needs to be reported. What's the hurry?" Ratiram asked, as the driver got out of the car to open the door for him.

Ratiram did not receive a response.

"Are you fasting on silence today?" He had another question for the driver now that they were driving to the office. It seemed that Ratiram's anger was desperately trying to find an outlet so that ABC weren't going to be the sole recipients.

"No," the driver responded.

"Is that the biggest favor your vocal cords have done to anyone this week?"

The driver did not respond.

Ratiram tried again. "I respect your reservations about speaking to a douchebag like me, but that doesn't mean you should behave like one, too."

The driver was as calm as a house is at two o'clock on a Monday morning.

"I tell you what: I bet you have been contemplating an essay in response to my questions! Please acknowledge my humble apologies for all the misunderstanding on my part that I wasn't very polite in expressing." It was another desperate attempt by his suppressed frustration to avoid having to pop open the lid of his mind.

"Sir…"

The driver couldn't help turning to look behind him, awed; Ratiram had imitated the driver's voice.

"Yes?" Ratiram answered to the imitated voice, acting very excited on finally finding company to converse with.

"I did not like it when you called me a douchebag. I agree, I am easily an asshole at times, but never a douchebag. I hope you are clear on the difference." Ratiram responded for the driver, in the same imitated voice.

"I understand. But being an asshole has nothing to do with not responding at all!" Ratiram said in his own voice.

"It doesn't. I am unusually quiet today because my tongue is tired from an overnight enterprise," the plagiarized voice said.

"I don't blame you," responded Ratiram to his other voice. "I would give up speaking forever for a constant indulgence of that nature."

"No, I didn't mean that. I had tons of relatives show up yesterday evening to surprise me for my birthday. They stayed overnight talking all through the night. The retards made me speak throughout the night," the pretend voice continued.

"I feel bad for you—having to entertain relatives the entire night and then coming and picking me up early in the morning. I hope this once-in-a-lifetime turmoil at least allowed you to rinse your overnight-smelling body?"

"Frankly, it did not. But don't worry; I emptied half a bottle of my wife's talcum powder this morning to cover every cell of my skin," the imitated voice said.

The driver was fuming with anger by now, but seemed handcuffed by some secret oath of nonviolence.

"Sorry, dude," responded Ratiram to his driver-voice, "doesn't seem like that helped even a tiny bit. Your overnight endeavor seems to be more pungent than you might have thought. That makes me take the story you told me with a pinch of salt."

"I am helpless, man," answered the imitating voice. "It's not easy to be born smelling like a skunk and remain that way throughout life. I tell you, my paychecks disappear in visiting doctors, trying all possible scents, blowing twenty talcum powder bottles every week. There is no way out. This skunk shit is worse than forever farting after garlic meals."

That was it. Stopping the car, the driver turned and punched Ratiram in the face. The driver's patience had fortunately allowed him to defer doing this until they reached the office.

"Get hold of yourself, buddy!" Ratiram shrieked as he put his handkerchief on his bleeding nose while getting down from the car. "What's your name? You can't duck it this time. I need to complain about you."

"Chela Ramani. Go file a complaint. Nothing will ever happen. You are going to be racing downhill in a few minutes to sink in a muddy pond at the bottom of hell. Enjoy the party."

Chela drove past Ratiram so fast that he had no chance to ace back with his wit. He merely turned and took the elevator to the second floor.

"What's up with your nose, sir?" a twentysomething girl in formal attire asked. "Are you OK?"

"I may just be on the outskirts of being OK," he said, hiding his frustration.

"Can I help you with something?"

"No, I am all right. Thanks for asking."

She ushered him to ABC's office.

Alone in the room, Ratiram sat on the lonely chair on one side of the table. He then lifted the napkin holder from the middle of the table and put it next to himself. He took a napkin out and gently dabbed his nose. The bleeding had stopped, finally.

"Care for some tea?" He heard the girl's voice.

"May I have a soda instead?"

"You got it," the twentysomething girl replied. "By the way, I'm also supposed to apprise you that the three big bosses are running about ten minutes late because of a prior engagement. So please feel free to ask me if you need anything else, too."

"Nothing, unless you can help reduce the wait."

"I am afraid I can't. Let me grab your soda."

Ratiram couldn't believe himself—he had been an entirely different man since he woke up this morning: arrogant, abusive, careless, and indifferent.

The girl left and locked the room from outside, so Ratiram got up and walked around to have a closer look at everything. Turn by turn, he picked up everything on the table—paperweight, table bell, pen holder, family photographs, a trophy—and turned them in all directions, examining each very closely before putting it back. He also opened all the drawers, one by one, and quickly read through many of the files, reports, and diaries.

Then the twentysomething came back with the soda.

"Do you need ice separately?" she asked him.

"I don't."

"Very well, then; good luck!"

"Thank you."

He took the soda can and walked to the mysterious door at the rear of the room, stood next to it holding the handle, contemplated for about two minutes if he should open it, and finally flung open the door.

The door opened to a long, narrow corridor that contained several other closed doors, equidistant from one another—like a hotel corridor. Ratiram couldn't assess his state accurately, whether he was afraid, nervous, or respectful, but he quickly came back into the room and closed the door again. He then sat on his chair.

All quiet.

ABC's appearance followed within a minute. They settled themselves on the three chairs on the other side of the table.

"Ratiram, first of all, a big thank-you for your flexibility in making this meeting on short notice," said Andar. "I am Andar; the gentleman on my left is Bandar; and to his left is Chandar." He took a puff from his pipe.

"Hello, everyone." Ratiram returned the greeting. "May I humbly request to have a nonsmoking discussion?"

"In all its history," Bandar said, "this has been a smoking meeting. We're not going to change it for you."

"Does the smoking bring some extra effects or what?" Ratiram knew his self-destructive state of mind too well but hardly cared about it right then.

"Without further ado," said Bandar, "things haven't been working very well. We have bad news for you."

"Put this smoke to rest first. Else we are not meeting." Ratiram's ultimatum shocked them.

"Will it work better if we stroll outside? You can get fresh air, and we don't have to compromise on how we run this meeting," Chandar said. He wasn't a smoker, but stood strongly by his two companions. It wasn't a matter of smoking, but a matter of a legacy.

"I don't think that would work. I would need to be standing next to you to be able to hear you. That would mean inhaling the smoke in almost the same way."

Andar and Chandar leaned toward Bandar, conferring in hushed tones so that Ratiram couldn't catch anything.

"Let's see if this works," Andar said, turning toward the rear door and pointing at it. "Bandar and I go behind that door, and Chandar will stay here. We will only open that door to a tiny slit, just enough to be able to participate in the conversation."

"We can try it," Ratiram said, "and see if it works for me."

"Thanks for your openness," Bandar said.

"We are here to relieve you from your responsibilities, effective immediately." Chandar wasted no time as soon as Andar and Bandar went behind the mysterious door.

"What else could you do? I mean really, wasn't that the easiest way?" Ratiram asked fearlessly.

"As you know, the whole Coinman thing was the most disreputable matter that has ever come to our table. A disciplinary action has been determined on the key engineers of the incident," Andar explained, without considering Ratiram's question.

"Being one of the chief architects of the debacle"— Bandar took it forward from Andar—"you are impacted by the decision, and it is our duty to let you know that your employment with the firm ends as of today."

Ratiram stood up suddenly and clapped. "Please accept my standing ovation on this marvelous move."

The three bosses were caught off guard by this. For nearly a minute they couldn't think of anything to say.

Andar broke the silence. "Are you all right? Hearing you're getting fired may be quite stressful to the mind. But please understand; we follow our disciplinary process very religiously here, because high productivity can't be expected without a healthy environment."

"Could you please repeat what you said? I couldn't hear because the door was accidentally closed fully for a second, it seems," Ratiram said.

"I heard it very clearly," Chandar responded.

"That's probably because you tell this to everyone here. You heard it from your own mind, not from Andar at this moment."

Andar repeated his previous words.

"Let's get to the point," Ratiram said, dabbing his nose with a napkin.

"The way it works," Chandar said, "is we provide you with a proposal with two options. You choose one of those two options, and then sign the respective contract. And we wrap this meeting up."

"Keep going, please." Ratiram was impatient to get to the meat of the matter.

"Also," Andar added, "we want to make you aware, in addition to terminating your employment with us, we strive to enforce an 'extinct relationship' policy."

"What the heck does that even mean?"

"In layman's terms," Bandar explained, "it means that once you are gone from here, you remain gone. Make sure that no one at the office is ever able to get in touch with you. If they do, you lose your funds per the contracts."

"Here is the deal," Chandar said. "The options we offer you are these. Option one: we terminate you and, as per our firm's rule, pay you six months' worth of severance. That's a normal termination. Option two: you resign and we give you a bonus equivalent to two years of your salary."

"And which one do you think I would take, if I may humbly ask?" Ratiram asked.

"Everything being said in this discussion gets recorded and could be challenged on legal grounds. Therefore, we are not entitled to respond on your behalf," Chandar replied.

"I will go with the third option," Ratiram said calmly.

"Have you lost captainship of your mind? There was no third option here." Bandar shouted from behind the door.

"I heard it. Maybe that was my own voice in my head. Let me state it anyway," Ratiram said with conviction. "Option three holds when the first two options are not applicable; specifically in a case where the firm is guilty of violence against its most loyal employee by breaking his nose, even when he helped senior management for years by spying on his own colleagues. Option three states that such an employee would be asked to resign with five years of salary, without the condition of losing touch with the firm."

The three big bosses couldn't believe it. It appeared that a deadly snake had just left each one of them—without biting, but after exploring each man thoroughly.

"Are you saying we are responsible for that miserable nose?" Andar finally found words.

"Yes, sir. Chela punched me in the nose."

"We gave no such instructions to him," Bandar protested.

Andar made a quick phone call in the meantime.

"He was working under your orders when he did it," Ratiram responded.

"Bandar, he is right. I spoke to Deena. She confirmed that Chela broke that nose because of Ratiram's obnoxious behavior," Andar quickly confirmed.

"What will you do if we don't agree to your demand?" Chandar asked.

"Well, I am not going to do much. I am just going to send a letter to all the employees here, telling them that their most dreaded big bosses have balls merely as big as mustard seeds and are the three biggest *fattu*s that ever dwelt in this world. I would tell them that Ramta received such a fat check that his family was able to settle in Hawaii forever. And the bosses used the driver to propagate a fake rumor about his nervous state."

"You seem to know more than what would suit our comfort level," Andar said, as he and Bandar walked into the room smoking, not caring about Ratiram's earlier protest.

"For your kind information, however," Bandar said, in a manner that was enough to send a chill down Ratiram's spine, "your research is not thorough. We have a fourth option that wouldn't even require us to pay out any money. We try to stay away from things we don't want to mix with business. But you have forced us to take that route."

Bandar had effortlessly converted Ratiram's grit into the smoke rings that he blew triumphantly in the air.

"We will be back in a minute," Chandar said as he walked toward the mysterious door, signaling to Andar and Bandar to follow.

It was only a minute before Ratiram's clothes were drenched in sweat from the fear caused by the gravity of their manner.

The three of them came back to the room after five minutes.

"We have decided that our best offer for you is the first one," Andar said. "The second one is not available to you anymore. And if you insist more on the third one, the first one will also slip from your hands. We would need to then force option four. The beauty of option four is, it's not discussed, just carried out."

"I will take option one," Ratiram said, wiping the sweat from his forehead.

"You may not have realized, and for reasons we can't reveal," Chandar said sedately, "this has been, and will remain, the most significant decision of your life. Deena will have your contract papers at the front desk. All the best for your future!"

Ratiram got up and left without wasting another second.

28. The Verdict

"*C*oinman," Jay said, addressing him in his office room, "I am so happy that you have found a solution entirely on your own. I have no awareness of Sage Mangal's capabilities, never heard of him, but I am very sure this will work more than the lousy solutions I forced on you."

Both of them laughed.

"And by the way, Sage Mangal's fee is not a problem," Jay said. "Management has always committed to invest a large sum on the personal development of its associates."

"I can never pay you back for this kindness and support, sir," Coinman said. "I promise you that when I come back after finishing at the ashram, I will dedicate myself even harder to the progress of this firm."

"I am very glad to hear that. I can't wait to see you come back. We will miss you here." Jay said, then paused for few seconds, as if he just remembered something important. He asked, "How is the investigation going? What does the officer have to say? What was his name, Mr. Kaatil?"

"Mr. Patil, sir. Everything is good. We received the final report yesterday. They have closed the case as suicide." Coinman took a deep breath and continued, "That was a big relief. I had almost decided that if it was to come to Shimla being charged with the murder, I was going to take it on me. That may not sound practical, but sometimes practical methods are not ethical."

"Whoa, that would have been some real sacrifice. May I know, only if it's okay, the reason behind such feeling?" Jay clearly looked confused.

"Because I have never seen anyone like Shimla in my entire life."

"Why would you say so?"

"After she joined our family, she hasn't, for a single moment, put her own interest above the family's. Even before that, all the trauma she underwent at her parents' house, and her still managing to be a fine person, without a single complaint about what life offered her, puts her at a godly status in my mind. It's very easy to be nice when you are affluent, but it's next to impossible to be nice when you are constantly in severe mental and bodily pain. Despite experiencing the darkest side of the human mind, her mind is still a clean slate for a fellow human."

"She is a phenomenal human. I can completely see now why you would have done the sacrifice."

"She is," Coinman said, with calmness. "Sir, if you don't mind, can I ask you something?"

"No, not at all. Please go ahead."

"Why don't we see Tulsi and Ratiram at the office any longer?"

"Shoot! That reminds me that I needed to put out an announcement to inform everyone of this. Actually, I am planning to have a town hall meeting with all the associates to inform and take any questions on this. It still is a good idea to put up a notice in the meantime, though, to prevent the speculation market from surging to an all-time high."

"That would be great. But I am leaving for Sage Mangal's ashram in two days. Can I get some answers to satisfy my curiosity? I don't think I can stand the suspense for a year."

"Why don't we do this," Jay said. "I can dictate the notice right now, and if you can note it down and type it for me later today, that would help both of us. You would learn about what happened, and I will have the notice ready for the bulletin board. I can then get it on the board as early as tomorrow."

"I am ready." Coinman picked up his pen and writing pad.

"Here we go."

To: Everyone
Date: July 09, 2007

From: Jay Tripathi, Unit Head

Two of our distinguished and old-time associates, Ratiram and Tulsi, have contributed immensely in multiple roles to the overall success of this unit over the past several years. They have been part of the team that laid a very strong foundation for our firm, upon which we have been building our future. The unit has gained immeasurably from their contributions.

The time, however, has come for some changes. It is with mixed emotions that I inform you that Ratiram and Tulsi have decided to look for employment elsewhere. We thank them for all the great support they have provided us and wish them all the best in their future endeavors.

We are working on finding replacements for these positions, and we'll soon have a follow-up announcement with details on filling their roles in the interim.

I also wish to inform you that one of our most experienced associates, Coinman, is undertaking a classified assignment. He will return to the office a year from now, upon the successful completion of this task.

Please join me in wishing Coinman, Tulsi, and Ratiram all the best for their future.

Jay Tripathi

P.S.: Guidelines for the usage of the cafeteria have changed. Please refer to the updated handbook.

29. The Unpleasant Divergence

"**B**y God's grace, good sense has finally prevailed over everyone and everything," Kasturi said to Coinman and Imli, who watched her prepare to leave with sadness.

"Why are you doing this? What will we do without you?" Imli had begun to weep.

"Don't feel sad, dear." Kasturi embraced Imli, patting her head lovingly. "Daulat and I had hardly talked during the past few years, yet his departure has left my life with an unimaginable hole. It's like missing a part of yourself you did not think existed until you lost it. There seems no other way to fill the void than to devote the rest of my life to the service of humanity."

"Mother," said Coinman, "I wouldn't stop you, yet request, for our family's sake, that you consider your decision once again. We will all be so lost without you."

"I have considered this from all angles before coming to this hard decision. You and Imli are going to be at Sage Mangal's ashram for the next year. What would I have done here anyway, without you both?"

"Shimla is going to be here," Imli replied. "She would be good company to you. Besides, how can the poor girl live alone in this house?"

"It's time she takes on the world all by herself," Kasturi said sincerely. "Our experiences from recent years have taught me that in protecting Shimla, we have actually hurt her more. She has grown up with one important side of her personality quite underdeveloped—which is going to be a dangerous thing for her future if it's not corrected immediately by training her in living on her own. If she doesn't start to handle things all by herself, she will never be ready to live life independently. And no one can be with her for the rest of her life. So in a way, this is the best plan for her. For a strong woman such as she is, I am very confident she will learn to cope without too much trouble."

"That's so right," said Coinman. "I admit that as a child I never understood when you and Dad didn't console me every time I wept or felt upset. As I grew, you purposely left more and more on me to tackle. You just wanted me to become strong by experiencing the mental maturity of handling disappointments in the early stages of my life. I am so grateful to you and Father for that because these things couldn't be taught in any schools."

"We were always so proud of you, Son."

"Thank you. By the way, what kind of humanitarian service are you going to do?" Coinman asked.

"To start with, I am going to work on the welfare of underprivileged kids and women. Instead of protecting the weak, society oppresses them. That's not good for humanity."

"I am sure the weak would be fine now. They are going to get you by their side. I wish you every success in this noble endeavor. Take good care of yourself, Mother," Coinman said, hugging her. "Call me when you get there. We are going to be out of touch for one year, sadly, because once we are at the sage's ashram, we will be cut off from everywhere else."

"I will. I will keep in touch with Shimla, too, to make sure she is doing well."

Seeing the taxi from the window, Kasturi started walking outside.

Coinman and Imli hugged Kasturi one final time, all of them with tears in their eyes.

Kasturi had chosen to leave at a time when Shimla was still asleep because she knew the gentle young woman couldn't have endured her departure.

Coinman and Imli gazed in the direction of the taxi, with vision blurred by tears, until it disappeared from their sight.

30. The Lonely Fracture in Time

*S*ometimes it's easy to forget about the most important factors governing the world around you. I bet you have forgotten about me already. It's me, your humble mate Sesha.

Actually, if you had really forgotten about me, then that only makes me extremely happy—because that tells me I haven't done a bad job making myself invisible through the story. On the other hand, if you do remember me, I would like to congratulate you on your phenomenal memory.

Sadly, I am not done testing your memory yet, not until we're done with this surprise quiz. Isn't life a collection of weird quizzes with no answers to half the questions? Well, here is my quiz: what was Coinman's real name?

I got you, didn't I? It was Kesar. Remember?

I'll be honest. Since coming back, I have only annoyed you so far. But that's not why I am back. I have reappeared, against my wishes, to keep a professional promise I made to Sage Mangal. As much as Sage Mangal strives to market his services to the world to help humanity out of complex problems, he doesn't want his detailed recipe to be discovered. It's not because he wants to retain the exclusive copyright, but because he doesn't want this knowledge to fall into bad hands. Knowledge that can make miracles happen needs to be guarded carefully. If it falls into the wrong hands, miracles become disasters in no time.

I am back to mend a fracture in time caused by our inability to divulge details of the rigorous journey in which

Imli and Coinman engaged. So we rather have to catch them after their journey is done, right at the point when they are preparing to leave the ashram.

Before I disappear again, let's kill the elephant in the room. I am as confused as you are on how Hukum could get away without meeting ABC! My explanation: the world isn't always fair.

31. The Spiritual Quest

Sage Mangal's ashram was located on the banks of the Ganges River, at the bottom of the mountains, well hidden in the mangrove trees. Covered with colorful flowers on all sides, the ashram was connected directly to the riverbank via a walking trail. On clear days one could see from the ashram the mesmerizing beauty of the falls, the mountain, and the river, as well as stunningly beautiful sunrises and sunsets.

It was the most serene place, miles away from the nearest highway and outside access. The timeless chirping of the birds during the day and the musical singing of the crickets at night added to its ambience. The pristine spiritual atmosphere was ideal for immersion in one's true soul and spending time in its rejuvenation.

It was the morning of their last day at the ashram. Still feeling tired from their previous night's packing, Kesar and Imli had woken up early to be ready on time for their last meeting with the sage.

"Kesar," Imli said, as she came back from the shower, "I was thinking, maybe we can talk to Sage Mangal directly when we meet him today and implore him to let us stay here for a few more months. I just can't leave this place."

"The reverend sage only takes a few students in each batch for a year. People wait for years before they can get in. Most people can't, despite being willing to pay any amount of money. Therefore, having completed the course successfully, I have no doubt that asking the holy sage to extend our stay would cause him ire."

"I know," Imli said. "It's just that once you have found heaven, you want to do anything to stay in it."

"Hey—do you know," Kesar asked Imli, "that I have finally been able to kill the deadly cobra I was after?"

"Really?" Imli clapped in excitement and came running to him. "I want to hear all about it. Did you do it during last night's dreams?"

"Yes. In my dream last night, I saw the same black cobra that's been troubling me for over two years. The dream started with the chase I always had with it—shifting all the stuff in the house to find him. The only change this time was that I could actually kill it."

"That is so wonderful. Don't stop. I can't wait to hear the details. Please!"

"So last night, in my dreams, I was helping you with chopping some vegetables, and I suddenly saw the cobra passing from beneath the couch in our drawing room to our bedroom. Without wasting a second, I hurled the knife at him with full force. I couldn't believe the accuracy of my aim. The snake was cut in two halves, bleeding over the rug."

Imli clapped again and hugged him. "To me, that symbolizes the final defeat of our adversaries."

"Maybe you are right. This cobra—it has surely caused me immense distress for two years. The very idea of having a deadly snake hiding in the house can make every moment of your time quite a challenge to live. Even if it was only in dreams, it seemed to affect my mind during waking hours, too."

"I am glad you were able to kill him."

"Last year when my father passed away, you know, I thought the cobra had represented the death hovering over the family. Turned out that wasn't the case. These dreams have perturbed me even more after that. So yes, I am really relieved."

"I am curious what may have changed to help us get rid of the cobra."

"Maybe it's the final lesson we had from the sage yesterday."

"The secret endowment?"

"Yes."

They looked at each other in silence for a few seconds before Kesar spoke again.

"Imli, this is the last time we have mentioned it. We are bound by our promise to Sage Mangal; we are not going to talk about it even between us. Like he said, it has to remain a secret, and, until he summons us, it stays undiscovered."

Imli nodded and said, "I am very intrigued by that—what in the world will make him summon us? Of what help can two ordinary souls like ours be to him?"

"I guess we need to wait to find out," Kesar said. "Let's get ready so we can leave in the next ten minutes for the final meeting. Let's not make *Mahatma* wait for us."

Imli nodded and rushed to the mirror to do her hair.

Hindi Word References

Adham – A mean and wretched person
Andar – Inside
Asana – A yoga posture
Ashram – A spiritual monastery
Bandar – Monkey
Barulay – A spicy snack from north India
Chandar – The moon
Cheela – A spicy snack from north India
Daulat – Wealth
Daya – Benevolence
Fattu – A person who lacks courage or is timid
Hukum – An order; a commanding instruction
Ida – Earth
Imli – Tamarind fruit that's used in cooking
Jay – A victory
Kasturi – Musk from a deer, which is used in perfumes
Katori – A small bowl, typically made of steel, used for curry
Kesar – Saffron
Mahatma – A grand soul; person with supernatural powers
Mangal – State of happiness, felicity, and contentment
Mujra – The dance form of courtesans
Panna – Emerald
Purdah – A veil that covers the face
Ramta – Wanderer
Rudra Tandava – Divine dance performed by the destroyer
Sanjog – Destiny
Saree – Traditional Indian female dress
Sawaal – A question
Sesha – What remains in the end
Sevak – A helper; an attendant
Shimla – A hill station in the northern part of India
Sukhi – Happy
Tulsi – The holy plant of basil

ABOUT THE AUTHOR

Pawan Mishra is a leader in the technology and finance industries. He completed his education at the Indian Institute of Technology, Kanpur. He spent the first eighteen years of his life in the small town of Aligarh in India where he discovered his love of storytelling, reading, and writing. In his debut novel, *Coinman*, Pawan Mishra plays to those who have ever felt stymied by the bureaucratic process of office life, successfully and mercilessly capturing the inertia and ennui that's inherit in most corporate cultures.

Pawan now lives in Morrisville, North Carolina, with his wife, Ritu, and two daughters, Mitali and Myra.

Visit him at:
www.pawanmishra.com
pawanmishrablogs.wordpress.com

CPSIA information can be obtained
at www.ICGtesting.com
Printed in the USA
LVHW032330281021
701820LV00008B/1172

9 780692 475676